Bakerloo Line

Steve Schach & Sharon Stein

Wandering in the Words Press

Requests for permission should be sent to Wandering in the Words Press: 2131 Burns St, Nashville, Tennessee, 37216
www.wanderinginthewordspress.com

All characters in this book are fictitious, and any resemblance to real persons, living or dead, is coincidental.

PUBLISHED BY WANDERING IN THE WORDS PRESS

WANDERING
IN THE WORDS

ISBN-10: 099091934X
ISBN-13: 978-0-9909193-4-6
First Edition

To Jackson and Mikaela

Also by Steve Schach

Old Bach Is Come
Highly Satisfactory
A Matter of Trust

Also by Steve Schach and Sharon Stein

Coopers Island

CHAPTER ONE

The London Underground train cut through the freezing January morning air as it hurtled along the Bakerloo line toward Waterloo station. But Suleiman Haroun, tightly gripping a vertical pole to keep his balance as he stood in the crowded fourth carriage, was oblivious of the weather. All he felt was a sense of specialness. His suicide vest contained ten flat bricks of top-quality Semtex, a gift to his terrorist cell from a multimillionaire banker in Saudi Arabia; less privileged homicide bombers had no choice but to use TNT of dubious provenance, scrounged from demolition sites. Also, instead of the usual old nails and screws, perfectly round small steel balls surrounded the bricks of the Czech-made explosive that his handlers had loaded into the compartments of his belt. When Suleiman detonated the Semtex, the deadly shrapnel would kill far more people than the blast from the explosive itself.

Suleiman was like a tightly coiled cobalt-steel spring as he awaited his immediate ascent into Paradise and his reward of seventy-two beautiful virgins. Despite the months of training and indoctrination, he was far more nervous than ever before in his twenty-four years, and he was sweating profusely. However, this did not seem unusual to his fellow passengers, tightly jammed into the overheated carriage for the morning commute to work, because everyone was bundled up in heavy winter outerwear as protection against the London mid-winter weather. Wearing a well-worn anorak to hide his suicide vest, Suleiman appeared to be just another passenger dressed far too warmly for the Underground ride, but adequately equipped to cope with the icy wind that he would have to face after arriving at his destination.

As instructed, Suleiman had carefully positioned himself near the door of the carriage to ensure that he would leave the train somewhat ahead of the bulk of the other passengers alighting at London's busiest Underground station. When he reached the middle of the platform, it would be crammed to capacity with hundreds and hundreds of commuters. He would press the red button on the controller in the pocket of his anorak. The resulting merciless carnage, with threats of unlimited bloody massacres to come, would force the British Army to stop killing his fellow Muslims and withdraw unconditionally from the Middle East and Afghanistan.

The Bakerloo line train slowed to a halt. The doors opened. Suleiman alighted at Waterloo station and shuffled along with the crowd of other passengers toward the center of the platform, taking the greatest care not to trip. When he reached the intended location, he pressed the button on the controller.

Nothing happened.

Suleiman pressed the button again and again. But his actions were futile; the Semtex stubbornly refused to detonate. Despite a rising sense of panic, Suleiman quickly realized that he needed to act like any other commuter, otherwise the police might arrest him and confiscate the irreplaceable Semtex. If he stayed calm, no one would notice what had happened, and he would have a second chance at a mass killing. So he forced himself to control his nerves and ride up the long escalator with the others. When he reached the street, the freezing cold air helped him to think more clearly.

He took out his good-luck talisman, the smartphone that he had kept with him throughout his training in the Khyber Pass region of Pakistan and then in Yemen. They had allowed him to keep the phone because the SIM card was useless outside Britain. Amazingly, his cell phone had worked when he returned to the United Kingdom six months later; his parents must have continued to pay his T-Mobile account while he was overseas. Standing against a wall to try to find some shelter from the icy wintry blast, he once again read the text message that Ali Musa the Bombmaker had sent the previous evening.

> *May Allah be with you tomorrow! But if anything goes wrong, go straight to 181b Elmwood Avenue, Kenton, opposite Kenton Underground station.*

Suleiman had no need to consult the map on the wall as he re-entered Waterloo station—his two years as a messenger for a large firm of solicitors had familiarized him with the London public transportation system in all its glory. He headed back to the Bakerloo line and took the next northbound train. Alighting at Kenton station, he crossed Kenton Road and entered Elmwood Avenue, where a three-minute walk brought him to Number 181b, a two-story house faced with red bricks. He knocked on the door.

Nothing happened for a while, so he knocked again. Then, out of the corner of his eye he saw a twitch in the lace curtain covering the window next to the door. He heard a muffled voice saying urgently in Arabic, "It's Suleiman."

The door opened, and there stood Yussuf, looking absolutely bewildered. Yussuf pulled Suleiman into the house, shut the door firmly, and asked, "Suleiman, what happened? What are you doing here? How did you find this place?"

Before Suleiman could answer, Yussuf dragged him down the stairs into the basement, where Ibrahim and Abubakar were standing. All three men looked shocked. Yussuf had instinctively appointed himself to be their spokesman, and he repeated his three questions sternly, without appreciating that Suleiman had undergone a transition from certain death back to life, and that his mental state was therefore extremely fragile.

Suleiman answered only the last question. "Ali Musa the Bombmaker sent me a text last night telling me to come here if anything went wrong."

"That's impossible!" Yussuf shouted. "Ali Musa couldn't know anything about this house. No one in Yemen has even heard of the London cell. There's no way that Ali Musa could know the address here. And his bombs always explode perfectly—the man doesn't know the meaning of the word 'failure.' You're making up all these lies to justify your cowardice, you treacherous dog."

Suleiman did not bother to reply. He just took out his smartphone, touched a few keys, and showed Yussuf the message from Ali Musa. Yussuf's mouth dropped open and his eyes widened.

Abubakar took up the aggressive questioning. "What happened? Why didn't you set off the explosion, killing thousands of infidels and sending you straight to Paradise?"

In an unnaturally calm voice Suleiman responded, "The detonator didn't work."

"That's nonsense, you worthless liar and son of a whore!" Abubakar yelled. "We use only Frishman detonators, the finest in the world."

"What? You sent me on a suicide mission with an Israeli detonator? Are you crazy? If that Semtex had exploded, I'd have gone straight to the blazing fires of *Jahannam* instead of Paradise. What kind of Muslim are you?"

"Suleiman, calm yourself," Ibrahim said. "Only the Zionists can make a detonator that's always one hundred percent reliable. We dare not use any other brand. In fact, all Muslim suicide bombers have always used Frishman detonators."

"Well, this Frishman detonator failed."

"What do you mean, 'failed'?" Ibrahim asked.

"I pressed the button on the controller, over and over, and nothing happened. The detonator is faulty. You didn't believe me about Ali Musa's text message, and I was right. Now you won't believe me about the detonator. Look here!" Suleiman drew the controller out of the pocket of his anorak and displayed it to the three men. Then he pressed the red button yet again, to convince them once and for all that the Frishman detonator did not work.

Six seconds later the Semtex exploded.

CHAPTER TWO

Abdul Rahman ibn Sultan walked swiftly through the Souq in East Jerusalem. On both sides of the lane, eager shopkeepers invited every passing tourist to enter and inspect their wares piled high to the ceiling in the small shops of the huge market. As always, people stopped and stared as the tall, handsome man hurried past them. He wore white flowing robes with a white *keffiyeh* on his head held in place by a golden rope circlet—the resemblance to Rudolph Valentino in *The Sheik* was remarkably close.

But Abdul Rahman wasn't a film star. He was the leader of the Islamic Front for Jihad and the Liberation of Palestine, and he was on his way to an emergency meeting of his executive committee to discuss the London Underground debacle that had taken place two weeks before. He turned into Souq Khan el-Zayit, where the throng of shoppers was particularly thick. Pushing his way through the crowd, he suddenly turned left into a small spice shop, hardly larger than a booth. Ignoring the shopkeeper, Abdul Rahman strode to the back wall, which was covered by an imitation antique Tabriz rug. Pulling aside the rug, he opened the back door of the shop and entered the cell-like storeroom, firmly pulling the door closed behind him. The smell of exotic spices in the confined space was even more intense than in the shop.

On Abdul Rahman's right was a decrepit-looking wooden door. He now took a ring of five keys out of his pocket, selected one, and carefully inserted it into a high-security lock. He turned the key. The door opened, revealing that the old wood was merely the front surface of a solid steel door. Equally thick steel also lined the outside of the rest of that wall of the storeroom. The door led to a flight of stairs. After meticulously locking the door behind him, Abdul Rahman climbed to the third floor.

The door at the top of the stairs was open, revealing a table littered with papers, small cups of Turkish coffee, and bottles of water and soda. Around the table sat nine men in Western dress. His salutation, *As-salamu alaykum* (Peace be unto you), was the prescribed way Muslims greet their brethren, as was their reply to him, *Wa alaykum as-salam* (And unto you peace). What was unusual, however, was the expression of cold rage on Abdul Rahman's face. All nine men were well aware of the reasons for their colleague's extreme displeasure: The suicide bombing had failed and their London cell was now nonexistent, but most of all the Pan-Islamist Global Jihadi movement had suffered a grave loss of face as a consequence of the debacle at Waterloo station.

Abdul Rahman took the empty seat at the head of the table and spoke, his voice under control. "*Bismillah* (in the name of Allah). What happened?"

There was a long silence, and then one of the men cleared his throat.

"Yes, Mustapha?"

A small man with a large moustache who was seated at the other end of the table spoke up confidently. "After the blast we sent someone we trust to London to investigate the situation."

"Do you mean Tarek?" Abdul Rahman asked.

Mustapha nodded. He seemed surprised that Abdul Rahman had known who had flown to London in the wake of the disaster.

"Go on, please," Abdul Rahman said. Even under such trying circumstances, Abdul Rahman was almost invariably polite.

"Tarek spoke to one of our informants in the Metropolitan Police. He told Tarek that Scotland Yard believes that there was a bomb-making factory in the bascment of the house in Elmwood Avenue, Kenton. The police have concluded that something went wrong and a suicide bomb went off prematurely. But they're puzzled by the fact that the explosion was far less severe than they would've expected from a typical suicide bomb. And that makes no sense at all to me. We provided Suleiman with enough Semtex for a major explosion that would kill hundreds of people on the platform and most of the passengers remaining on the train, as well. But the explosion in Elmwood Avenue was tiny. In fact, were it not for the small steel balls, with so much greater penetrating power than nails and screws, the four people in the basement would probably be alive today."

"So, what happened to the rest of the Semtex?" Abdul Rahman asked. "It couldn't have been in the suicide vest, and it wasn't in the house on Elmwood Avenue. Did Suleiman unload the explosive before he left the Swinderby Road safe house in Wembley that morning and, if so, why?"

"Tarek went to check out the Wembley safe house. Everything was exactly as he expected to find it. In particular, there was no Semtex."

"So, I ask you again," Abdul Rahman said, "what happened to the rest of the Semtex?"

"So far, they've found nothing," Mustapha replied. "The London police are frantically searching for it to try to prevent us from setting off a second suicide bomb. But this time we shall succeed, *Inshallah!*"

"The situation is incomprehensible: Why would Suleiman dispose of all but a tiny fraction of the explosive, keeping just enough to kill himself and Yussuf, Ibrahim, and Abubakar? And where would he hide the remainder of the Semtex?"

The silence around the table was palpable. Abdul Rahman tried a new tack.

"Well, what do we actually know?"

Mustapha spoke again. "Tarek discovered that Suleiman, or someone looking remarkably like him and wearing the clothes found on Suleiman's body at the house in Elmwood Avenue, travelled by train from Wembley Central station on the Bakerloo line to Waterloo station. Three passengers identified him: one on the platform at each of the two Underground stations I just mentioned, and one in his carriage on the train. In addition, Tarek found a man who thinks he saw Suleiman in the street outside Waterloo station, but that identification is somewhat dubious. Finally, a man standing outside Kenton station waiting for a taxi to arrive is certain that, about ten or fifteen minutes before the explosion, he saw Suleiman emerge from the station and cross the street toward Elmwood Avenue.

"And what do the police make of this?"

"They know nothing about it. Our police informant told Tarek that Scotland Yard thinks that the four men were in the house working on the bomb, so they haven't yet investigated when and how Suleiman or any of the others arrived."

"But what about the three train passengers and the men standing outside the stations? What have they told the police?" Abdul Rahman asked.

"It took Tarek a week to gather the information. He started by going to Wembley Central station around the time that he thought that Suleiman had gone there and speaking to Muslim commuters. One man said that he'd noticed Suleiman standing on the platform a few days earlier. Another stated that he'd stood near Suleiman on the train and had alighted with him at Waterloo. So Tarek took the next train to Waterloo and continued his inquiries there—I won't bore you with all the details of the rest of the investigation. Tarek approached only men with the beards and clothing of devout Muslims, and swore them all to secrecy. A *Mu'min* (true believer) always keeps his word. So the police, and especially the Counter Terrorism Command, are in the dark regarding Suleiman's movements, and this situation is unlikely to change in the future."

"What else do we know?" Abdul Rahman probed further.

Once more there was a long silence. Abdul Rahman turned to Mustapha and said, "Tell me what you know, no matter how bad it is."

The silence resumed. From the look on his face, Mustapha seemed to be coming to a decision. Suddenly the words poured out.

"Tarek went to visit Suleiman's parents. They are largely assimilated Palestinian immigrants who came to England about thirty years ago, about five years before Suleiman was born. They are totally mystified. Suleiman had been living with them and his younger sister in Ealing. By all accounts there was a warm family relationship. Then suddenly, about six months ago, Suleiman told them he was going to travel to Palestine to 'discover his roots.' They had no idea what he meant, but they had no objection to his travelling to the land of their birth. On the contrary, they hoped that he might meet a bride there. The fact that he was still unmarried at the age of twenty-four was starting to irk them—they wanted grandchildren.

"Then Tarek asked if he might examine Suleiman's room. His parents said that the police had gone through his belongings many times, but Tarek was welcome to look, too. They were desperate and were most willing to co-operate with this friendly stranger who appeared to be as eager as they were to uncover what had happened.

"Tarek got up to accompany them to Suleiman's bedroom. As he did so, he spied an envelope lying on the dining room table, a bill from T-Mobile addressed to Suleiman. Tarek asked Suleiman's father if he could see the bill. On receiving permission, he opened the envelope and discovered that Suleiman had owned a smartphone. He copied down the number. That was the only thing of any value that his visit yielded.

"Later that evening Tarek enlisted the help of a T-Mobile employee and examined Suleiman's telephone records. Among the messages there was a text from Ali Musa the Bombmaker in Yemen. The message read:

> *May Allah be with you tomorrow! But if anything goes wrong, go straight to 181b Elmwood Avenue, Kenton, opposite Kenton Underground station.*

On hearing this, Abdul Rahman for once could not contain himself.

"Lies, I tell you! All lies!" he shouted. "I know Ali Musa. I met him years ago in Afghanistan where he was born, and I saw him a few months ago in Yemen. He would never write, 'If anything goes wrong' because he is the supreme bombmaker. His bombs never fail."

Abdul Rahman continued in a somewhat calmer tone. "And he's working for the Islamic Front of Yemen in a base situated in a remote location in the Rub' al Khali desert, what the infidels call the Empty Quarter. There's no way he could've heard that we even have a London cell, let alone the address of the house in Elmwood Avenue, no way at all, because he moved to Yemen months before we sent Yussuf, Ibrahim, and Abubakar to London to establish the cell. This is all nonsense."

He paused for a while and then continued in a soft, puzzled voice. "And just how did he send the text to Suleiman? For security reasons, there's no way to send a message from the base other than by courier. The text has to be a forgery of some kind. There's no question whatsoever about it."

He turned to Mustapha and asked, "Please continue."

But Mustapha blushed, looked away, and did not answer. His confident air seemed to have drained away.

"Mustapha, what has happened?"

Again there was no response.

"Speak!"

Finally, Mustapha pulled himself together. "Our people at the camp in Yemen interrogated Ali Musa. He denied sending the message. He said he knew nothing about London, let alone about Elmwood Avenue. He even denied knowing how to text. Then they accused him of using a courier to send the message, perhaps via Aden. Again he denied everything. And then ..."

"Yes, yes, go on. What happened then?"

"They refused to believe him. After all, his bombs have never failed. And the events in London had abjectly humiliated them in the eyes of the infidels. So ..."

"So?"

"So they applied the electrodes. He continued to deny everything. They turned up the current. He wouldn't admit to anything. They increased the current once more. And then—then he died. *Inna lillahi wa inna ilayhi raji'oun* (Verily we come from Allah and to Him we shall return)."

Once more there was silence around the table. Finally, a despondent-looking man with sparse, rust-colored hair who was seated next to Mustapha spoke up. "So now we have no cell in London that can organize bombings to force the British into leaving Afghanistan and Iraq. We have no bombmaker. We have no Semtex. We have nothing."

Mustapha replied, "We still have the agricultural college."

CHAPTER THREE

Ilan Gilboa sat at the foot of the long table in the main conference room in the Tel Aviv headquarters of the Mossad, the Israeli national intelligence agency. Senior members of the agency sat on each side and Haggai Eshkolot, the Director, sat at the head of the table, directly opposite Ilan. Haggai was wearing a blue casual shirt and khaki trousers. He refused to wear a jacket and tie, even for his weekly meetings with the Prime Minister.

The mood in the room was clearly positive—everyone wanted to know all the details of what had occurred in London and how each of them could contribute to the continuing success of the ongoing operation. The Director opened the meeting. "Ilan, please give us your report of exactly what happened."

Ilan, who was equally informally dressed, ran his fingers through his long hair, leaned forward in his chair, and began to speak in a quiet but confident voice. "Thank you, Haggai. Two weeks ago, a CIA agent in Yemen sent a message to MI5 regarding a British citizen named Suleiman Haroun. The message stated that Haroun had trained to be a suicide bomber in an Islamist camp situated in the

Federally Administered Tribal Area of Pakistan near the Khyber Pass. Thereafter the Islamists had flown him to a camp in Yemen, where Ali Musa the Bombmaker taught him.

"The purpose of the CIA message to MI5 was to inform the British that Haroun was about to board a plane in Istanbul to fly home to London on a suicide bombing mission. The message even specified the Turkish Air Express flight number. We intercepted the message."

The other participants essentially ignored this last remark of Ilan's; everyone in the room was fully aware of Israel's capabilities in that regard.

Ilan continued. "An unusual feature of the message was that the CIA agent encoded it in RSA++, a coding system we developed two years ago by extending the Rivest–Shamir–Adleman cryptosystem. All the major intelligence agencies now use RSA++ from time to time.

"As soon as our computers had decoded the American message, two Mossad teams sprang into action. Here in Tel Aviv, a team of four analysts tried to determine why the American had chosen to use an Israeli coding system for a message that he sent to the British. The analysts came to the conclusion that the CIA agent wanted to be sure that we'd be able to read his message even though he sent it to MI5. It was a somewhat crude approach— MI5 analysts would almost certainly come to the same conclusion that we did. But it's likely that the CIA agent in the field in Yemen simply did the best he could under extreme time pressure.

"The second Mossad team assembled at once in our London office. Field operatives made a detailed plan with the aim of quickly discovering Haroun's intended target without tipping off the British that we were taking action in response to the CIA message. I led that effort.

"The first step in our operation was to watch what happened when Haroun handed his British passport to the immigration official at Heathrow. We achieved this by giving one of our agents a British passport, getting him on the Turkish Air Express flight in Istanbul and making sure that they seated him near Haroun. As always, the Turkish authorities were extremely cooperative when it came to a matter of security.

"Then we considered the highly likely possibility that the British would decide not to arrest Haroun at Heathrow, but rather follow him when he left the airport. That way he would lead them to the terrorists in London who were responsible for organizing the suicide bombing mentioned in the CIA message, and MI5 officers could lay their hands on the explosives, as well. Accordingly, we arranged for a team of six cars, two vans, and four motorcycles to follow Haroun from the airport in such a way that they wouldn't tip off the British that we were interested in Haroun. After all, as we understood the situation, the British weren't supposed to know that we'd received and decoded the American message from Yemen. But what actually happened was somewhat surprising.

"Our agent who'd been on the Turkish Air Express flight reported that the immigration official treated Haroun like almost every other British citizen returning from abroad, that is, with total disinterest. She didn't even bother to stamp his passport; she just waved him through. Next, as Haroun exited from the Customs Area of the airport, three men who appeared to be Arabs emerged from the large crowd of people waiting to meet arriving passengers. They shook hands with Haroun; two of them also hugged him warmly. Then they escorted him to their car, a red Ford Fiesta, which is a popular subcompact car assembled in Britain. I stress that there was no attempt at secrecy—the four members of the group acted at all times as if everything was normal and completely above board.

"At this time, our twelve vehicles started executing our standard procedure for shadowing a person of interest without letting any other followers know that we were there. It was a wasted effort for two reasons. The British made no effort at all to follow the car containing the four men, so we could simply have followed them with a much smaller team. And second, the driver of the Ford Fiesta didn't take even the most elementary precautions against being followed, let alone any evasive action. He simply drove directly from Heathrow to 235 Swinderby Road, Wembley. He stayed just under the speed limit all the way. He parked the car in the driveway of the house—he didn't even bother to put it in the garage—and the four men went inside. This was at about two forty-five in the afternoon.

"Our first reaction was that the total lack of subterfuge was a brilliant way of disarming the suspicions of anyone who was watching Haroun. After all, what sort of terrorist drives a bright red car and never even glances in his rear-view mirror? Then we wondered if perhaps their blatant disregard for security was some sort of clever trap. So we parked one of our surveillance vans four houses away and waited. About three quarters of an hour later, the three men who had met Haroun at the airport left the house. They got back into the Ford Fiesta and the same driver as before drove them straight to 181b Elmwood Avenue, Kenton. Again, he took no precautions whatsoever against being followed. He didn't even wait until it was dark before driving to Kenton. And when he arrived there, he parked in the street directly outside the house.

"Once more their actions raised our suspicions. This had to be an extremely clever trap of some kind; no terrorist could possibly be that obliging. So we parked the second surveillance van a few houses away and waited.

"In the meantime, another team of analysts had assembled here in Tel Aviv to try to determine why the British had ignored the CIA warning regarding Haroun. The conclusion that the team arrived at— and I emphasize that it was a unanimous decision— was that there's a pro-Islamist mole in MI5, a traitor who's willing to allow suicide bombings in Britain so that the Islamists can achieve their aims. And the only persons who could possibly have ordered MI5 officers to let Haroun move around in Britain unhindered so that he could detonate his suicide bomb are the Director General of the British Security Service and the Deputy Director General. The analysts decided that it's going to be necessary in the near future to run a sting operation to uncover which of the two men is the mole. And then they wondered whether the real reason that the CIA agent used RSA++ to encrypt the message was that the CIA is fully aware of the Islamist mole at the top of MI5 and was concerned that the British might not take action against Haroun.

"Returning to the first van, the one we parked in Wembley, we set up the usual surveillance equipment, including the appropriate microphones. Around ten o'clock that night we knew that Haroun had been sleeping for half an hour, so two agents left the van in order to enter the house. Because all the members of our team were so certain that the terrorists had set a trap, the two agents took every precaution. They didn't walk to the back door of the house from the van, but rather walked around the block to Scarle Road and approached the back door of 235 Swinderby Road from the backyard of the house located behind it. They were on the lookout for booby traps, trip wires, and alarms of all kinds. But they found nothing whatsoever of that sort. Naturally, that made them even more suspicious and careful. Twenty minutes after leaving the van they unlocked the back door of the house and walked into the kitchen.

"The downstairs of the house appeared to be deserted. In the dining room, a suicide vest loaded with Semtex bricks, each wrapped in blue plastic film, was draped over the back of a chair. Outer compartments of the vest contained small steel balls for shrapnel. A standard Frishman detonator was embedded in one of the flat bricks, its wires waiting for Haroun to connect them. The controller, a gray plastic tube about five inches long and an inch in diameter, with a large red plastic button on the one end, lay on the dining room table.

"Next they walked slowly upstairs, expecting that the Islamists had modified the staircase to creak loudly and so wake Haroun, but once more our people were surprised to find no security precautions at all. They walked carefully into the room where their microphones had led them to believe that Haroun was sleeping. They expected to see some recording device playing sleeping noises, but to their relief Suleiman Haroun really was asleep in a bed against the wall, snoring away. They quickly sprayed him with an ether-like gas to ensure that he wouldn't wake while they searched the premises—we used the same gas that the Russian Mafia thugs use when they rob train passengers sleeping in their compartments on the overnight Moscow–St. Petersburg express. Next to his bed they found a smartphone, which they took with them.

"They returned to the van and called Israel. Our people in Tel Aviv then phoned Amir Frishman at his home. It was the middle of the night, but that didn't bother him at all. Within an hour, a slightly modified detonator controller, identical in outward appearance to the one in the house in Wembley, was on its way to London by air. On the same plane were a number of bricks made from a substance that we developed some years ago. It looks like Semtex. The flat bricks have the same dimensions as the bricks of the genuine article. As I'm sure you know, to aid in detection the Czechs now add a taggant to Semtex that emits a distinctive vapor signature. Currently they're using 2,3-dimethyl-2,3-dinitrobutane, or DMDNB for short. Our Semtex lookalike is not only visually indistinguishable from the actual explosive, but it contains the same amount of DMDNB as genuine Semtex. Now, dogs are extremely sensitive to DMDNB, and ion mobility spectrometers can identify the tiniest quantity of the taggant. But to help humans to detect the explosive, they're now also adding a chemical with a strong bitter almond smell to Semtex, and the lookalike contains the same chemical. But best of all, in an explosion the lookalike just burns away without leaving a solid residue, just like the ashless paper that all the agencies give to their spies to use in case they need to burn a message to prevent the enemy from reading it.

"Our explosives team in Israel had wrapped all ten bricks of the inert Semtex lookalike in blue plastic film. In addition, they'd fastened a strip of red paper around one of the bricks. That brick contained a small amount of genuine Semtex, just enough to kill the suicide bomber when he detonated his vest. They'd also sent us a supply of various other blue plastic films, just in case the Israeli bricks looked different to what we'd found in the suicide vest. We were lucky; both sets of wrappings looked pretty much identical.

"Now, once the smartphone was in our hands we were able to extract sufficient information from the stored data to put together a text message apparently from Ali Musa the Afghan Bombmaker. Forging the message header to make it appear to have come from Ali Musa was simplicity itself.

"Six hours later when we re-entered the house on Swinderby Road, we gave the sleeping Haroun another dose of the gas to make sure he wouldn't wake. Our first task now was to pull the Frishman detonator out of the top of the Semtex brick where Haroun had inserted it. Then we removed the ten flat Semtex bricks wrapped in blue plastic from the inner compartments of the suicide vest, removed the red paper strip from the Israeli brick that contained the small quantity of genuine Semtex, and placed that brick in the compartment of the suicide vest that had contained the Semtex brick with the detonator. Then we inserted the inert lookalike into the other nine compartments. Finally, we embedded the Frishman detonator in the corresponding place in the special brick. No matter how closely Haroun or anyone else inspected the vest, there was no way that anyone could tell that we'd switched all the bricks.

"Next, we took the genuine controller from the dining room table and put the modified controller in exactly the same place. Amir Frishman had removed the standard mechanism from the modified controller and replaced it with a radio-controlled mechanism. The result was that, if Haroun pushed the red button on the controller, nothing at all would happen. But if one of our people sent the appropriate radio signal, the Semtex would detonate. We placed miniature video cameras in each of the rooms, including Haroun's bedroom and especially the dining room, where the suicide vest was located. Finally, we replaced the smartphone exactly where we'd found it earlier.

"Two hours later the alarm in his smartphone woke Haroun. He got up, said his prayers, put on the suicide vest, and then his anorak. On the screen in our van we saw him take the two wires that came out of the top of the detonator and pass them through a hole in his anorak pocket. He connected the wires to the controller, which he put into the pocket of his anorak. Finally, he checked in a mirror to see that the wires that now linked the detonator to the controller via the hole in his pocket weren't visible. We followed him as he walked to Central Wembley station and took the southbound Underground train on the Bakerloo line. When he got off the train at Waterloo station, we continued to follow him. As he stood on the platform and repeatedly pressed the button in his pocket, a look of anguish grew on his face. When he realized that there was no way that the bomb would detonate, he rode up on the escalator with his fellow train passengers. Presumably he was trying to pretend that he was just another commuter.

"We next saw him standing outside the station, looking intently at his smartphone, and we realized that he was re-reading the text message that Ali Musa the Bombmaker had ostensibly sent to him. Sure enough, Haroun re-entered the Waterloo Underground station and took a northbound train on the Bakerloo line to Kenton.

"Now returning to the events of the previous night: After our two agents had successfully entered the Wembley house in which Haroun was sleeping, four agents in the other van entered the house at 181b Elmwood Avenue, Kenton. We'd informed them that the two agents had found no security precautions of any kind at the Wembley house, but they obviously entered the Kenton house as circumspectly and warily as possible. But they, too, couldn't find any alarms at all. I'll return to this perplexing issue later.

"They sprayed the three Islamists with the same gas we'd used on Suleiman Haroun. Our agents photographed a variety of interesting-looking documents that they immediately forwarded to Israel for analysis. Finally, they planted video cameras and bugs in each of the rooms including, fortuitously, the basement. Then they waited. The next morning the three men woke and, after breakfast, they all went into the basement to watch television and listen to the radio—clearly they were awaiting news of the impending explosion at Waterloo station. Instead, Haroun arrived at the house an hour or so after the scheduled time for the suicide bombing.

"At that point I made a mistake," Ilan continued. "Thanks to the bug in the basement, we were able to hear Haroun's conversation with his three handlers.

As they interrogated him, I suddenly realized that the handlers would eventually catch on to the fact that we'd switched the detonator. Furthermore, they might even have taken the 'Semtex' for laboratory analysis, and that would have told the world that Israel had developed a Semtex lookalike and smell-alike. So it was essential to explode the suicide bomb before the handlers could examine it too closely. One valuable property of the lookalike is that it has a surprisingly low flash point.

"I had no qualms about killing Haroun in the process. We'd witnessed his attempt to blow himself up on the platform at Waterloo station, together with hundreds and hundreds of innocent people. The MI5 mole was sheltering Haroun, so there was no alternative to killing him—the British would never arrest him. But what we didn't know was the status of the three handlers. Were they also under the protection of the mole? If not, it was important to keep them alive so that the British could interrogate them. I knew that the small amount of Semtex we'd placed in Haroun's suicide vest was enough to kill him, but it was probably insufficient to give the small steel balls enough kinetic energy to do any serious damage; the shrapnel would merely injure his three handlers. MI5 would be able to interrogate them once they'd recovered from their fragmentation wounds, and that process could lead to our uncovering the Islamist mole.

"So, when Haroun pushed the red button to demonstrate that the detonator didn't work, I made the decision to destroy the bomb by detonating the

Semtex via radio. However, I'd overlooked the fact that the basement had been used as a bomb shelter during World War II. In short, the thick walls of the basement contained and reflected the blast, and the explosion instantly killed all four men.

"Finally," Ilan said, "I return to the issue that the four Arabs took absolutely no security precautions of any kind, notwithstanding the sophisticated skills that so many Islamist terrorists have consistently displayed for the past few decades. I've discussed the issue in depth with a number of Mossad personnel. The consensus of opinion goes something like this: The MI5 mole was sheltering Haroun from above. But what if someone had accidentally discovered the activities of the terrorists from below? For example, suppose a burglar alarm had gone off in the Wembley house and a policeman on the beat had investigated the situation. Suppose further that, in the course of checking the premises, he'd found the suicide vest loaded with Semtex and small steel balls. The result would have been catastrophic for the Islamists. In short, they wisely did all they could do to keep an extremely low profile and act like law-abiding citizens in every way.

"That explained why they drove straight to their destinations, why the driver stayed just below the speed limit, why they parked in the driveway in Wembley and then on the street in Kenton, and why there were no alarms, trip wires, or booby traps in either the Wembley house or the Kenton house. Not even an off-the-shelf household burglar alarm."

Ilan sat back in his chair with a satisfied expression on his face. Haggai Eshkolot's poker face betrayed nothing.

CHAPTER FOUR

Sir William Hartsford-Knipe, the Director General of MI5, known throughout the organization as "D," invited Admiral Albert Marsdon, the Deputy Director General, to sit opposite him at the large table in the private dining room on the sixth floor of MI5 headquarters in London.

"Albert, I'm so glad you could join me. I know how busy you are with this Underground bomber."

"Well, I'm glad you asked me to have lunch with you today. I need to discuss the situation with you. Either we have a full-scale crisis situation on our hands, or it's a genuine instance of 'Peace in Our Time' just for once."

"What have you discovered?" D asked.

"Well, William, the whole thing started with a major snafu, and I'm not sure we can prevent a similar situation arising in the future."

"Oh?"

"As you know," Marsdon continued, "we automatically send all incoming signals to two independent supercomputers for decoding. One of the supercomputers is in the basement of this building; the other is in Cheltenham, at Government Communications Headquarters. The idea is that, if one machine is out of commission for whatever reason, the other one will perform the decryption."

"And we had a problem with that? Here, let me pour you a glass of this really excellent hock. Now tell me more."

"I think that the best way to describe what happened is that we had a stroke of bad luck. Yes, I know that neither you nor I believe in luck, but I can't think of a better way to explain what happened. By the way, you're quite right, this hock is absolutely delicious."

Admiral Marsdon went on speaking. "The supercomputer in this building, like every other huge mainframe computer, needs to be serviced on a regular basis. At the time that we received the message from our American cousins, our machine was undergoing its scheduled monthly maintenance."

"You're referring to the message from Yemen?"

"Yes, that one. Anyhow, before he did anything to our machine, the technician followed the protocol we've laid down and phoned Cheltenham to get confirmation that the second supercomputer was in full working order. On being told that by the operator there that all was well, he switched off our machine and started the monthly maintenance. Now, here was where the bad luck occurred. It seems that just after the Cheltenham operator checked her machine, its central processing unit was struck by a high-energy cosmic ray. Our scientists tell me that destructive events of this kind are somewhat rare. I understand that various sorts of cosmic rays from outer space continuously bombard the earth. Almost all of them pass right through without doing any harm. But occasionally a cosmic ray will interact with something. In this case, it damaged the central processing unit, causing a problem."

The waiter had entered the room and was approaching their table with their Dover sole *meunière*, so Marsdon stopped speaking for a moment. The waiter filleted the fish expertly and served it with boiled new potatoes. He firmly closed the door as he left the private dining room. Then, and only then, did Marsdon resume his narrative.

"The problem with this type of fault is that the way we detect it is that the output from the machine is garbage, in whole or in part. But the operator in Cheltenham didn't have the security clearance to read deciphered messages. So it took a while before the problem was noticed. When the cipher clerk tried to read the message, he realized that it was incomprehensible, so he asked the operator to run it again. This time the output was different, but still unreadable. The situation was finally resolved when our machine downstairs came back online. But by that time, the Haroun fellow had left Heathrow for parts unknown. We couldn't blame anyone and, quite frankly, there doesn't seem to be a way of preventing this sort of problem from occurring again."

"Would it help to have a third supercomputer, situated in Aberdeen perhaps?" Sir William asked.

"Yes, of course, but our information technology wizards have told us that the next occasion that they expect a cosmic ray to damage one machine while the other is being serviced will be in about two hundred years' time. And I'd therefore be most surprised if, under those circumstances, the Minister would be prepared to authorize funding for a third supercomputer—they're awfully expensive. I think we're just going to have to live with the current situation."

"Hmm, I see what you mean. Here, have some more of this hock. Good, isn't it? For once they've chilled it to just the right temperature. Now tell me the rest of the facts," Sir William said.

"Well, now things start to get interesting. Interesting but perplexing. As I said, Suleiman Haroun had left the airport, and we had no way of finding him. The next morning an explosion took place in a house at 181b Elmwood Avenue, Kenton. The police found four bodies in the basement. Three of them were easy to identify from their driver's licenses. They were British-born Muslims of Palestinian ancestry. They grew up together in Saltley, in Birmingham. They'd travelled together to Pakistan, where they'd stayed for nine months. We strongly suspect that they trained there with Al Qaeda, but as of now we've no proof of that. The fourth body had no identification papers. He was wearing the remains of a suicide belt.

"As you know only too well, both the Islamist terrorists and the Israelis have infiltrated the Metropolitan Police. So we ordered the ambulance driver to take the bodies to the morgue in this building, where our pathologists conducted the autopsies and our investigators analyzed everything found on the bodies. And when the people from the Major Crime Team of the Specialist Investigation Department had finished gathering evidence from the scene of the explosion, we arranged to have everything brought here, too."

"Didn't anyone notice that everything was being spirited away to MI5?" Sir William asked.

"I don't think so. We've done this several times now, and we're getting to be quite good at it. After all, the crime scene personnel, including the police on the beat, aren't in any way interested in who performs the autopsies, and they clearly don't care which lab analyzes the evidence. Anyhow, as I said, the body with the remains of the suicide belt had no identification papers in its pockets. But it did have an Oyster Card. So we assumed that he'd used London public transportation. We had one of the Transport for London experts check the microchip on the Oyster Card. Someone had bought it from a ticket machine at Piccadilly Circus Underground station two days before Haroun arrived in London. It had been used only twice: first for a trip on the Underground from Wembley Central station to Waterloo, and about twelve minutes later for a trip from Waterloo to Kenton. That train arrived at Kenton about ten minutes before the explosion, which took place in a house about three minutes' walk from the station. Finally, dental records proved that the body of the suicide bomber belonged to Suleiman Haroun, the subject of the message from the CIA man in Yemen."

"So," D said, "you concluded that Haroun went from Heathrow Airport to a location in the vicinity of Wembley Central station. The next morning, he took a southbound train from there to Waterloo, exited the station there, and about twelve minutes later re-entered the station to take a northbound train to Kenton. What do you think he did for twelve minutes outside Waterloo Underground station?"

"That's the Sixty-Four Thousand Dollar Question, as our American cousins would put it. I don't know, nor does anyone else in our organization. What we do know is that a nurse saw him on the southbound Bakerloo line platform at Waterloo, so some people have suggested that he was trying to set off a suicide bomb on the platform. But there's a problem with that, a big problem."

"And that is?" Sir William asked.

"The Semtex. Our people are absolutely positive that there was only a small quantity of Semtex in the basement room in Kenton when the bomb went off. But the shreds of cloth remaining from the suicide belt were thoroughly impregnated with the taggant for Semtex: 2,3-dimethyl-2,3-dinitrobutane."

"Do you mean DMDNB?" Sir William enquired.

"Dammit, I can never remember that name," Marsdon replied, trying to keep a straight face. "And there were also traces of that new chemical that smells like bitter almonds. So, it seems incontrovertible that at one time the suicide belt was packed with Semtex, which is unusual in itself— most of the terrorists can't afford anything better than second-hand TNT. But by the time Suleiman Haroun reached the house in Elmwood Avenue, Kenton, all but a tiny quantity of the explosive had disappeared. Where's that Semtex?"

"Could it be at the location near Wembley Central station where you think he spent the night?" D asked.

"Possibly, but what suicide bomber would go on a mission with just a minuscule fraction of his explosive, Semtex no less? And why didn't he explode even that small remaining amount of Semtex at Waterloo station? We've been looking at this question in depth, and we've come up with a few ideas. One possibility is that he got cold feet. He got to the platform, changed his mind, and went to his friends in Kenton."

"But there's a contradiction there," Sir William said. "If he went to Waterloo with only a limited quantity of Semtex, he'd already made up his mind not to be a suicide bomber. And in that case, why would he go to Waterloo at all? If he'd decided to back out and stay alive, he'd have travelled straight from Wembley Central to Kenton without his suicide belt. Instead, he went to Waterloo with just a small amount of Semtex, and from there he went to Kenton where he blew himself up. That makes no sense at all. Also, if he went to Waterloo station with just a fraction of his Semtex, where's the rest of it?"

"Precisely!" Marsdon agreed. "But the other possibility is equally bizarre. In that scenario, Suleiman Haroun travelled to Waterloo station with all his Semtex. However, when he got there he decided not to blow himself up. So, he dumped almost all the Semtex either somewhere outside Waterloo station during the time he was away from the Underground, or between leaving Kenton station and entering the house in Kenton, but he left just enough explosive material to blow himself up together with his friends. In other words, we have a suicide bomber who decides not to kill himself and hundreds of people with him. Instead, he goes to his friends' house with just enough explosive to kill himself and his three friends."

"If your first theory is correct," D replied, "which it obviously isn't, there's a load of Semtex stored somewhere near Wembley Central station, but no one has a clue as to where it is. And if your second theory is correct," he continued, "which it obviously isn't either, there's a cache of Semtex somewhere near Waterloo station or near Kenton station that no one has been able to find, even though the timeline indisputably defined by the Oyster Card makes it impossible for Haroun to have been anywhere other than in the immediate vicinity of Waterloo station or the immediate vicinity of Kenton station. As Alice put it so well, curiouser and curiouser."

"In the meantime," Marsdon said, "we're trying to find the location near Wembley Central where we think he spent the night. The problem, of course, is that we have no clues at all, other than the information on the Oyster Card. We're asking people if they saw Haroun, but we don't have enough personnel to do a thorough job, and we can't involve the police. In short, the good news is that the suicide bomber and his associates are dead. The bad news is that we're desperately short of information of all kinds in this case, precisely because the four people who could help us are dead, and we can't find the Semtex that we know has to be somewhere."

"So, where do we go to from here?" D asked.

Before his deputy could answer, the waiter re-entered, this time bearing two chocolate soufflés and a bottle of Château d'Yquem. When the waiter had left, D repeated his question.

"I really don't know," Marsdon said. "We're absolutely at our wits' end. As always, we're doing everything in our power to defeat the Islamist terrorists. I certainly don't need to remind you that fifty-two people died in the bombings on London Underground trains on the seventh of July 2005, and that a double-decker bus was also destroyed. Over seven hundred people were injured. Then, as we both know, there were four more attacks two weeks later, on the twenty-first of July. Three stations and a bus were attacked. Thankfully, even though all four of the detonators fired, for some reason none of the explosive charges ignited. We heard that Al Qaeda executed the bomber who was responsible for the failure and replaced him with Ali Musa. Since then, there's been nothing in London until two weeks ago, when Suleiman Haroun apparently tried to set off a bomb at Waterloo Underground station—maybe."

"I agree," Sir William said. "We don't yet know what Haroun was supposed to do in London, and we don't even know what he actually did do. We may never know. But one thing is for sure—this chocolate soufflé is truly sublime."

D then went on. "Unfortunately, another thing that we do know for sure is that somewhere in London there's a cache of Semtex large enough to fill every compartment of a suicide vest. We have to find that Semtex if we're to successfully defend Britain against Islamist terrorists.

"We've had one failure in this case already," he continued. "It wasn't anyone's fault—we have no control over cosmic rays. But we cannot afford another failure. So please keep me informed at all times. I obviously don't have to tell you that this is really, really important. The lives of hundreds of our fellow countrymen are at stake."

CHAPTER FIVE

Mustapha, the rector of the New Palestinian Agricultural College, was seated behind his antique Syrian desk, a vast expanse of walnut wood with exquisite mother-of-pearl inlay, when the door of the luxuriously appointed office silently opened about a foot. Abdul Rahman ibn Sultan put his finger to his lips as he stuck his head into the gap. He then pushed the door wide open and entered the room. He took a small notebook and pencil out of his pocket, scribbled a brief note and handed it to Mustapha. The note read: *"Bismillah.* Don't say a word. Follow me outside."

Mustapha pursed his lips in exasperation, but allowed Abdul Rahman to lead him out of the building and across an olive grove and then an orange grove, both just starting to display the first signs of spring. When they were about two hundred yards away from the building, Abdul Rahman spoke for the first time.

"Mustapha, I think that you know very well why I asked you to come outside with me on this chilly March morning. As I have repeatedly told you and your colleagues, I believe that the agricultural college building is bugged."

"Abdul Rahman, we all appreciate that you are extremely security-conscious, and we are most grateful to Allah for giving us a chairman who takes every precaution to protect the safety of the IFJLP. But as we have insisted many times, what you are suggesting is just not possible. When our executive committee took the decision to convert the abandoned high school into an agricultural college, one of the first things you did was to warn us that in 1979 the KGB embedded hundreds of listening devices within the walls and ceilings when the Soviets built the new American Embassy in Moscow. Yes, we all paid careful attention to what you said that day, and we took every precaution to ensure that the Mossad couldn't plant any sort of bug when we remodeled the high school."

"Every precaution? Don't make me laugh!" Abdul Rahman replied. "As you well know, about six months ago I visited the agricultural college in the middle of the night to check on security. The major part of the work was almost complete at that stage. I drove up at about two in the morning. No one came out to see what was going on. Yes, the gate was securely locked, but there was a hole in the wire mesh fence about ten yards from the gate that was large enough to drive two tanks through. I marched up to the building, expecting a squad of armed young men to challenge me. Instead, I found that the front door was open. I walked in. Yes, there was a night watchman there, a one-armed man about seventy-five years old. He was fast asleep on the floor, snoring loudly. I tried to wake him, with no success. Then I noticed the empty bottle of Stock 84 brandy, Israeli brandy no less, lying on the floor next to the unconscious guard. Mustapha, when I saw that bottle of Zionist alcohol in the building that would soon house the secret training headquarters of the IFJLP, I realized that this was the American Embassy in Moscow all over again.

"I called an emergency meeting of the executive committee. I told you and the others what had happened. To a man, you brushed aside everything I said. You all insisted that the Mossad couldn't possibly have bugged the building. When I suggested that, at the very least, we should all be extremely careful with what we say inside the building, you claimed that the Israelis had no cause to plant listening devices inside the agricultural school, and therefore there were no listening devices. You weren't even prepared to admit that the building was inadequately guarded that night."

"Yes, that's all true, Abdul Rahman. But to convince you that there are no listening devices, Mahmoud ibn Laban bought a bug detector when he was in the United States two months ago. When he returned, we swept the entire building and discovered nothing. And we did it again two weeks later, and once more we couldn't find a single listening device anywhere in the Agricultural College."

"Mustapha, he bought that bug detector for fifty dollars at some dubious electronics store I've never heard of. I told you at the time that the Mossad uses highly sophisticated surveillance equipment and that the contraption Mahmoud purchased was a useless cheap toy, but yet again none of you were prepared to listen to me. In any event, if finding bugs is so easy, do you really think that the KGB would have bothered to embed so many listening devices within the American Embassy in Moscow? The Americans ended up demolishing what the Soviets had constructed and then rebuilding the embassy with American labor using American materials they imported via Finland. That was twenty years ago. Since then, experts at the Israeli national intelligence agency have developed an all but foolproof bug detector they call Juke Box. But do you really think the Mossad would lend us a Juke Box to sweep the college?

"I was honored that you asked me to preside at the opening ceremony, but since then I have stayed away from the school on security grounds—this is my first visit since the opening. I firmly believe that this school is a Zionist Trojan horse."

"But Abdul Rahman, how can you say that? The Israelis have been so supportive from the start. They expedited the paperwork, rushing our development application through all the relevant boards and committees. And don't you remember that the Israeli Minister of Agriculture even sent a letter of congratulation when the building was opened? And you know as well as I do that, every two weeks, one of the professors from the Hebrew University Faculty of Agriculture in Rehovot comes to visit us, with graduate students in tow, to give a lecture to our students. They cover all expenses, and our students greatly look forward to the highly informative and interesting talks."

Abdul Rahman lowered his voice. "Mustapha, one way of interpreting the facts as you have just laid them out is that the Israeli government wants the Palestinian people to be self-sufficient food-wise. It's undeniable that they have done many things to assist us. They've trained our farmers, they've provided us with seeds of the highest quality, and they've even showed us how to grow more crops with much less water using drip irrigation. But there's another way of looking at the situation here. Suppose, just suppose, that the Israelis have found out that our 'agricultural college' is a cover. Perhaps they knew from the beginning that our idea was to start an educational institution where most of the students would be farmers who wanted to learn how to improve their yields, lower their costs, and increase their profits. However, those students would be there to provide cover for the real students, the handful of jihadis whom we would train for the armed struggle, for Holy War."

"That's absurd!" Mustapha said. "How could they possibly find that out?"

"In many ways, Mustapha old friend, in many different ways. For example, there may be a Zionist spy on our executive committee."

"Impossible!"

"Why 'impossible'? How do you know that no one on the committee is reporting to Tel Aviv on a regular basis?"

"Impossible!"

"So you say, but you haven't explained why."

"It's just … impossible. That's all."

"No, it isn't. And it would explain all sorts of otherwise inexplicable events, like the Suleiman Haroun disaster. If the Israelis had known he was coming and why, that would have changed everything, wouldn't it?"

"Abdul Rahman, what you are saying is beyond belief."

"Is it? Are you really so sure that the college building isn't bugged? And how do you know that none of the graduate students who come along with the various professors they send here every two weeks are Mossad agents?"

"Well, at least I can reassure you on that point. We surreptitiously photographed the whole group who came from Rehovot last week, and compared the photographs we took with their pictures on their pages on the Hebrew University Faculty of Agriculture website. All of them are precisely who they said they were: A professor of agronomy and four of his graduate students, one woman and three men."

Abdul Rahman rolled his eyes, being careful to turn his head away from Mustapha as he did so. He paused and then chose his words carefully. "Mustapha, isn't it just possible that the Mossad asked the Hebrew University to add four additional pages to its Faculty of Agriculture website? In other words, even though the professor of agronomy is the real thing, couldn't his graduate students actually be Mossad agents masquerading as students?

Couldn't they have constructed their web pages with the precise aim of convincing you that they are genuine agronomy graduate students? Have you checked further back than, say, six months?"

From the start, Mustapha and his colleagues had stubbornly refused to admit even the possibility of eavesdropping devices in the agricultural college. Their experience of covert listening was restricted to bugging scenes in movies and TV shows, and they treated Abdul Rahman's attitude toward surveillance as paranoia caused by overexposure to the American entertainment industry. But Mustapha had extensive first-hand experience of using the web to spread disinformation, and he knew from personal knowledge how quick and easy it would be for the Israeli national intelligence agency to create convincing false personae for their agents on the Internet. Suddenly he understood that Abdul Rahman might just be correct. A wave of abject terror passed through Mustapha as he realized what the Mossad might have overheard. The thought of what the Israelis could have learned through his pigheaded obstinacy nearly made him retch.

Finally he regained control of himself and responded. "Abdul Rahman, are you saying that the Israelis know everything that's going on in the New Palestinian Agricultural College?"

"As I've told you repeatedly for half a year, I believe that the whole building is bugged."

Mustapha shuddered. "What do we do about it?"

"As I've just explained to you, sweeping the building for listening devices isn't going to work. I think we need to set a trap."

"What sort of trap?" Mustapha asked. He had lost his usual self-confident air, and was clearly desperately worried now.

"Let's choose one of our agricultural students, someone with no political agenda whatsoever. Accordingly, he'll have no record at all with the Israelis."

"What about Hassan Ali ibn Bakran Al-Husseini? The man walks around all day in a daze. I'm not sure he's even aware that he's living in Palestine. The man has no political awareness whatsoever."

"Fine, let's pick Hassan Ali. Next, contact the Queen Victoria College of Agriculture in Tricester, United Kingdom, and ask them if you can send Hassan Ali there for three weeks on an exchange visit at our expense. I have no doubt that they'll agree—the British universities are great friends of the Palestinian people."

"And what's he going to do there for three weeks?" Mustapha asked.

"If I'm correct, he's not going to get there, so it doesn't matter."

"What are you saying? Is something going to happen to him? I don't like this at all."

"Be calm, Mustapha, be calm. It's not what you think."

"I hope not."

"Just give me a chance to explain. The key thing is that Hassan Ali has to be 'clean' at all times."

"What exactly do you mean by 'clean,' Abdul Rahman?" Mustapha asked.

"There must be no excuse whatsoever for either the Israelis or the British to arrest him. We agree that Hassan Ali is totally apolitical. We'll buy him new clothes in Israeli shops for his trip, give him an Israeli-made suitcase, fly him to London on El Al, and—"

"What are you saying? No Palestinian ever flies on the Zionist airline. Apart from the political implications, can you imagine the searching he'd undergo before they'd allow him to get on the plane, assuming they'd ever let him on board? No, what you suggest is impossible. They would strip-search Ali Hassan, X-ray his luggage, put every part of his clothing under a microscope, and—"

"Precisely!"

"What do you mean by 'precisely'?"

"I mean that what you just said is precisely what will happen to Hassan Ali. And in addition, they'll subject everything he brings with him to exhaustive testing for explosives, including the clothes he'll be wearing. We'll make sure that he arrives early at Ben Gurion International Airport near Tel Aviv to give the Zionists plenty of time to be one hundred percent certain that Hassan Ali is 'clean' and no possible threat to the plane."

"But why?"

"Because we're going to make sure that every step, every aspect of the visit is above board in every way. As I said, we're going to ensure that neither the Israelis nor the British have any grounds whatsoever to cancel Hassan Ali's trip, let alone arrest him. With one exception."

Abdul Rahman paused. Mustapha looked at him in anxious anticipation.

"Yes, with one exception. We'll arrange for Hassan Ali to fly to London on a Friday morning. At some stage, you'll tell him that, as a reward for being such an outstanding student, he'll be able to enjoy a weekend in London, at our expense, before travelling to Tricester early on Monday morning for his three weeks of study there. You'll tell him that we are arranging accommodation for him in London, and we'll give him the address later. Then, two or three days before he's due to depart, you'll call him into your office and you'll say to him as follows: 'The address in London is 235 Swinderby Road, Wembley, where Suleiman Haroun stayed.' And you'll shoo him out of your office before he can ask you who Suleiman Haroun was. Do you see the point?"

"I think so," Mustapha said. "Everything about Hassan Ali will be 'clean,' as you put it, except that I'll tell him that he's staying where Suleiman Haroun stayed. If the Israelis are listening, it will put them on the spot, in two different ways. First, the whole world knows about Suleiman Haroun—except Hassan Ali, of course—but no one but ourselves know about 235 Swinderby Road, Wembley. So, either the Mossad will rush to that address to investigate, or they'll tell their good friends at MI5 to do it. And we'll have our people watching the house. If investigators turn up, that will prove conclusively that the Israelis are listening in. Second, the way you've described it, the Israelis cannot conceivably have a reason to stop Hassan Ali unless they're listening in. Similarly, the British won't possibly have a reason to refuse to admit him, again unless the Mossad are listening in and they tell their British counterparts what they've heard. If Hassan Ali is allowed to visit the Queen Victoria College of Agriculture, after spending a weekend in London staying at 235 Swinderby Road, Wembley, that will mean that the Israelis aren't bugging the school. But if they stop him anywhere en route—"

"Precisely!" Abdul Rahman said. "And now let's bait the trap."

"Just a minute," said Mustapha. "Let's think about this a little more carefully. The most we can gain from your trap is that we can prove to ourselves that Mossad agents are listening in. The price we pay for this is that we tell the Zionist enemy the address of our safe house in London. That doesn't seem like much of a trade-off to me. If you're so worried about the possibility that they've bugged our college, all that's needed is for us to issue an instruction to everyone in the college, genuine agriculture students and jihadis alike, to discuss any sensitive issues outside."

"Mustapha, with all due respect, I think you are overlooking the key point."

"Which is what?"

"If we know for certain that the Israelis are listening in, we can deliberately give them false information. That power over the Zionists is worth much, much more than the address of the safe house, which is useless in any event. Who do we have in London now? Nobody. And we have no explosives there, no suicide vests, no detonators and, most importantly, no way of transporting to Britain the items that we need there. The operation in London is finished. But by trading the address of the now useless safe house for the certain knowledge that we can use our agricultural college for disinformation, we gain a big prize, *Inshallah*."

Mustapha had an uneasy feeling that there was a flaw somewhere in that argument. But he somehow just could not put his finger on it, so he kept silent.

CHAPTER SIX

"We have a huge problem," Ilan said to the three Mossad agents crowded into his tiny office in Tel Aviv. "Hassan Ali's trip to Tricester has just taken a turn for the worse. I'm meeting with the Director in fifteen minutes' time, but I called you in here to see if one of you can come up with a good idea."

"What's the complication?" Miri asked. She was one of the cleverest agents in the Mossad, who frequently fooled enemy operatives by playing the role of a 'dumb blonde' with great success.

"We've just overheard Mustapha tell Hassan Ali that, when he arrives in London on Friday, he's to stay at '235 Swinderby Road, Wembley, where Suleiman Haroun stayed.' Which means that—"

But Miri quickly interrupted him. "We all know exactly what this means. If we impede the trip in any way, Mustapha and his comrades in the IFJLP will know for sure that we're listening in on them. But now, with Swinderby Road thrown into the equation, there's a good chance that Hassan Ali may not be the innocent that we all thought he was. After all, the IFJLP has lost everything in Britain, with the exception of their safe house in Swinderby Road. In fact, they've lost that, too, but they don't know it

52

yet—they still don't seem to have realized that we followed Haroun and his three handlers to the Wembley safe house."

"Well, they're half right," Ilan added. "The British don't yet know about Swinderby Road— we're the only people who do."

"Yes, of course," said Miri impatiently, "but you don't play your last remaining card just to prove that we're bugging your agricultural college. Now it seems much more likely that they're unaware of the fact that we're listening in, and what they're really doing is sending a suicide bomber to London, someone who up to now has kept well under the radar, playing the role of a political halfwit to perfection."

"Why don't we tell the British about all this and let them handle it?" asked Yossi, a tall, heavy-set agent with a bad smoker's cough.

Before Ilan could answer, Miri shot back a sarcastic reply. "Yossi *motek* (sweetie), have you already forgotten what happened when the IFJLP sent Haroun to London? The CIA informed the British that Haroun was on his way, and MI5 did precisely nothing. The British didn't stop him at Heathrow, and they certainly didn't follow him when he left Heathrow for Wembley. If we were to tell the British what's really happening, the traitor in MI5 would do exactly what he did the last time, and Hassan Ali would get a free pass. In fact, I wouldn't be surprised if the MI5 traitor were to arrange for an armed escort of police cars, with sirens blaring, to accompany Hassan Ali all the way from Heathrow to

235 Swinderby Road. And talking about Swinderby Road, just what do you propose telling the British about the safe house? Would you tell them that everything was perfectly kosher regarding the visit of Hassan Ali to the Queen Victoria College of Agriculture, until the Palestinian terrorists just happened to mention Swinderby Road? And just how do you propose to introduce the subject of 235 Swinderby Road into the conversation? Would you say something like, 'We followed Suleiman Haroun and the three stooges to their safe house in Wembley, we broke in that night, we replaced the Semtex with the lookalike stuff that vaporizes when the bomb goes off, we got Amir Frishman to give us a radio-controlled detonator that Ilan set off in the Kenton house the next morning, but we somehow forgot to tell you about all this, because there's a mole in your organization, and the traitor is probably you?' Is that what you want to tell the British? Yossi *motek*, you're a Category Five moron, but only because there's no Category Six."

Yossi was clearly getting angrier by the second. His face was red, he was breathing heavily. He tried to reply to Miri's onslaught, but his years of heavy smoking got the better of him, and he started coughing uncontrollably. Ilan suddenly jumped to his feet, shouting, "Yossi, you've got it! You've got it! Yossi '*motek*,' you're a genius!" and ran out of his office in the direction of the Director's suite.

Miri just sat there shaking her head. Having to work with Yossi was bad enough, and now Ilan was equally crazy.

Ilan strode into the Director's suite and looked expectantly at his personal assistant sitting behind a small desk. She waved him through with a cheery "Haggai is waiting for you."

Unfortunately, the Director was a lot less cheerful than his personal assistant. Before Ilan had a chance to take a seat, Haggai barked at him, "What are we going to do now?"

"Don't worry, I've got a great plan."

"It had better be great," Haggai grumbled. "If we stop Hassan Ali, the inevitable result is that we totally dry up the flow of information that we so desperately need to protect ourselves against the IFJLP. And if we don't stop him, hundreds are going to die in London. Maybe thousands."

"Don't worry. In the first place, there is a ninety-nine percent chance that this is just a trap to prove that we've got listening devices in the agricultural college, and that Hassan Ali is merely a pawn in the terrorists' game and poses no threat."

"And what about the other one percent? What if he's a true blue, honest to goodness, dyed-in-the-wool violent jihadi and suicide bomber? We dare not follow him and the British won't follow him. The man has a Get Out of Jail Free card of the highest order. Hundreds are going to die, and thousands will be injured."

"Relax. I've got a foolproof plan."

"Don't make me laugh—no plans are foolproof, not even yours."

"Wait until you hear this one."

***

"Sir William, how good of you to see me at such short notice."

"Not at all, Ambassador Yaroq, not at all," D replied. "Whenever an Israeli Ambassador has previously requested an urgent meeting with MI5, there was no question that the security of the United Kingdom was at stake."

"Which is what we believe to be the case in this instance as well, Sir William. Have you met our new Second Secretary, Gabriella Lapid?"

"Delighted to meet you, Ms. Lapid. I hope your stay in Britain will be most productive."

"Thank you, Sir William."

"Won't you sit here? My assistant will bring us afternoon tea in a moment. Now, what can I do for you?"

The two Israeli diplomats sat together on a plush sofa. Sir William Hartsford-Knipe sat opposite them on an upholstered wingback chair. Between them was a low wooden table. Before the ambassador could reply, the door opened and two assistants entered. One carried a tray with a teapot, milk jug, hot water jug, teacups, saucers and cake plates, all in matching Royal Albert bone china. The other carried an oversized tray with serving platters, also in the same bone china pattern. The platters were filled with cucumber sandwiches, smoked salmon sandwiches, scones with clotted cream and jam, and a wide variety of different cakes and pastries.

Gabriella was able to identify only the fruitcake and the chocolate éclairs.

Anxious as they were to get to the matter at hand, both Israelis were fully aware that the demands of etiquette were such that only small talk was permitted until the afternoon tea ritual was complete. Eventually Sir William put down his cup and saucer, and turned to the diplomats, an expectant smile on his face. Ambassador Ze'ev Yaroq spoke.

"About two months ago, the Islamic Front for Jihad and the Liberation of Palestine—or IFJLP for short—sent Suleiman Haroun to London. Fortunately he didn't succeed in detonating his suicide bomb at Waterloo station, if that was what he intended to do; we still haven't found that out. As you well know, there were many other puzzling features of that incident. In particular, the Semtex is still missing, and we still don't know where Haroun stayed in Wembley. As a result, we've kept an especially close watch on that organization."

The ambassador paused for a few seconds before continuing. "A reliable source has informed us that the IFJLP will be sending a second suicide bomber to London. He'll arrive at Heathrow Airport tomorrow, on the morning El Al flight."

"Are you sure about that, Ambassador Yaroq? As a matter of principle, Palestinians won't fly on El Al. And your security precautions are by far the best of any airline in the world, so why would they take the risk of sending a terrorist through Ben Gurion

Airport, where the personnel would detect any last trace of explosives?"

"That's the beauty of their scheme, Sir William. They've chosen a man called Hassan Ali ibn Bakran Al-Husseini. He's a veritable *rara avis*, an apolitical Palestinian."

"Yes, indeed. But if he's so uninvolved in the struggle, why is he prepared to become a suicide bomber and give up his life?"

"Here's how we see the situation. We believe that the IFJLP is convinced that they have a mole in their executive committee, an Arab who's collaborating with us. In order to expose the informant, they've come up with a clever scheme. Hassan Ali is a student at their new agricultural college. They've arranged for him to spend three weeks visiting the Queen Victoria College of Agriculture at Tricester. All the evidence shows conclusively that he's totally apolitical. As someone put it, it's as if Hassan Ali isn't even aware that he's living in Palestine. Not only is Hassan Ali totally 'clean,' but every aspect of his trip is equally clean. They've provided him with new clothes and a new suitcase, all bought in Israel. I've no doubt that he'll pass through security at Ben Gurion International Airport tomorrow morning with flying colors, pun not intended. As far as we were concerned, until this morning we had no objection whatsoever to Hassan Ali's visit to Britain.

"But earlier today," the Ambassador continued, "we learned that the real purpose of Hassan Ali's visit was to retrieve the Semtex that Suleiman Haroun hid somewhere in London and use it to stage a suicide bombing. Our first reaction was that this was just a clever ruse to show up their mole. After all, neither your people nor our people have the slightest grounds for stopping Hassan Ali, other than the information that the mole passed on to us today. So, if either party were to cancel the visit or arrest Hassan Ali, that would provide conclusive proof to the IFJLP that they have a mole on their executive committee, which would inevitably mean immediate execution of the person they suspect. And we certainly wouldn't want that to happen. We need to know what's going on in the IFJLP. And, in view of the fact that they seem to be targeting London, you indubitably want to keep the mole in place, too. So, we decided to do nothing, in order to protect our mutual source."

"Very wise, Ambassador Yaroq," Sir William purred.

"However," the ambassador continued, "our analysts are concerned that the terrorists are playing a much more subtle game. They know that we won't do anything to implicate the mole, and neither will you. That is, Hassan Ali has the terrorist equivalent of diplomatic immunity, if you get my drift—neither the British nor our people would dare to interfere with him in any way, or even have him followed. As a result, he's the ideal suicide bomber."

"But you said he's totally apolitical," Sir William protested.

"True, but what if they've brainwashed him in the three months he's been in the agricultural college, and he has all the zeal of a new convert?

What could be better for the terrorists than having someone ready to travel to Britain and explode a suicide vest packed with Semtex on the platform at Waterloo station, *who positively won't be stopped?*"

D's mouth dropped open. "That's fiendishly clever," he breathed. "If we stop him, or even interfere with him in any way, they'll kill the mole and the information ceases, which means that hundreds of Londoners will die in the near future. And if we do nothing, hundreds of Londoners will die very soon indeed."

"Exactly, Sir William. But our people have come up with a plan that we think will outmaneuver the terrorists."

***

The Ambassador and the Second Secretary left MI5 and were driven back in the ambassador's car to the Israeli Embassy at 2 Palace Green, Kensington. They did not speak a word from the time they left Sir William's office until they were seated in the ambassador's private office, which they both knew was regularly checked for listening devices using a Juke Box.

Finally Gabriella turned to the ambassador and spoke. "Ze'ev, I have four questions."

"Go ahead."

"First question: Does Sir William know that I'm the Mossad representative in London?"

"He's no fool, so he must have worked that out. Why else would I bring my Second Secretary to a security meeting unless she's really a top Mossad executive?"

"Fine. Second question: MI5 totally ignored the American warning and let Suleiman Haroun run free in Britain. What makes you think that the traitor in MI5 isn't going to protect Hassan Ali, too?"

"In this case, their hands are tied. With Suleiman Haroun, whoever it is who protected him will come up with some sort of story to explain what happened and they'll probably believe him. However, one of the reasons I brought you along this afternoon is that, with two diplomats briefing Sir William, or 'D' as they call him for some unknown reason, the traitor would be hard pressed to find a way of justifying any actions he may think of taking to protect Hassan Ali. And what's your third question, Gabriella?"

"Who's the mole on the executive committee of IFJLP?"

"There isn't one."

"I knew that. So why did you tell Sir William that there is?"

"We don't want anyone to know that we're getting all our information from the listening devices we planted in the agricultural college. Also, with any luck, the story about the mole will reach the ears of the executive committee, and they'll kill someone on the committee, just like they killed Ali Musa the Bombmaker. A good technique for destroying our enemies is to give them sufficient encouragement to murder one another. After all, facts don't matter to terrorists. All they need is the slightest suspicion, and that's good enough for an assassination."

"That makes sense. And my fourth and final question is this: You told Sir William about a nonexistent mole in the IFJLP. Am I correct that the primary reason that you did so was to alert him to the fact that we know that there's a pro-Islamist terrorist mole in MI5?"

Ze'ev Yaroq said nothing, but he grinned broadly.

CHAPTER SEVEN

The taxi dropped Hassan Ali at the departure hall at Ben Gurion Airport at five o'clock in the morning, more than four hours before his 9:15 flight to London. Passengers are usually not allowed to check in more than three hours before their scheduled departure time, but El Al personnel had received instructions to open flight LY315 at midnight. Consequently, when Hassan Ali looked up at the departures board, he saw that he could check in at Desk Twenty-Six.

As he neared the desk, a young security agent approached him. Mustapha had warned Hassan Ali that a security agent asks every El Al passenger a series of questions before check-in. The answers to the questions are not really important; what the highly trained security personnel are trying to determine is whether the passenger is unduly nervous and, if so, why. Hassan Ali had nothing to hide and nothing on his conscience. He handed over his Israeli passport.

"Mr. Al-Husseini, where were you born?"

"In Ayn Al-Ba'id—it's a small farming village in the Galilee."

"So you were born in Israel?"

"Yes."

"And where do you live now?"

"Still in Ayn Al-Ba'id, but I'm currently studying at an agricultural college."

Ilan's team was ensconced in a room in the basement of the airport terminal building. The moment the security agent started talking to Hassan Ali, a technician directed the appropriate video camera mounted in the ceiling of the departure hall on the pair, and homed in on them. At the same time, a second technician adjusted a shotgun microphone to point directly at Hassan Ali, so that they could hear and record every word he said. Ilan and his team were then able to watch the interchange on the video screens in the basement room while listening intently on their headphones.

"Mr. Al-Husseini, what is your destination today?"

"I'm flying to London."

"Thank you. And the purpose of your visit?"

"I'm spending three weeks at the Queen Victoria College of Agriculture at Tricester."

Hassan Ali had, perhaps not surprisingly, mispronounced "Tricester," but his interlocutor was none the wiser.

"Are you going straight to the Queen Victoria College of Agriculture?" The young man was sensible enough not to even try to pronounce "Tricester."

"No, I'm spending the weekend in London."

"And where in London are you staying, Mr. Al-Husseini?"

This was the question that Ilan's team had been waiting for. They had intensely coached the security agent as to how to ask the question. If he posed it too casually, Hassan Ali might reply, "At some house in northwest London." On the other hand, if the agent put too much emphasis in his voice, Hassan Ali might realize that the purpose of all the questioning was really this one single issue. In that case, he might well lie.

When push came to shove, the young man asked the question exactly as they had instructed him, and received the forthright answer from Hassan Ali, "I'm staying at 235 Swinderby Road, Wembley."

Ilan and his team were stupefied. Here was a suicide bomber blatantly giving away an address that MI5 and the Metropolitan Police had been trying to uncover for two months, with no success whatsoever.

"He's clean," Ilan insisted. "No Palestinian terrorist is going to tell an Israeli security agent the address of his safe house in London. This whole exercise is just a terrorist trap to discover whether or not we're bugging their agricultural college."

"I'm not so sure," Miri said. "My suspicion is that they're trying to send a suicide bomber to London by portraying him as totally clean and politically naïve. An excellent way of convincing us of that is to encourage him to give away the address of their safe house. After all, we can't follow him there and we can't stake out the safe house—that would give away the fact that we're listening in. So they lose nothing by giving away the address."

"You may be right," Ilan said, with obvious reluctance in his voice. "But either way, we continue with the plan."

While the two Mossad agents were discussing the various sides of the issue, the security agent had directed Hassan Ali to Desk Twenty-Six, where a smiling check-in clerk tagged his suitcase, handed him his boarding pass, and pointed in the direction of the emigration officers.

The border policeman seated in his booth hardly glanced at either the passport or the boarding pass that Hassan Ali handed him. He perfunctorily stamped both documents and handed them back, displaying the total lack of interest that characterizes so many members of his profession all over the world.

Hassan Ali now approached airport security. He put his new briefcase on the belt in front of the X-ray machine and walked through the metal detector. He was amazed that the agents treated him like every other passenger. He picked up his briefcase once it had passed inspection and looked for a seat in a waiting area. He had arrived more than four hours early at the airport in order to be sure that he would not miss his flight as a consequence of unending searches, but a glance at his watch showed that the complete check-in process had taken less than twenty minutes. Fortunately he had a book in his briefcase, so he sat and read it while waiting.

The boarding announcement eventually roused him from his reading. "Passengers in Economy Class will board by group number. Please look in the bottom right-hand corner of your boarding pass and check your boarding group number now."

Hassan Ali looked down and examined his boarding pass for the first time. He saw that he was sitting in seat 19B, and he was in Group Four. He waited patiently until the first three groups had boarded the plane and then lined up with the other passengers in his group. He handed his boarding pass to the pleasant-faced woman standing by the door to the jetway. She put it in the scanner, which emitted a soft approving beep. The woman reached across to another boarding pass lying next to the scanner. She handed it to Hassan Ali, saying, "This is your new seat," and immediately turned her attention to the next passenger standing in line.

Hassan Ali walked along the jetway, taking as little notice of the second boarding pass as he had of the previous one that the check-in clerk had issued to him. After all, one seat was as good as another. As he reached the door of the plane, one of the cabin crew asked him for his boarding pass and then escorted him to seat 1A, the window seat in the front row of the First Class cabin of the aircraft. Hassan noticed that there were only two rows of black leather seats in this part of the plane, all unoccupied so far, and he wondered why El Al had chosen him to sit in this luxurious area. He took his seat and, as he did so, a flight attendant proffered a tray brimming with glasses of champagne, orange juice, and water.

Hassan Ali had often wondered what champagne tasted like. He looked around again, saw that he was still alone in the First Class cabin and quickly took a glass of champagne. He drank it quickly, wanting to get rid of the glass before any other passengers entered the cabin and saw him breaking one of the precepts of Islam.

As he was drinking the last of the wonderful bubbly liquid, a tall, heavy-set man entered the First Class cabin and sat down next to him. A second or two later, he started coughing. Smoker's cough, thought Hassan Ali. But the coughing continued. The flight attendant with the tray reappeared. He offered the other passenger a glass of water, which he gratefully accepted to try to stem the coughing. The flight attendant then took Hassan Ali's now empty glass and offered him a second glass of champagne. Feeling guilty at having been caught consuming alcohol, Hassan Ali reluctantly refused.

A few minutes after finishing his glass of water, Hassan Ali's fellow passenger started coughing again. Hassan Ali looked at him, and saw that he was red-faced and sweating heavily. He looked feverish. He stole another glance and reached an inescapable conclusion—the passenger next to him was seriously ill. The flight attendant had noticed this as well and asked the sick passenger, "Sir, are you sure that you're well enough to fly?"

Trying to nod while coughing, the passenger indicated that there was no problem. The flight attendant did not seem convinced, but he wandered off in the direction of the First Class galley without taking the matter any further.

Nearly five hours later the plane neared Heathrow Airport. The other passenger had been coughing all through the flight. Several times he left his seat to go to the lavatory, apparently to throw up. On one such occasion, Hassan Ali had looked around the First Class cabin, and noted that only four of the eight seats were occupied; there were two middle-aged women in the row behind him, one in each window seat. When the aircraft landed and was approaching the gate, the pilot made an announcement.

"Ladies and gentlemen, please remain seated until the aircraft has come to a complete standstill at the gate and I've turned off the seatbelt sign. Quarantine officials will be coming aboard, and no one may leave the aircraft until they have cleared us. If you stand up and block the aisles, this will only slow down the process. So please remain seated until the medical authorities have cleared the aircraft. Thank you for your co-operation, and thank you for flying El Al."

Soon the door of the plane opened, and two men in uniform entered. They walked to the First Class cabin. The older man turned to the four passengers and said, politely but firmly, "Ladies and gentlemen, please take all your possessions and come with us."

Hassan Ali, his sick neighbor and the two women gathered their belongings and followed the older man. The younger official brought up the rear of the short procession. They walked from the aircraft to a flight of stairs that led down from the jetway onto the apron, and from there to an inconspicuous entrance to the terminal building. The entrance led to a corridor with numbered doors on each side. Each of the four passengers was asked to go to a different room. Hassan Ali was assigned Room Three, which seemed to be some sort of hotel room. Another quarantine officer followed him into the room. He was wearing a protective gown, gloves and mask.

"Sir, may I please see your passport?"

Hassan Ali handed it to the official, who looked through it.

"Sir, as I am sure you noticed, the passenger who was seated next to you is a very sick man indeed. In fact, the Israeli authorities should never have allowed him to board the aircraft in his condition. We are greatly concerned that he may have a communicable disease, one that he may have passed on to you."

Hassan Ali suddenly felt cold shivers going down his back. The official continued, "The next step will be to determine exactly what's wrong with your seatmate. As soon as I know anything, I promise you that I'll get back to you. In the meantime, I'm afraid that you'll have to remain here, in this quarantine room. I assure you that the bed is comfortable, I'm certain that the TV works, and there are books and magazines on the shelf over there. There may even be some films you haven't seen yet in the pile of DVDs in that cabinet on the right. The en suite is behind you. You'll get three excellent meals a day, all strictly halal, of course.

"We'll stay in constant touch with you, updating you as soon as we have any definite information.

We'll deliver your luggage to you here just as soon as it comes off the aircraft. Feel free to let your family know the situation—your cell phone should work in here and there's Wifi, of course, for your laptop or tablet. The network name is 'quarantine-station' and the password is 'blackdeath'—just a tasteless inside-joke, sir, I assure you.

"Of course, sir," he added, "we're extremely sorry for the inconvenience but, as I explained, this unfortunate eventuality is not of our doing. Let's just hope that you haven't caught whatever it is that your fellow passenger has."

Hassan Ali was utterly bewildered at his change of fortune. He had been looking forward with the greatest of eagerness to his weekend in London. And he had been determined to learn as much as possible from his three weeks at the Queen Victoria College of Agriculture. And now he was in prison. A luxurious prison, certainly, but a prison no less.

Toward evening the quarantine official re-entered the room. Hassan Ali had spent the day glancing fitfully through magazines and channel surfing on the wide-screen TV, interrupted only by attendants bringing in his meals and removing the trays afterward. For their protection, all the attendants were also gowned, gloved, and masked, thereby increasing Hassan Ali's feeling of isolation and alienation. His mood was low. He felt powerless. At one stage he wondered if his drinking the glass of champagne had caused his predicament. He tried to put that thought out of his mind, but it kept coming back. By the time the official returned, Hassan Ali was thoroughly racked by guilt at the sin he had committed on the plane.

The quarantine officer wore a mask over most of his face, but his body language made it obvious to Hassan Ali that the official did not have good news. He invited Hassan Ali to sit down. Then he told him what had transpired.

"Sir, we've taken your fellow passenger to an isolation hospital. For reasons of confidentiality I cannot tell you what he's suffering from but, having sat next to him for five hours, you know as well as I do that it's a serious condition. When he recovers, El Al will fly him straight back to Israel."

Hassan Ali was glad to hear the words "when he recovers"—clearly this was not a fatal disease, should he have caught it. But the official was still speaking.

"Now we come to you. The quarantine period for the disease is thirty days. That is, if he's infected you, we would know within that time. So, sir, I can offer you two choices. First, you can stay in this room for thirty days. If you're well at that time, you'll be free to enter Britain."

"But I'm only here for a three-week visit."

"In that case, sir, I suggest you take the other choice. The next El Al flight back to Israel is tomorrow night; as I'm sure you know, El Al does not fly on the Jewish Sabbath. You'll stay in this room until then. When the aircraft is ready, you'll fly back to Israel, first class of course. And El Al will refund you the cost of your ticket in full. Then, if you wish to return to Britain after thirty days, you'll need to undergo a medical examination by one of the doctors on the list at the British Embassy in Tel Aviv. Of course, El Al would have to pay for the examination—the whole situation is entirely due to their carelessness. If I were in your position, sir, I would sue El Al, but don't tell anyone I said so."

And the quarantine officer left the room. He walked to the end of the corridor, turned left and entered a room where Yossi was sitting. Yossi had removed the make-up that made him look ill, and was no longer wearing the woolen clothing under his shirt that had caused him to sweat so profusely. The quarantine officer took off his protective gear, offered a cigarette to Yossi and lit up one himself.

"Other than having coughed your lungs out, how are you doing?" he asked.

"Working for the Mossad is no joke, I can tell you that. You MI5 boys just wear fancy uniforms and pretend to be quarantine officers, but I had to act sick for five hours at a stretch."

"It's all for a good cause," said the MI5 officer, soothingly. "And there are a lot worse situations for people in our profession."

"That's for sure," replied Yossi. "Now tell me, what's with our friend in Room Three?"

"As we both knew would happen, he's chosen to fly back tomorrow night. Not surprisingly, he didn't really fancy thirty days in quarantine."

"Does he suspect anything?"

"Not a thing. By the way, the only part of this performance that I don't understand was your giving him a seat in the First Class cabin," said the MI5 officer. "Why did you put him there?"

"There were only two other passengers with seats in that section, two older women. After your colleagues had escorted them off the aircraft, they were kept in quarantine for about fifteen minutes. Then we told them that we'd determined that the sick man wasn't infectious, and gave each of them a free limousine ride to their respective destinations in London for their trouble. If we'd had to quarantine the whole Economy section, it would've been a nightmare."

CHAPTER EIGHT

"What now, Abdul Rahman?" Mustapha asked. The executive committee was meeting in the third-floor room over the spice shop in Souq Khan el-Zayit, in East Jerusalem. The overall mood of the meeting was anger. Two of the members, Mustapha and Mahmoud ibn Laban, were boiling with rage.

"Your plan," Mustapha continued, "was a total disaster. First, you still have no proof that the Israelis are listening in. I, for one, have never believed that they bugged the college, and I still don't believe it."

Heads around the table nodded in agreement.

"Furthermore," Mustapha added, "for all our time, effort, and money we have gained nothing."

"But we have lost nothing," Abdul Rahman retorted.

"Not so," Mustapha answered. "The experience has politicized Hassan Ali."

"*Subhan Allah* (Allah is glorious)!" Abdul Rahman exclaimed. "That's wonderful news!"

"Not exactly," Mustapha replied drily. "He's been politicized *against* the Palestinian cause."

"What, two flights in First Class at no cost to him, and two days in a luxury hotel room, and he's against us? How can that be?"

"He's not stupid, Abdul Rahman, and his adventures have opened his eyes as to how utterly incompetent we are. First, look at our truly marvelous achievements. We set up a cell in London at 181b Elmwood Avenue, Kenton, with a safe house at 235 Swinderby Road, Wembley. We somehow managed—and I still haven't been told how we did it—to transport an explosive vest, fully loaded with top-quality Semtex and small, perfectly round steel balls, to our London cell. But then what happened? Suleiman blew himself up at the Elmwood Avenue house, taking Yussuf, Ibrahim and Abubakar with him and destroying our cell. And where did he hide all but a tiny fraction of the Semtex? We don't know, and we haven't been able to find out."

"But Scotland Yard can't find it either," Abdul Rahman interposed.

"That's of no relevance to us. Our Saudi benefactor provided us with the finest Semtex, and we've lost it. He's never going to give us any more Semtex, or any more money either, for that matter. *Yela'an* (dammit)!"

"Mustapha, I agree that the Suleiman Haroun operation was a disaster. But what happened to Hassan Ali was just kismet—we are all helpless against the unseen hand of fate."

"Fate? What's fate got to do with it? We were once again outsmarted by the Israelis."

"Outsmarted how?" Abdul Rahman asked. "El Al decided to be nice to the first Palestinian passenger they've had for years, if ever, and upgraded him to First Class at no charge. It was just bad luck that he happened to sit next to that sick passenger."

"Oh, it was bad luck, was it? Don't you realize that the Israelis deliberately sat the sick man next to Hassan Ali?"

"Mustapha, old friend and colleague, we Arabs are prone to seeing a conspiracy under every bed, but even for a loyal Arab nationalist and jihadi like yourself, that's a bit of a stretch. A sick passenger, holding a First Class ticket, turns up at Ben Gurion Airport. On the spur of the moment, the Israelis say, 'We rewarded that Palestinian with a free upgrade not just to Business Class, but to First Class. Now let's punish him by seating him next to that sick passenger.' And tell me this: How could the Israelis have known that one of the women sitting behind Hassan Ali would phone her husband in London just before the plane took off and tell him about the sick passenger? And, fiendishly clever as you think the Zionist dogs are, how could they possibly have been aware that her husband is the head of a major London hospital, and that he would immediately contact the airport health authorities? An Israeli conspiracy is one thing, but you're going much too far. I know that, as a loyal Palestinian, you're as upset as we all are, but enough is enough."

"Precisely, Abdul Rahman, enough is enough. One humiliating defeat is more than enough. This second disaster is more than I am prepared to tolerate. And I think that I speak for all of us."

There were emphatic nods around the table.

"My friends," Abdul Rahman responded, "we've had two reversals. I freely admit that. But that's no reason to get despondent. We can establish a new cell in London, find the Semtex, and have an even greater triumph there than we had on 7 July 2005, *Inshallah*."

"How, Abdul Rahman? How? How exactly do you propose to establish a new cell? And we've been looking for the Semtex for months, to no avail. And don't tell us yet again about Scotland Yard—that's old news, and it's of absolutely no interest to us. Repeating yourself over and over like an old beggar in the Souk pleading for alms doesn't help matters.

"Instead, explain to us in detail how you're going to find the Semtex. And how you intend to transport the material we need for a suicide bomb to London. Are you going to give Hassan Ali every bit of equipment he would need and tell him to take it with him to London on an El Al flight?"

"Mustapha, I understand how you feel, but please be reasonable. The Israelis have continually humiliated our people since the *naqba*, the catastrophe of 1948. But now the tide is turning. We must fight back, not just here in Palestine, but all over the world, *Inshallah*!"

"How exactly do you want us to fight back? With suicide bombers who kill their handlers instead of the enemy? With naïve students who have now turned against their own people and are telling their fellow students how wonderful the Zionists are? Abdul Rahman, you're finished. Hand over your keys and leave this room forever. *Yaqta omrak* (may Allah cut your life short)!"

Abdul Rahman ibn Sultan looked around the table. All he saw were looks of hatred and contempt. Trying to retain his dignity, he stood up, took his keys out of his pocket, laid them carefully on the table and walked slowly out of the room.

Mahmoud ibn Laban stood, too, saying, "I'll unlock the door to let him out." They both left the room. Two sets of footsteps descended the stairs. A few seconds later, the sound of a shot broke the heavy silence. Neither man returned.

"Should I take the chair?" Mustapha asked the remaining executive committee members.

The seven other men all nodded, but some did so more enthusiastically than others. Mustapha moved from the foot to the head of the table.

"Now," he said, "where do we go to from here?"

There was a long silence.

"I have an idea I'd like to bounce off you," Mustapha said. "Here's how I see the situation. We're fighting on two fronts: As Palestinians, we're engaged in reconquering Palestine from the Zionist enemy, and as jihadis we're involved in a world-wide all-out Holy War against non-Muslims to re-establish the Caliphate everywhere. Our weakness is that we don't have any sort of base outside Palestine from which to wage war on the infidels. We used to have a base in London but, thanks to Abdul Rahman, we no longer have it. It's easy to establish a base anywhere in the world—all we have to do is raise the funds and buy or rent a house in the desired location. The problem is getting the tools of war to that base."

The other members of the executive were totally engaged. Seven pairs of eyes were focused on Mustapha as he continued to lay out his plan.

"It's essentially impossible to transport explosives by plane. Governments are scrutinizing passengers and their luggage like never before, and now they're examining air freight equally carefully."

The men nodded.

"We used to be able to transport explosives on ships. However, it's become impossible to obtain explosives like Semtex without a taggant. And the latest taggants emit some sort of vapor that sticks to the ship, leaving behind a traceable signature. So modern explosives are out. And no captain, not even a jihadi, is prepared to carry second-hand TNT. It's one thing to die for the glory of Islam. It's quite another to have your ship blow up in mid-ocean."

"Surely it's not that dangerous," one of the men interjected. Mustapha fixed him with a long stare before answering.

"Imagine this," he said. "At the bottom of the hold of a ship a wooden crate filled with inferior TNT lies hidden. Because it has so many impurities, residue continually oozes out, leaving cracks and small holes that greatly increase the shock sensitivity, until finally a big wave hits the side of the ship and …"—he made an explosive gesture with both hands—"… *boom!*"

Mustapha shook his head. "No. Transportation of explosives in cargo vessels is now out of the question, too."

He paused for a few seconds, and then resumed his lecture. "Well, what about transporting explosives in a car from the Arab world to Europe? There are two problems. The first is the border guards. They're becoming exceedingly clever, and these days they're aided by dogs and electronic sensors that can detect a taggant even in the tiniest of quantities, especially the DMDNB in Semtex. The second problem is that, if you think transporting explosives on a cargo ship is perilous, wait until you drive on the bumpy roads of Eastern Europe.

"The dilemma seems hopeless. But I think I've found a way. The problem is this: Where in Europe can we establish an explosives cache? And the answer is simple: the Greek islands. We can acquire whatever we need in the way of weapons and explosives in Lebanon, and then transport our supplies in a fast motorboat to our island. From the island we can easily travel by boat to the Greek mainland, as well as to other Mediterranean countries, in order to wage violent jihad against the infidels. So, I propose that we establish a base on one of the thousands of Greek Islands." Mustapha sat down.

This speech was met with several seconds of stunned silence. Then the other members of the executive committee rose to their feet and applauded enthusiastically. The clapping finally stopped and everyone sat down again.

A man seated near the far end of the table raised his hand. "Have you chosen an island?"

"Not really. I need your advice here. One possibility would be to select one of the numerous uninhabited islands. But that would lead to major logistical problems—issues with food, water and electricity—in addition to inviting unwanted suspicion. After all, why would a sane person build a house on an uninhabited island when there's no shortage of fine homes available at reasonable prices on the inhabited ones? The only explanation we could offer would be to achieve total isolation, and that in turn would lead to lots of really undesirable questions being asked. So that cuts the choice down from thousands to two hundred or so. For the same two reasons, logistics and averting suspicion, I think we should choose from those islands with at least a hundred inhabitants. That reduces the number of suitable islands down to about seventy-five. But then there's the converse problem: the larger the population of the island, the more prying eyes."

Once more, the members of the executive committee were totally absorbed by Mustapha's presentation.

"Then there's another issue. From what I've been able to determine, small islands all over the world breed a close-knit community. In particular, strangers are generally unwelcome. And when the strangers are Arabs, there can be open animosity, or worse. So, we need an island with a population of reasonable size that will not react too violently when we purchase or rent a large house on the island. And that brings me to Ziyad bin Abu Dawud, that *ibn al-kalb* (son of a dog).

"I am fully aware that many of you seated around this table know my no-good ex-brother-in-law only too well. If there was a major scandal, he wasn't just involved, he was usually the instigator. There was no criminal endeavor that he didn't want to participate in, usually as the leader. Eventually things go too hot for him in the Arab world, so he took his millions—or more likely, billions—and moved to Krotonos. It's one of the Cycladic Islands."

Mustapha stopped speaking for a moment when he saw the puzzled expression on his colleagues' faces. He then explained. "The Cyclades are a group of over two hundred islands arranged in a rough circle around the sacred island of Delos—the Greek word for a circle is *kyklos*, or something like that. The Cyclades lie to the southeast of Athens, and not too far away from that city. We've all heard of Santorini, of course. Well, that island in the Cyclades is one of the furthest from Athens, and yet it's only about a hundred and fifty miles away. And Krotonos is about ninety miles from Athens, an easy trip in a fast motorboat.

"Anyhow, Ziyad bin Abu Dawud tried to use his huge fortune, every last piastre obtained illegally, to buy acceptance from the islanders. First, knowing how conservative the islanders are, he made sure never to appear in public with more than one woman at a time, and she had to be exceedingly modestly dressed. He built a huge house, but he surrounded it with a high wall. Also, he made sure

that the rooms were all soundproofed, so the
islanders never learned about the wild, drug-fuelled
orgies that went on inside.

"Ziyad turned the island of Krotonos into a sort
of botanical paradise. He paid for the planting of
indigenous trees everywhere, especially in the
squares. He built a municipal auditorium and
subsidized the fees of top performers. No, there
were no rock stars or anything like that; it was only
ancient Greek plays and traditional Greek music. He
used to joke that Krotonos had become the
bouzouki capital of the world—that's a time-
honored Greek musical instrument, something like
our own oud. But none of that worked. Ziyad bin
Abu Dawud was treated as a total outsider, or worse.
You know how the Greeks feel about the Turks.
Well, Turks are Muslims and Arabs are Muslims, so
the islanders referred to him as 'The Turk' and
treated him accordingly.

"Finally he came up with the answer. You all
know how crazy the Greeks are about soccer—
they're even more fanatical than us, and that's saying
something. Anyhow, Ziyad built a soccer field with a
grandstand, he paid for uniforms and boots, and he
brought in top soccer coaches from Athens. That
did the trick. Ziyad went from pariah to local hero
overnight. They even elected him to the island
council, and you usually have to be a tenth-
generation islander just for someone to nominate
you for the council, let alone get elected. There was
even some talk of him becoming the mayor, but

Ziyad bin Abu Dawud was much too smart to fall for that.

"Having said that, I don't want you to get the idea that every islander loves Ziyad. He has several opponents. Some of them are just xenophobes— they hate all foreigners no matter what. And a few of the local inhabitants of Krotonos are sufficiently intelligent to be able to see through Ziyad and his tricks. But the vast majority of the 2,500 or so islanders seem to like Ziyad bin Abu Dawud, and are grateful for what he has done for Krotonos and its people.

"Anyhow, what I am getting at is that, as a result of Ziyad's machinations, Arabs are not entirely unwelcome on Krotonos. But we have to be careful. We don't want to get involved with Ziyad bin Abu Dawud in any way. He'd befriend us and turn us into the authorities in the same breath."

Another hand went up. "How do we buy a house there without interacting with Ziyad?"

"We don't have to worry about that for now, because I've heard that Ziyad mysteriously disappeared about two months ago. The rumor I heard is that an executioner from the Russian Mafia is responsible, but that may just be wishful thinking. In any event, I strongly suggest that we use a realtor. We'll tell him we need a house outside the main town, right on a sandy beach. In that way, we can easily bring the shipment ashore at night, but the locals won't be watching us as we do so. And the house has to have a cellar, of course, that we can securely lock. When our realtor has found what he thinks is a suitable place, we'll pay a visit to Krotonos. If he's come up with what we need, we'll give him a power of attorney to close the deal, acting on behalf of a company we'll establish in some obscure offshore tax haven. And we'll have our base from which to wage jihad, *Inshallah*."

CHAPTER NINE

Pantelis Papakostas was sitting at their usual outside table at the café overlooking the fishing harbor on Krotonos when Heracles Stavridis joined him for their daily early morning cup of coffee. As Heracles reached Pantelis, they greeted one another the way that the men of Krotonos have greeted one another for centuries: They shook hands while leaning forward to touch their lips lightly to their friend's right cheek and then their left cheek.

An observer standing nearby watching this performance would not be able to see the second ritual that simultaneously took place as they kissed each other, because their bodies hid the secret handshake. The two young men did not grasp one another's palms, but rather grabbed each other's wrists. Furthermore, the observer would not have been able to hear them whisper in each other's right ear as they kissed: "Death to all Muslims." Pantelis and Heracles were active in the Hellenic Spartan League, an extreme right-wing organization with the aim of ridding Greece of all "non-Greeks."

The two of them had been inseparable friends since early childhood, both born on Krotonos, the sons of fishermen. They had been in the same class in the local school. During their compulsory military service, they had served in the same platoon of a light infantry battalion. After six months, they had volunteered for the *Evzones*, the Greek Presidential Guard; neither had any trouble in meeting the stringent minimum height requirement of six feet, one and a quarter inches to join that elite ceremonial unit. As passionate nationalists, they had reveled in parading in public in the traditional Greek uniform: scarlet fez with a long black silk tassel; long navy-blue tunic in winter, khaki in summer; white cotton kilt with four hundred pleats, representing the four hundred years of Ottoman occupation; long white woolen stockings; black garters; and heavy red leather clogs with black pompoms and up to a hundred nails under the right sole. The highly formalized marching style, which included goose-stepping and striking the ground forcefully for several paces with the nailed boot, was another aspect that they both loved, and when they left the Guard at the end of their service they did so with the greatest reluctance.

They had joined the Hellenic Spartan League soon after returning home. The whole island had thrown a party to welcome the handsome heroes back. Toward dawn, when the celebration finally seemed to be winding down, Sergeant Kyrgiakos, the head of the four-man police force on the island, took them aside.

"You two are true patriots," he said.

Pantelis and Heracles just nodded. They were extremely drunk by this time and weren't really listening to what the sergeant was saying, or to anyone else for that matter.

"Come to my house tomorrow night at nine," Sergeant Kyrgiakos said.

The two ex-soldiers just nodded again.

At nine fifteen that night, a policeman knocked on the door of the Stavridis house. Heracles's father opened the door.

"Where's your son?"

"What's he done this time?" was the reply. "He's been back only one day, so he can't have gotten up to too much mischief yet."

"Heracles and Pantelis were supposed to be at the sergeant's house at nine o'clock this evening. They weren't there, so Sergeant Kyrgiakos sent me to fetch them."

"They're both here, watching soccer on TV. I'll call them."

Five minutes later Heracles and Pantelis crammed into the main room of the Kyrgiakos house, together with the sergeant and the three burly policemen under his command. There was no sign of Mrs. Kyrgiakos or their three daughters—Sergeant Kyrgiakos had presumably ordered them to visit friends until the meeting was over.

After making sure that everyone had a full glass of retsina, Sergeant Kyrgiakos opened the gathering with a virulent diatribe against all immigrants living in Greece, but especially Muslims. He ascribed all the ills of Greek society to aliens. His pitch was far more than just nationalistic in tone; it was racist and xenophobic. As he spoke, the other three policemen nodded approvingly. Perhaps it was because their heads were still aching from their severe hangovers, or perhaps because they had occasionally heard similar views expressed considerably less forcefully by a few of their fellow soldiers, but Heracles and Pantelis found themselves nodding approvingly, too. An hour later they had joined the Hellenic Spartan League.

Weekly meetings followed, usually held at the Kyrgiakos home. Most of the time the sergeant read the latest League bulletin out loud, and the five other members of the Krotonos branch of the League enthusiastically endorsed the hateful propaganda emanating from party headquarters in Athens. On one occasion there was a guest speaker from a nearby island, but he was by no means as passionately xenophobic as Sergeant Kyrgiakos, so the exercise was not repeated. Week after week the two men were exposed to this neo-Nazi ultranationalistic poison, and eventually it infected them at a time when they were in the process of changing their way of life.

When they came back to Krotonos after their national service, each had returned to working for his father on the family fishing boat, but they soon felt constrained by that occupation. In the words of the highly popular song about farm boys returning to America at the end of World War I, it was a classic case of "How Ya Gonna Keep 'Em Down on the Farm (After They've Seen Paree)?" But although they both decided that the life of a fisherman was not for them, neither was prepared to even think about leaving the island; Krotonos was in their blood. Each day after the boats had returned to the fishing harbor, they discussed the issue at length. Finally they decided to set themselves up as guides, offering walking tours of the town to the many tourists who visited the picturesque island by ferry. At the start, their high school English was barely adequate, but their extreme good looks and tanned muscular bodies hardened by military drills and repeatedly pulling heavy nets out of the water seemed to make up for their limited vocabulary and a multitude of grammatical errors, at least with women visiting Krotonos. And interactions with a considerable number of attractive young female tourists on a more intimate level led to a steady improvement of their English language skills.

After a year, they had earned enough money to pay a substantial deposit toward the cost of a home of their own, a typical one-room island house consisting of a living/dining room with kitchen in the rear, and a stepladder leading to the sleeping loft. Each month they paid the bank not just their required mortgage payment, but also a further sum to reduce the principal. Even on winter days, when tourism slowed to a trickle, they were almost always able to find at least one couple to engage their services. When business was slow, they conducted the walking tours together.

Living in their own home, rather than with their parents, meant that they never had to explain to anyone where they were going or why. This made it easier for them to devote a large part of their limited free time to the Krotonos branch of the Hellenic Spartan League. The primary target of the local branch was Ziyad bin Abu Dawud. At the second meeting they attended, Heracles and Pantelis were astonished to hear a stream of vile invective directed against their island's benefactor. They learned, much to their surprise, that the true purpose of Ziyad's philanthropy was to soften the islanders so that they would not object when he introduced his real objective, Sharia Law. That was why, they discovered, he now served on the island council.

Heracles pointed out that pious Muslims abstained from alcohol and pork, whereas Ziyad indulged freely in both. This observation was met with mocking laughter.

"Of course he breaks Islamic Law in public— he's just lulling us all into a sense of false security. Once the Muslims take control again, there'll be no alcohol and no pigs on this island, and we won't be able to eat and drink whatever we want. That's how it was when the Ottoman Turks ruled Greece."

Heracles tried again. "But what about the soccer field and the uniforms and everything? And the theatre and the music and the plays?"

"Muslims love soccer, too—he built the field for his co-religionists, for when the time comes. And haven't you noticed that some Arab music sounds suspiciously like Greek music? The Arabs stole our music, too."

The forceful way with which the sergeant spoke convinced Pantelis and Heracles that Ziyad was indeed bent on Muslim reconquest of the island.

Soon they started to implicitly believe other equally preposterous declarations from Sergeant Kyrgiakos and his three colleagues, who seemed to spend most of their time working for the Hellenic Spartan League. Fortunately for the local inhabitants, there was almost no crime on Krotonos, so the lack of wholehearted commitment to law enforcement on the part of the island constabulary went largely unnoticed.

A Coast Guard patrol boat policed the waters around Krotonos and the neighboring islands. If the patrol boat was moored in Krotonos Harbor on a Wednesday night, the weekly gathering was held on board the vessel. Lieutenant Cosmatos and his crew of five were as enthusiastic about the Hellenic Spartan League as the police force on Krotonos. But they were more bloodthirsty in their hatred of Ziyad bin Abu Dawud. Every meeting of the League had to end with the cry, "Death to all Muslims." However, when meetings were held on the Coast Guard patrol boat, this was followed in addition by the shout, "And death to Ziyad bin Abu Dawud."

Accordingly, when Ziyad suddenly disappeared from Krotonos, neither Heracles nor Pantelis was at all surprised. Nor were they in any way shocked when the unavoidable police investigation into Ziyad bin Abu Dawud's disappearance lasted less than ninety minutes. And they fully understood why subsequent meetings on the Coast Guard patrol boat had concluded with only the standard "Death to all Muslims" cry. Sadly, none of this bothered them, and they continued to sleep well at night.

CHAPTER TEN

"The distance from here in Beirut to the island is almost exactly six hundred miles," Mustapha said to Sheikh Mansour ibn Aziz Arabiya. "Does your price include shipping?"

The sheikh laughed. "*Habibi* (my friend), once the shipment leaves this warehouse, that's it. You inspect the goods inside my warehouse, you give me the cash, and then you and your men take the goods to your truck. What happens after that does not concern me."

"Can you sell me a fast cabin cruiser? And what about hiring a truck to get the shipment from your warehouse to the port?"

Sheikh Mansour laughed again. "*Habibi*, I'm an arms dealer, not a shipping agent. If you want to buy a reconditioned military transport plane to fly your goods to your island, I can sell you one. But I strongly advise you against trying that; the Greek Air Force will shoot you down long before you reach your destination. I can supply you with a couple of different fast attack boats. I have an American World War II PT boat in really excellent condition. I even have a missile boat ... much faster than the PT.

But either would be a terrible idea. The Greek Coast Guard is equipped with superlative radar, and they'd blow you out of existence the moment you crossed the six-mile limit. No, what you need is a fast civilian cabin cruiser to transport your purchases to your island, but I don't sell those."

Sheikh Mansour smiled broadly and waited for his unspoken message to become evident to Mustapha. It took the IFJLP leader less than a second to receive the signal and process it correctly.

"Sheikh Mansour, I was wondering if you have a cousin who could sell me a suitable vessel, with an inflatable dinghy, like a Zodiac, on board, to get our shipment ashore."

"Of course I do, *habibi*, and he's ready to do business with you. And he has a cousin who will rent you a truck and a team of three men to load your purchases into the truck and unload them from there into your new boat. The three men will then crew your boat, and unload your purchases when they've taken you to your island."

"And those three men are his cousins, of course?"

"Of course, *habibi*, of course they are. And all the contracts are on my desk, ready for you to sign. And you have to pay for all this in cash, of course."

"Of course."

***

From Beirut, Mustapha flew to Athens, and from there he took a ferry to Krotonos. The realtor was waiting at the ferry port. His navy-blue blazer, crisp white shirt, and striped rep tie clashed with the weathered white houses, blue shutters, and cobblestone streets.

"Welcome! I have my car here if you would like me to drive you to the house," said the realtor, "but I would strongly suggest that we walk there. That will give you a better idea of the location of the property in relation to the town and, perhaps more importantly, you'll be able to experience for yourself how gloriously isolated the site is."

"Walking will be fine," Mustapha replied.

"It's the only house on the island that meets all three of your requirements: It's on a sandy beach, it's isolated, and it has a cellar," the realtor continued. "Here on Krotonos we have to build our houses directly on the solid volcanic rock of the island, so it costs far too much to dig out a cellar. The previous owner went to enormous expense to construct his cellar, and you'll reap the benefit. Of course, you'll immediately notice that the house has a most undesirable feature, a high wall surrounding it on all four sides. That's a major reason why the current owner, a Lebanese woman, I understand, is so anxious to sell. In fact, the whole situation is rather strange. By the way, I'm telling you all this because that's how we do business here—full disclosure even to the point of possibly losing a sale, but then no comebacks afterward."

"I like to do business that way myself," Mustapha replied.

"I'm delighted to hear that," the realtor said. "As I was telling you, the house was occupied by a Mr. Ziyad bin Abu Dawud, an Arab gentleman like yourself. He was the island benefactor, and then some. He built a beautiful auditorium for us, he brought out actors and musicians who attracted an audience from all over the Cyclades—Krotonos became a center for classical drama and traditional Greek music. Why, people sometimes even came all the way from Athens for some of the performances he sponsored. He paid for a wonderful soccer field, too, and he even hired top coaches to train our children. The coaches have left, of course, with no one to pay their salaries, but we still have the soccer field and the uniforms. And did I mention the grandstand? He must have devoted tens of millions of euros and countless hours to beautifying Krotonos and improving our resources.

"Anyhow, one day Mr. Zeta just disappeared. We all called him that, because 'zeta' is the first letter of the name Ziyad when it's written in Greek. His disappearance was most peculiar. He was last seen walking by himself on Argos Beach directly in front of his house. That was strange in itself; I can't recall ever seeing him without an assistant and a bodyguard. Anyhow, that was the last anyone saw of him. At that time, the local Coast Guard patrol boat was fortunately located somewhere not too far from Krotonos, and Lieutenant Cosmatos—he's the skipper—was able to look back through some radar records and determine definitively that there were no boats near Argos Beach at the time of the disappearance. Sergeant Kyrgiakos and his three police constables searched the island, but with no success. Finally, about two weeks after he vanished, the police in Athens instructed Sergeant Kyrgiakos to make detailed inquiries; it seems that some important people were concerned about the whereabouts of Mr. Zeta. The police broke into the building, but it was deserted. It seems that a day or two after Mr. Zeta disappeared, all the other people living in the house had taken the ferry for Athens, and that was the last anyone has seen of any of them. The conclusion we all came to is that Mr. Zeta had committed suicide by walking into the sea. That would explain why he was all by himself when he left the house. However, bodies of drowned people usually end up on shore, possibly on a neighboring island, but they've found nothing so far."

"I see," Mustapha said, hoping that the realtor would change the subject. Unfortunately for Mustapha, the realtor seemed to think that "full disclosure" included every detail of the apparent death of the previous owner.

"Sergeant Kyrgiakos," he continued, "made a report to his superiors in Athens, and that was that—or so we all thought. But about ten days later two detective inspectors arrived from Athens. They went to the house and found that Sergeant Kyrgiakos and his men had not secured the gate and the front door properly, because the whole building was now totally empty. We all assumed that the thieves had arrived by sea from other islands, beaching their boats in front of the house, and had helped themselves to the contents of the villa. One thing is for sure. Nothing from inside the house has turned up here on Krotonos, thank goodness. We certainly wouldn't want to be living here with anyone dishonest."

"Of course not," Mustapha said, wondering if the realtor ever realized that the "island benefactor, and then some" was as crooked as they came.

The realtor continued the saga. "With the house stripped of all its contents and its occupants having left for parts unknown, there were few clues for the detective inspectors. So they left for Ermoupoli, on the island of Syros. Ermoupoli is the capital of the South Aegean region of Greece—that's the Cyclades, the island group where we now are, plus the Dodecanese Islands, like Rhodes and Kos, which are situated next to the coast of Turkey. All the official records for the whole region are stored in their beautiful huge white marble city hall—it's around the corner from the Cathedral of St. Nicholas—so the detective inspectors went there and asked to see the title deeds for Mr. Zeta's house. It went without saying that we all had assumed that a billionaire like Mr. Zeta owned his own house; people who have unlimited money buy their permanent residence, they don't rent. But much to everyone's surprise, it turned out that some woman who lived in Beirut owned the house. The detective inspectors from Athens then contacted her. She told them that she'd known Mr. Zeta socially, but she hadn't seen him for years and years, and she knew nothing about a house anywhere, let alone on some obscure Greek island. Her reaction to the phone call was that this was a practical joke of some kind. The police, however, don't make jokes when billionaires disappear, especially billionaires who spend tens of millions on improvements to our beautiful Greek islands. The detective inspectors sent an official report to the Beirut police, and a few days later the owner arrived here, accompanied by the two detective inspectors from Athens. By that time either the Lebanese police or the Greek police had managed to convince her that she indeed owned the house. We later learned that Mr. Zeta had bought the house, paid for it in cash and put the purchase in her name without telling her anything at all about it. Weird, isn't it?"

"Yes, it certainly is," Mustapha replied.

The realtor, pleased that Mustapha tended to agree with him, persisted. "I was told that she took one look at the house and announced, 'Sell it!' I'm now the only realtor left on the island, so the inspectors escorted her to my agency. It's on the other side of the square over there, next to that butcher shop—we can go there on our way back. Anyhow, the owner was a woman of about fifty, I reckon. Twenty years ago I'm sure that she was truly beautiful, but today ...

"Perhaps it was alcohol that did the damage, perhaps it was drugs. Anyhow, she told me that she wanted to sell the house. I pointed out to her that she could get much, much more for the house if she demolished the outside wall and put picture windows in all the rooms, especially those that would then overlook Argos Beach, one of the most glorious beaches in the Cyclades. She just said, 'Sell it as is.' I suspect that she's destitute. Anyhow, I drew up the necessary papers, she signed them and she left the island. I put a color photograph of Argos Beach that I took standing in front of Mr. Zeta's house—or, more correctly, in front of what we all thought was Mr. Zeta's house—in the plate glass window of my agency. I labeled the photograph 'Glorious Location of Beach House' in English, in the hope that a visiting millionaire—or better still, another billionaire—would recognize the potential of the site, knock down the house, and construct either a palatial home for himself, or perhaps a hotel. To tell the truth, as I strive to do at all times, of course—"

"Naturally," Mustapha interposed.

"I wasn't expecting to sell the property. I felt sorry for the owner, obviously, but I certainly wasn't anticipating that she'd be able to sell the house in the near- or even medium-term future. My concern was that, when the annual property taxes fell due, she wouldn't be able to afford to pay them, so she'd lose the house to the municipality. In the long term, I had visions of the house being unoccupied for decades and eventually falling into ruin—and that would be very bad for a picture-perfect island like Krotonos. And then your associate contacted me. That was why I was able to tell him, right away, that I had just the house he was looking for and that it was priced for a quick sale. We're almost there, it's just around this bend."

Mustapha breathed a sigh of relief. The "full disclosure" had clearly come to an end. Now he could examine the property and decide whether to buy it as a base for the IFJLP. The realtor, however, having cleared his conscience, now started on the hard sell.

"Just look at that incomparable beach—the white sand goes on forever in both directions!"

"Yes, it does," Mustapha said, taking the line of least resistance. Unfortunately, that didn't work. The realtor had done his homework and was determined to close the sale then and there.

He continued: "For some reason, no one thought of buying the land from the farmer who owned it until Mr. Zeta arrived. Most surprising, because this piece of land has the greatest possible potential. As I indicated, an investor could build a luxury seaside hotel here. Another excellent idea would be to construct a block of condominiums—you could sell them to Americans for a lot of money. A yacht harbor would be perfect—there are no rocks except on the far ends of this white, white beach. Or a marina. I once took the liberty of suggesting to Mr. Zeta that he develop the site. He was scrupulously polite, of course, as he always was, to me and to everyone else, but he made it unambiguously clear that he valued his privacy and that was why he had built his house here. I never raised the subject again, naturally. If you want to live here yourself, I've taken the liberty of asking a local builder to provide a rough estimate of what it would cost you to demolish the outside walls and put in picture windows. When we return to the town and go to my agency, I can show you the figures, if you like. That would help you to settle on a fair price for the property, I think."

They arrived at the house. Mustapha assumed that the realtor would now allow him to inspect it on his own, but this was not to be.

"Here we are. I've put a chain on the gate, to prevent any further damage to the house. Please come through. This is the front door—I've repaired the unavoidable damage the police caused when they broke in. In fact, it's not just the front door, it's the only door. That's also unusual—a huge house with only one outside door. But it would be easy for you to put in a door to the kitchen, as well as a door leading to the beach. Even better, you could build a beautiful patio facing the beach, with palm trees and everything. And what about an infinity-edge swimming pool with crystalline clear water? It would be spectacular if your builder positioned the pool so that the infinity edge appears to merge into the deep blue sea behind it—it would give the illusion of the water from your pool pouring into the ocean. And of course, your beautiful pool would have a diving board and exquisite marble fountains."

"I don't mind looking through the house by myself," Mustapha said.

The realtor chose to ignore that remark. "Here on the first floor," the realtor continued, "are four entertainment rooms, the kitchen, and Mr. Zeta's study. On the roof are various aerials and things for satellite communication; I was told that Mr. Zeta was always in contact with his business associates in other countries. Now let's go upstairs. There are five bedrooms here, each with its own private bathroom. This one was Mr. Zeta's bedroom. Huge, isn't it? And just look at the fittings in that bathroom."

Mustapha tried again. "You know, it's probably better if I examine the house on my own."

Again the realtor took no notice. "Oh, I forgot," he went on, "your associate specified a locked cellar. There's a wooden door leading downstairs from the kitchen. Let me show you. Please follow me down this flight of stairs. This is more than a cellar, I can tell you; it's an underground strongroom. Here we are at the foot of the stairs. But look at that door in front of us—I've seen safes in some banks with considerably less impressive thick steel doors! Fortunately we found it open, because there's no indication anywhere of the combination. If you want to lock it, you'll have to bring a locksmith in from one of the larger islands, or perhaps from Athens— that's a very fancy lock. By the way, back at the agency I also have a copy of the plans of the building for you to take with you. For some strange reason, this cellar isn't on the plan; Mr. Zeta seems to have added it after the building was finished. Odd."

"Yes, isn't it," Mustapha replied.

"If you've seen everything you want to see inside, let's go to the beach. I hope you don't mind a little sand on your leather shoes! Actually, there's no need to walk all the way down to the water's edge, you can see everything relevant from up here. Notice how the sand slopes down gradually to the water. Also, I would like to draw your attention to the fact that boats can easily beach here. As I said before, there are no rocks, and the water is quite deep only a few yards from the waterline. So, if you were to build a harbor or a marina, you wouldn't have to dredge. If you like, I can get you a topographical map showing the depth of the water. It would be in Greek, I'm afraid, but I'm sure that you'd quickly understand the gist of it. The point is that many islands in the Cyclades have virtually no continental shelf of any kind—the deep water starts almost as soon as you enter the water."

This time Mustapha tried saying nothing. But that approach, too, failed miserably.

"Now that I come to think of it, I can understand why Mr. Zeta decided to commit suicide here on Argos Beach. Apparently he couldn't swim, so if he just waded out into the deep water, that would've been that. Though it beats me why a man with all the money in the world, living on beautiful Krotonos, would want to kill himself."

Maybe, just maybe, Mustapha thought to himself, Ziyad bin Abu Dawud had committed suicide because it was the only way to get a moment of silence on Krotonos.

CHAPTER ELEVEN

Mustapha stood at the head of the table in the third-floor room above the spice shop in East Jerusalem and addressed the executive committee of the IFJLP.

"I've called this meeting in order to give you the latest information regarding our new base in the Cyclades. The big news is that I've visited the wealthy Saudi banker who's been supporting our cause so generously. I went to his office in Jeddah and explained to him in detail everything we know concerning the disastrous London Underground suicide bombing. I also told him everything that occurred with Hassan Ali. I kept nothing whatsoever from him. And it's a good thing that I was so absolutely frank."

Mustapha paused, waiting for someone to put the obvious question. There was no response. In the growing silence, Mustapha continued.

"You're probably wondering why my openness was so important. Well, he'd learned about the London fiasco in detail from his contacts in London and Riyadh, and he'd heard rumors about Hassan Ali's visit to Britain, all of them extremely negative. I gathered that, based on the information he'd received, he'd decided to entirely wash his hands of our organization.

"I explained to him that both the Suleiman Haroun bombing and Hassan Ali's visit were conceived and organized by Abdul Rahman ibn Sultan who, as we all know, is no longer associated with the Front. I then told him about my plan for setting up a base in the Greek Islands and what I've already achieved. His initial reaction was skepticism. He asked me to come back the next day. I gathered that, in the interim, he'd made extensive inquiries—like all top bankers, he has excellent sources all over the world—and discovered that I'd in no way exaggerated regarding the progress we've made. On the contrary, the next day he was most interested in the details of our new base on Krotonos. I had the impression that he's supporting at least one other jihadi organization financially, and that if they were to copy my idea of a base in the Greek Islands, this would solve their major problem, too. At our first meeting he was cold and unfriendly, to say the least. But the next day he gave me a check that will cover all our setting-up costs, with plenty over for operational expenses. It seemed to me that he wants to determine if a base in the Greek Islands is feasible, and is using the IFJLP as a guinea pig."

Now there were broad smiles all around the table.

"What can you tell us about this generous Saudi banker?" Mahmoud ibn Laban asked.

"Well, for one thing, he's a Qutbist."

Almost all the men nodded. Sayyid Qutb was a leader of the Muslim Brotherhood in Egypt. In 1966 he was hanged for plotting the assassination of President Nasser. Like the members of the IFJLP, Qutb promoted violent jihad.

"So, on the one hand our banker friend is an ardent follower of Qutb philosophy. That's why he supplies loads of money to enable jihadist groups such as ourselves to further our aims. But on the other hand, as a successful banker, he doesn't want to waste money, so he's extremely careful to fund only successful groups with a proven record. And that was why he was so unfriendly the first time I met him. But once he'd discovered our successes in Greece, the next day he changed his tune and presented us with far more money than I'd hoped for."

"So what's the next step?" Hashim bin Baba asked.

"Now that we have the funds, we'll buy the house on Krotonos. Our Saudi friend and supporter asked me to register the purchase in the name of a subsidiary of one of his banks, and I had no choice but to agree. The banker reminded me that the Greek authorities were somewhat disconcerted when they discovered that Ziyad had purchased the house in the name of his former mistress, a notorious Lebanese whore. The banker insisted that, when it came to ownership of real estate, nothing inspires more confidence than a major bank, because a huge bank is rich and conservative, and does everything it can to suppress scandals, unlike the former owner.

When he said that, the distaste on his face was palpable—those Qutbists insist on the highest standards of morality at all times.

"Once the sale has gone through," he continued, "I'll visit Krotonos again. I'll get the house ready to receive the shipment. In particular, I need to arrange for a locksmith to come from Athens to reset the combination on the strongroom door. In that way, we'll keep complete control of the contents. Any attempt by any other organization to blast open the door would set off the explosives inside—as I'm sure they'd realize."

"Mustapha," a man seated to his left asked, "Just what are you hinting at? What other group is going to steal the explosives we're going to store in our base?"

"I'm just a little concerned about the organization in Yemen that our Saudi friend is also bankrolling— I believe they call themselves the Islamic Front of Yemen. I don't yet completely trust our benefactor, and I'm still not sure that he entirely trusts us. On the one hand, he's given us everything I asked for, and more. But on the other hand, he may be paying us to set up a base for that other organization. By keeping the explosives under lock and key—our lock and our key—we can frustrate his knavish tricks, as the British sing with such enthusiasm in the second verse of their national anthem.

"And talking about the British," Mustapha went on, "we have some unfinished business in England. Once we have everything in place on Krotonos, I'll fly straight back to Lebanon to organize the shipment of our goods from Sheikh Mansour ibn Aziz Arabiya's warehouse in Beirut. And then we're going to bring down the British government by paralyzing transportation in London and spreading unlimited fear, panic and terror."

***

As soon as his plane landed at Rafic Hariri International Airport in Beirut, Mustapha grabbed his valise from the overhead bin and headed apprehensively for the immigration booths. The Lebanese government of the day decides whether a leader of a specific terrorist group is warmly welcomed, unceremoniously marched onto the next plane out of the country, or thrown into prison, and its attitude toward an organization can change suddenly with the prevailing political wind. As a result, a number of previous attempts to visit Beirut had not gone smoothly for Mustapha.

He had to stand in line for more than thirty minutes, which greatly increased his nervousness. Finally he presented his passport to an immigration agent, who scanned the travel document and waited patiently for the software to analyze the resulting image. After what seemed an age to Mustapha, the immigration agent looked up at his computer screen, nodded, stamped the passport with a flourish, and returned it to Mustapha with a broad smile.

Our Saudi banker must have greased the wheels, Mustapha thought as he rode downtown in a taxi on his way to the local branch of his backer's bank.

Three armed bodyguards in short-sleeved khaki shirts and blue jeans were waiting for him in the lobby. They were built like nightclub bouncers, and they looked reassuringly vicious. Mustapha greeted them politely and then went to the inquiries desk and said he had an appointment to see the manager. The receptionist, a smiling young man, asked for Mustapha's passport and disappeared for about fifteen minutes. During this time, Mustapha sat in a leather chair in the lobby; his team of bodyguards stood in a protective semicircle some three yards from him. Finally the receptionist returned, smiling. He returned Mustapha's passport to him and invited him into the manager's office; the bodyguards remained in the lobby.

The bank manager was a small man, even shorter than Mustapha, dressed in a well-cut, dark gray pinstripe suit, a gleaming white shirt, and a tie with a discreet red and blue pattern. He shook hands with Mustapha and invited him to sit down. On the manager's desk, a compact leather suitcase was waiting. The manager opened it and carefully took out all the bundles of used hundred dollar bills and invited Mustapha to check them. First he counted the bundles. Next he chose a bundle at random and removed the paper strip holding the package of banknotes together. He slowly counted the notes and made sure that there were a hundred in the bundle. Then he pulled a note out of the middle of the bundle, held it up to the light and checked that there was a watermark of Benjamin Franklin on the right side of his portrait. He carried out the same steps on a second bundle. Satisfied, he packed the money back into the case and signed for the cash. The three bodyguards were waiting in the lobby to escort Mustapha to an armored black Cadillac and drive him to Sheikh Mansour ibn Aziz Arabiya's warehouse. One of the bodyguards drove the car carefully. The other two had removed their large handguns from their holsters and were hungry for an excuse to fire them. Disappointingly for them, no one attempted to interfere with their progress.

Carrying the suitcase with the money in one hand and his valise in the other, Mustapha walked through the narrow front door into the warehouse. Two bodyguards preceded him, the third one followed. All three now openly brandished their handguns, presumably fearing some sort of treachery on the part of the sheikh's many men who stood around. But again the bodyguards were frustrated—Sheikh Mansour came out of his office with a big smile on his face and invited Mustapha into his office. This time the three bodyguards came inside with Mustapha, taking defensive positions around the large room. Sheikh Mansour simply ignored them and behaved throughout as if there were just two people in his office. Mustapha handed over the suitcase. The sheikh, too, counted the bundles, but then he chose three bundles at random and counted the notes. He nodded at Mustapha and, still smiling broadly, handed over a number of documents for Mustapha to sign.

"Sheikh Mansour, the last time we met you mentioned contracts. I thought you were joking."

"*Habibi*, why would you think that?"

"Well, to put it bluntly, I'm not too happy about creating a paper trail explaining in graphic detail what you and I are doing."

"*Habibi*, what you do is your business. But what I do is my business. And my business is strictly legal. I have permits for everything I buy and sell, I keep scrupulous books and I pay my taxes in full to all the various authorities, just like every other honest businessman. And each one of these contracts that I've drawn up for you, they're all with honest businessmen: the bodyguards, the firm that rented you the armored Cadillac, the boat dealer, and so on. No one wants any trouble with the authorities. If you want to do business with me and my associates, *habibi*, then you will sign the contracts. All the contracts."

With the greatest reluctance, Mustapha added his signature to the others already on the several documents that Sheikh Mansour laid in front of him. The look on Mustapha's face revealed that, with every signature he penned, he felt that he was signing his own death warrant. When Mansour was finally satisfied, he took the pile of signed papers over to a large Xerox machine, made copies of all the pages and handed them to Mustapha, who reluctantly put them into his valise.

"*Habibi*, I assure you that some day you will be most grateful for the copies of all these contracts." Mustapha didn't bother to reply.

With the paperwork complete, the sheikh escorted Mustapha to the back of the warehouse where the items he had ordered were waiting. The weapons and ammunition were still in the original boxes in which the factory workers had packed them. The Semtex was stored in compact ammunition boxes made of galvanized steel; each box held five of the bricks. Other ammunition boxes contained the detonators as well as suicide vests with compartments for ten flat Semtex bricks.

Sheikh Mansour signaled to an assistant to open the back gate, which was heavily reinforced, like the rest of the warehouse. Outside a truck was waiting. The driver of the truck, a tall, swarthy man with a captain's peaked cap on his head, drove the truck into the warehouse and stopped. Mansour's assistant closed and bolted the back gate of the huge warehouse. The rear door of the truck opened, and two armed men jumped out. All three men had a vaguely nautical air. The two men who had been in the rear of the truck loaded the Semtex, the detonators, and the suicide vests while the driver stood idly by. Then they loaded the weapons and all the ammunition; again the driver did not assist them. Mustapha kept careful count of his order, ticking off each item on the list provided by Sheikh Mansour ibn Aziz Arabiya. Finally everything was loaded into the back of the truck. The driver got back into the cab. One of Mustapha's bodyguards stood next to the vehicle; the other two bodyguards and the two men who had loaded the goods climbed into the rear of the truck, which the third bodyguard helped to close. Mustapha checked the list, and was not surprised to find that the sheikh had provided everything that the IFJLP had specified. He nodded to the sheikh, who provided yet another piece of paper for Mustapha to sign, this one stating that he had received all the goods as ordered. An underling took the paper to the office and returned with the original plus a copy, which Mansour handed to Mustapha. The sheikh made sure that Mustapha put the copy in his valise together with the copies of the rest of the paperwork. Satisfied that all the documentation was complete, the sheikh shook hands with Mustapha, who climbed into the cab of the truck and sat next to the driver. The remaining bodyguard then sat beside Mustapha and slammed the passenger door of the truck shut. The sheikh gave another signal, the same assistant unbolted and opened the back door, and the driver reversed out of the warehouse.

Being only too aware of the contents of the truck, the driver handled the vehicle with extreme care, so driving to the port took longer than Mustapha had anticipated. The Lebanese customs officer at the gate had received a liberal bribe earlier that day, so he waved the truck straight through. The driver took the vehicle to the small-boat harbor and stopped next to a fifty-foot long cabin cruiser. Mustapha had never seen a boat quite like that before, which was not surprising, given the extent of the alterations that Mansour had organized to add additional fuel tanks and a hidden reinforced hold under the deck. The wheelhouse was in front, and behind the wheelhouse were the saloon and two small cabins. A hatch in the saloon floor could be raised to gain access to the hold. The floor of the saloon was covered with a fitted carpet to conceal the hatch cover. Notwithstanding first appearances, the carpet could be rolled up to reveal the concealed hatch.

First the three bodyguards climbed out of the truck. Once they had given the all-clear, Mustapha and the two porters joined them; the driver remained behind the wheel. Then the two porters rearranged the furniture in the saloon, rolled up the carpet, opened the hatch and loaded the weapons into the cavity. Then they brought out the Semtex.

"What's that odor?" Mustapha asked. "I've been smelling bitter almonds ever since I got in the truck."

"It's the Semtex," one of the bodyguards replied. "In addition to the usual taggant, they're now adding this scent to Semtex."

"But the Semtex is packed in ammunition boxes," Mustapha said.

"Yes, they're supposed to be airtight, but it seems that at least one them is defective. It's probably caused by a fastener for those drop-down handles they use for easy stacking—they haven't got the technology quite right yet."

"So are we going to have this bitter almonds smell the whole way to the island?"

"Yes, I'm afraid so. The hatch covering the hold will help to reduce the odor, but if it bothers you, I suggest you stay in your cabin and out of the saloon as much as possible."

The two men replaced the hatch and rolled the carpet back. They returned to the truck and brought out three compact duffel bags. The driver finally emerged from the truck, straightened his captain's peaked cap and strolled importantly onto the cabin cruiser. The three bodyguards waved goodbye and climbed into the truck. The captain effortlessly took the cabin cruiser out of the harbor and into the Mediterranean Sea; the two crewmen, the former porters, carried out his orders. When they had covered about a kilometer, the captain told one of the crew to take the wheel, and he called Mustapha into the saloon.

"I've plotted a course that will ensure that we get to your island in two days' time at eleven o'clock at night. We'll anchor the cabin cruiser offshore from your beach. That will give us plenty of time to inflate the Zodiac, load the explosives and detonators into the inflatable, get the Zodiac to the shore, and unload the goods into your house. Then we repeat the operation with the weapons and ammunition. Everything should be finished well before sunrise. Then the three of us will walk to the ferry station and disappear. You'll have the Zodiac lying on your beach and your cabin cruiser moored offshore ready for you to move to the port when you're ready. Is that acceptable?"

"Yes, captain, that's what we agreed."

"I have more than enough fuel to take us to your island, so that will obviate the problem of trying to refuel in a foreign port where some wise guy might smell the Semtex." The captain returned to the wheelhouse.

The captain and his crew took turns at the wheel. As they entered the Cilician Sea between Cyprus and Turkey, they overtook a small, rusty freighter. Soon after, they saw a huge tanker on the horizon. The tanker was followed by what seemed to be an endless parade of vessels of all kinds. The helmsman on duty had to keep careful watch, especially at night. The corner of the Mediterranean in which they were sailing was clogged with a wide variety of ships, and they certainly didn't want any officials to inspect the cabin cruiser in the wake of a collision.

The sea voyage proceeded uneventfully. The three men tended to avoid Mustapha, who stayed in his cabin and read or slept. The only time he came into the saloon was when they told him that his next meal was ready; Mustapha ate alone. About an hour before the evening sun was due to touch the horizon for the third time, the captain called Mustapha to the saloon again.

"We're still a few hours away from the island, but I like to plan ahead—I don't like surprises. Look at this navigation chart. Here's your island. Now, where's your beach?"

Mustapha examined the chart carefully. The island that the captain had indicated looked totally unfamiliar. It had the wrong shape; it had towns and villages with strange names. He looked again. The island was situated right next to Turkey. He looked at the chart heading, which read "Dodecanese

Islands." And then he read the three large letters labeling the island itself. The letters spelled "Kos."

"Captain, that's the wrong island."

"Nonsense! I agreed to take you to Kos, and this is Kos. It's a beautiful island. Of course you want to go there. You want to have your photograph taken next to the statue of Hippocrates, the father of medicine, who was born there—everyone who visits Kos does that."

"No, Captain, my island is Krotonos in the Cyclades."

"I've never heard of Krotonos. There's no such place."

"There certainly is. I've been there, and I own a house there," Mustapha insisted.

"There's no such island. Show me on a chart."

It took Mustapha a quarter of an hour to find the correct chart and locate Krotonos on it. Those fifteen minutes were the longest in his life, because he remembered only too vividly what happened to Abdul Rahman ibn Sultan when his plans went awry. Dripping with sweat, Mustapha pointed to the island. The captain looked at the chart, and read the name aloud: "Krotonos." Then he added, "Okay, so there's an island called Krotonos. But I can't possibly take you there, because it's in the Cyclades. Kos is only three miles from Turkey, so neither Turkey nor Greece patrols that area. But the Cyclades are quite close to Athens, and the Greek Coast Guard monitors everything. If you sneeze on a boat in the Cyclades, within three minutes a patrol vessel arrives with a box of tissues. No, Krotonos is out of the question."

"But that's what the contract says," Mustapha said.

"Contract, what contract are you talking about?"

Mustapha returned to his cabin, rummaged through his valise, and extracted the pile of copies of the contracts he'd signed so unwillingly. He quickly found the correct one, and brought it to the Captain. "Here, Captain, here's your signature. And there's where it states that you and you men agree to take me and my cargo to Krotonos."

The captain studied the contract slowly. It seemed to Mustapha that the captain was looking for some way to get out of his obligations, because he read every single clause. Finally the captain spoke. "It seems that, as a man of honor, I have to take you to Krotonos. Now let me do some calculations."

Mustapha returned to his cabin, put the copies that Sheikh Mansour had given him back in his valise, and waited. About ten minutes later the captain called him back into the saloon.

"You've obviously noticed that we're travelling at full speed now. Fortunately we have enough fuel to get to Krotonos—there's no way I'd dare to put into any port with all this Semtex aboard. But even though we're going to travel at full speed from now on, we're going to arrive well after midnight, and we may not have enough time to unload everything before dawn. But let's try. We'll go as fast as we can, and we'll certainly have time to unload the Semtex and store it in your house on your island. But if we

can't unload the other stuff, we'll sail out to sea
before sunrise, spend the day offshore well outside
the limits of Greek naval jurisdiction—their
territorial waters extend six nautical miles from the
low-water mark. We'll return after midnight to
unload the rest. That's the best I can do for you, I'm
afraid. Now show me your beach on that chart that
you found." This time, Mustapha had no difficulty
indicating precisely where he needed the captain to
make the delivery. The captain studied the depths
off the coastline, made a mark on the chart with a
pencil, and returned to the wheelhouse.

Well after midnight the cabin cruiser dropped
anchor off Argos Beach; the walled house that Ziyad
bin Abu Dawud had built was in clear sight. During
the preceding hour, the crew had inflated the
Zodiac, rolled back the carpet and opened the hatch.
Consequently, as soon as they had securely anchored
the cabin cruiser, they were able to lower the Zodiac
over the side and start loading it with the boxes
containing the Semtex, the detonators, and the
suicide vests. The captain stayed on board while
Mustapha and the two crewmen clambered into the
Zodiac and headed for the shore. The soft sand and
gentle slope made it easy for them to beach the
inflatable boat. Once the Zodiac was on the sand,
they quickly carried the contents to the house.

Mustapha raced ahead to unchain the gate and
unlock the front door. He ran down the stairs to the
strongroom. When he reached the door, he suddenly
remembered that the combination was in his valise
back on the cabin cruiser. He decided to tell the

crew to leave the Semtex boxes in the kitchen; when they returned with the weapons and ammunition, he would unlock the steel door and they could load everything into the strongroom. A few seconds later, the two crewmen arrived with the first load. Mustapha indicated where they should leave the ammunition boxes containing the explosives and the detonators. Soon the entire cargo from the Zodiac was stacked in the kitchen. Mustapha locked the front door and the gate, and the three men returned to the cabin cruiser.

The captain was waiting impatiently at the stern rail. "Sorry, but we don't have time to unload the rest of the cargo in the darkness. Get the Zodiac on board, and let's get the anchor up and sail out to sea where we'll be safe until tomorrow night. I want to be outside Greek territorial waters as soon as possible."

***

Sheikh Mansour ibn Aziz Arabiya went into his office. He closed the door behind him, locked it and then bolted it shut. Next he opened one of the safes that lined the room and took out a smartphone equipped with a digital encryption device.

He pressed a button. After a few seconds of crackling, a voice said, "Speak."

"The shipment left my office three days ago. It should be on Krotonos by now."

"Message received and understood. Out." The connection was cut.

***

The Saudi banker called his confidential aide into his office. "Contact Salim in Athens the usual way. Tell him I need to know the status of the shipment. In particular, I want to know exactly where the Semtex is."

CHAPTER TWELVE

"Pantelis, I hear an outboard motor coming in our direction," Iphigenia Koteas said, rolling toward him over the blanket that covered the long grass just behind the crest of the ridge overlooking Argos Beach.

Pantelis looked at his luminous watch with sleepy eyes. "It's three o'clock in the morning. No fishing boat could possibly have set sail this early. Go back to sleep. Or, better still, let's make love again."

"No, Pantelis. Listen."

Pantelis turned his head slightly to the side and listened intensely. The noise was getting louder. "What's going on?" he wondered aloud.

"Let's get dressed and find out," Iphigenia suggested, beginning to stand up.

"Stay down!" Pantelis hissed. "Who knows what's happening here? First we have that one Muslim here, Zeta or whatever his name is. He disappears, and a second Muslim comes here, this little guy, Mustapha, and he buys the same house Zeta lived in? Then Mustapha disappears? This could be dangerous. Yes, get dressed at once, but stay flat on the ground until I can find out what's happening."

Pantelis quickly threw on his clothes while lying down and then headed up the ridge using the leopard crawl that he had learned in the army. He moved forward on his right elbow and left knee and then alternated with his other elbow and knee. His instructors had drummed into him that this ensured the smallest possible silhouette. He stopped when he reached the ridge and slowly raised his head. Below him he could see the walled house on the white beach gleaming in the light of the half moon. Out to sea he clearly saw a stationary boat that he did not recognize. Between the boat and the beach a black inflatable was heading in the direction of the shore, probably a Zodiac.

Pantelis watched as the crew beached the inflatable boat. They stepped onto the sand and two men started unloading the items in the Zodiac and carrying them toward the house. In the meantime, a short man rushed ahead of the two porters. Pantelis saw him unlock the gate and enter the walled compound. Soon the two porters carried their loads through the gateway and returned empty handed. Pantelis deduced that the short man must have unlocked the front door so that they could leave the goods inside. He suddenly realized that the short man must be Mustapha, and cursed himself for not realizing sooner that the Arab had come back to Krotonos.

The porters seemed to be Arabs, too. All three men left, the short man chaining shut the high metal gate behind him. They pushed the inflatable back in the water and headed back to the boat. The moonlight was sufficient for Pantelis to see the crew haul the inflatable on board, after which the boat headed off to sea.

Pantelis raced back to where he had left Iphigenia.

"Iphigenia, there's big things happening down there on Argos Beach, I'm not sure what. You'll have to go home now."

"But when I come inside it'll wake my dad and he'll kill me for staying out this late. I know he will. Last time I waited outside until I heard his alarm clock ringing. Then I sneaked in while he was in the bathroom."

"All right, stay with me, but keep out of things."

"Fine. I promise to stay in the background. I won't say a word."

Pantelis escorted Iphigenia back to the town. As they neared Sergeant Kyrgiakos's home, he told Iphigenia to wait around the corner. Pantelis knocked on the door, and a furious sergeant came out to see what was happening. "What do you mean by waking me at this hour?" he whispered as loudly as he dared without rousing his whole family.

Pantelis told him what he had seen. "Give me two minutes to dress and we'll go to the police station," said the sergeant, and closed the door.

Pantelis returned to Iphigenia. "Don't let Mrs. Kyrgiakos see you," he muttered. "But the sergeant won't tell your dad. When he and I start to walk to the police station around the corner, just join us and walk with us without saying anything. Kyrgiakos will understand and he won't ask any questions. We'll think up a story to tell your father later." Pantelis went back to the front door to wait for the sergeant.

A few minutes later Sergeant Kyrgiakos reappeared, buttoning his shirt over his beer belly. He closed the door as quietly as he could, and the two of them started out, shortly joined by Iphigenia. As Pantelis had predicted, the sergeant said nothing. As they reached the police station, Kyrgiakos said, "I have to contact Lieutenant Cosmatos. I know his boat docked in the port last night. I just hope he hasn't left on patrol." He speed-dialed the lieutenant, who arrived at the police station ten minutes later.

"Okay, where's the fire? It's nearly half past three, and I was fast asleep. This had better be really, really important," Cosmatos stated. Pantelis told him almost the full story, claiming that the outboard motor had woken him, and not Iphigenia. Cosmatos was a man of the world and immediately grasped the true facts, but he didn't want Iphigenia to be involved any further in the affair. So he offered to escort her home, promising to smooth things over if her father heard her coming in.

A few minutes later the lieutenant returned. "All's well," he reported. "She'd sprayed the creaky back door hinges with WD-40, so she was able to get to her room without making a sound. Now let's get down to business."

"Good," Sergeant Kyrgiakos said. "First and foremost, what are they smuggling? Drugs, I assume."

"I agree. No question about it," Lieutenant Cosmatos replied. "The only issue is: What do we do next? Pantelis said that all three men left the house, so there's no one there. The last time we visited the house we took everything we found and sold the items in Athens. That brought tens of thousands of euros into the party's coffers. But drugs are another matter entirely."

"Do we have to decide now?" Kyrgiakos asked. "We need to break into the house, remove the drugs, and store them elsewhere. That old warehouse by the port will be ideal—no one ever goes there. Once the drugs are safely hidden, we can decide at our leisure what to do. Even better, we can consult the party high-ups. The main thing is to get them out of the hands of the Muslims."

Pantelis spoke up. "There may be one little problem," he said. "The drugs are probably hidden in the cellar. Do you remember that steel door? I heard that Mustapha brought in a locksmith from Athens to get the combination changed. I'll bet that they're locked away where we can't get at them."

"If that's the case," Sergeant Kyrgiakos said, "You can make a sworn declaration about what you saw, and I can then use it to get a search warrant."

"Yes, but then everything becomes public, and the government gets the drugs," Pantelis protested.

"True, but that would be better than Mustapha having them. In addition, I can arrest Mustapha when he sets foot again on Krotonos, which is going to give me the greatest possible pleasure."

"But when we return with the search warrant, the constables are going to see that someone cut the chain and smashed the front door lock. Isn't that going to be a problem?" Pantelis asked.

"No, it won't." Kyrgiakos replied. "This time I'm going to use my large collection of skeleton keys."

After a few more minutes of spirited discussion, the three men finally agreed on a course of action. They got into the police jeep, and Kyrgiakos drove them to the house. It took about a minute for the sergeant to open the padlock on the chain and then unlock the front door. They headed for the cellar door in the kitchen, but before they reached it they smelt an unfamiliar odor. Then they saw the ammunition boxes lying on the floor.

"What's that smell? It seems to be coming from those boxes," Kyrgiakos said.

They each opened a box at random.

"Holy Panagia!" Pantelis shouted as he looked inside the box he had opened. "That stuff is orange and it smells like bitter almonds. We learned all about it in the Presidential Guards, and what to do if we found a backpack that contained it. That's Semtex—there's no question about it."

Sergeant Kyrgiakos and Lieutenant Cosmatos shrank away, but Pantelis had no fear. "Semtex is as safe as sand unless there's a detonator," he declared smugly.

"We both know that," the sergeant said. "And what do you think that box contains?" he asked as he pointed to the Frishman detonators in the ammunition box he had opened. Even Pantelis looked worried now.

"So," Lieutenant Cosmatos said, "the Hellenic Spartan League was right all along about Muslims, and this cache proves it." The other two men nodded wisely.

"What are we going to do now?" Sergeant Kyrgiakos asked. "We can't sell this Semtex."

"No," Cosmatos replied, "but we can use it to overthrow the communist–socialist government that's bleeding our beloved country to death. We'll start with a major explosion in Athens."

There was total silence for about fifteen seconds. Then Kyrgiakos spoke up. "We need get all this into the warehouse. It'll take one or two trips in the jeep. The sun's already up, and we certainly don't want anyone to see us carrying the Semtex boxes in, so shouldn't we wait until tonight before moving the boxes?"

"Keeping the stuff hidden from prying eyes won't be a problem," Pantelis suggested. "You can drive to the warehouse. I'll open the big doors in front, you'll drive the jeep in, and then we'll all unpack it with the doors tightly shut so no one can see a thing. And I think that it's going to need two trips."

"Hold on, there's something I don't understand at all," Cosmatos stated. "The Arabs have this superlative strongroom under the house with an impenetrable door, but they leave the Semtex lying on the kitchen floor, and they just lock the front door that they know someone broke into before. Does that make any sense to you? C'mon, no terrorist with an ounce of brains would do that. You don't leave gold lying around, and this stuff is worth its weight in gold, if not more."

Again there was total silence. This time Pantelis spoke. "This must mean that they're coming back. They must have been interrupted. Perhaps a really early fishing boat approached their cabin cruiser. No, that's too unlikely. Anyhow, something interrupted them, so instead of bringing the rest of their stuff from the cabin cruiser to the house and then locking everything away in the cellar, they went back to their boat and sailed out to sea. And that must mean—"

"That they'll be coming back tonight!" Lieutenant Cosmatos interrupted excitedly. "Only this time, we'll all be waiting for them. The police will stay just behind the crest of the ridge, so they can watch the house and the beach and the coastline with binoculars. And my crew and I will be waiting on the other side of the island, using our radar to detect the cabin cruiser as it approaches Krotonos. Of course, we'll all stay in radio contact."

"And Heracles and me?" Pantelis asked.

"One of you will be with me," the sergeant said, "and the other will be on the Coast Guard patrol boat."

"Not a good idea," the lieutenant replied. "If there's a fight, non-naval personnel are just going to get in the way, and probably fall overboard to boot. Here's a better plan: Pantelis and Heracles will put on their Army Reserve uniforms. You'll issue them with weapons, preferably semi-automatic rifles, but regular rifles will do in a pinch; I know that they're both really excellent shots. You and your men will have your handguns, as usual. Then, together with Heracles, you'll set up a command post just behind the top of the ridge; your three constables and Pantelis will hide inside the walled compound. My crew and I will try to prevent the Arab terrorists from landing at all. But if for some reason they get onto Argos Beach, the four men will appear from inside the compound when you give the command. And with one sharpshooter on the ridge and the other emerging from the house with the three constables, that will be the end of the Arabs on the beach."

"How do we make sure that the authorities don't find out about all this?" Pantelis enquired.

"They didn't find out about Ziyad, did they?" Cosmatos said, and there was a nasty overtone in his voice. "My job is to patrol the waters around Krotonos and the neighboring islands, and that's exactly what I'll be doing tonight. And that's what I'll tell Commander Eutropius when I next meet with him."

"As you well know, Pantelis," Kyrgiakos added, "I've been the police sergeant here for more than fifteen years. And the only time that anyone in Athens has interfered with me and my men in any way at all was that Ziyad business. Those two detective inspectors came here, threw their weight around, came back with that Lebanese whore, threw their weight around again, but that was the last we saw or heard of them. The worst that can happen is that they'll come back a third time to find out what happened to Mustapha, but that's not going to be any sort of problem, is it? They'll find the gate chained, the front door locked and the house completely bare, and that will be that. In the unlikely event that anyone from Athens comes here to snoop around, do you seriously think that they'll check the house for traces of Semtex? Get real!"

"Just a second," the lieutenant said. "Who knows about this? Just the three of us, plus Iphigenia Koteas? How much does the girl know?"

"She was the one who woke up when the Zodiac with the outboard motor neared the beach," Pantelis confessed. "But I told her to stay hidden on the ground behind the ridge, so she couldn't have seen anything. She walked back to town with me, but I didn't tell her anything. And the sergeant and I didn't say a word in front of her. So all she knows is that there was a boat with an outboard motor in the vicinity of Argos Beach, and that the three of us are extremely concerned about it, for some reason that we haven't shared with her. But that's it."

"You're quite sure about this? You know what would happen if she talks?" Lieutenant Cosmatos asked.

Pantelis thought for a moment and then replied, "Sergeant Kyrgiakos will tell you that she didn't say a word or ask a single question the whole time she was with him. Clearly she has no idea what's going on, so even if she tells people about the outboard motor she heard, she can do no harm. But I'm certain she's going to keep her mouth tightly shut, for a really good reason: She doesn't want her father to find out that she was out with me late last night."

Sergeant Kyrgiakos nodded. "We all know her father. She has an exceptionally good reason to say absolutely nothing."

Lieutenant Cosmatos cocked his head to the left and raised his eyebrows. "Do you think we have to scare her into silence?"

"She's absolutely terrified of her dad," Kyrgiakos said. "So there's nothing more that we need to say to her." And turning to Pantelis, he asked, "By the way, how did you convince her to spend the night with you? Wasn't she worried that her father would find out?"

"Of course she was, but she desperately wants to marry me, and she thinks that sleeping with me is the best way to achieve that."

"And is it?" Cosmatos asked.

"You know the answer to that," Pantelis replied with a laugh. "There's no shortage of pretty girls on this island, and as for some of the tourists ..."

"There's one other thing," Cosmatos said, with a grim expression on his face. "What are you going to tell her if she asks you what's going on?"

"She won't. She didn't ask anything this morning, and she won't ask anything now."

"But if she does?"

"I'll think of something."

"And what are you going to say to her when you tell her that you can't spend tonight with her?"

"That one's easy. I'll tell her that I have army reserve duties tonight. That's what I tell everyone on those evenings when we have our meetings."

It was clear that Cosmatos wasn't satisfied. "Do you realize that if Iphigenia starts asking awkward questions, she poses a threat not just to the three of us, but to the whole Hellenic Spartan League?"

"She's not that kind of girl. That sort of thing doesn't interest her."

Lieutenant Cosmatos shot a quick glance at Sergeant Kyrgiakos, who just stared back at him.

Pantelis tried again. "Look, Lieutenant, if she asks me any questions, I'll tell her that it all turned out to be a false alarm, that the captain of the boat lost his way and sent the inflatable ashore to find out where he was, and that will be that."

"Yes, that should certainly do it," Lieutenant Cosmatos said to Pantelis. But it was obvious to the sergeant that the lieutenant didn't mean what he had just said. And Sergeant Kyrgiakos began to get seriously concerned about what might happen to Iphigenia Koteas.

CHAPTER THIRTEEN

"Is that Lieutenant Cosmatos?"

"Sergeant, what's going on there? I've been trying to raise you on the radio for the last half hour."

"That's why I'm phoning you. The new radio set won't even switch on. The communist–socialist government can't even provide us with a radio that works. We've been communicating here using our cell phones. How far out does yours work?"

"No more than a kilometer offshore, usually. So if we're out to sea and we spot that boat, we probably won't be able to tell you about it."

"That may not be a problem. From this ridge I can see if the boat approaches the island, and I'll certainly see the Zodiac if it heads for the beach. If that happens, I'll use my cell phone to warn the men in the compound."

"Sounds good to me. Now you'd better hang up to conserve the battery. Out."

By one o'clock in the morning, the men on the shore were utterly bored. They had been waiting for four hours and absolutely nothing had happened. As for the Coast Guard crew, soon after Cosmatos had positioned his patrol boat at a point on the other side of the island from Argos Beach, they had watched the stragglers of the fishing fleet limping slowly into port. Since then, however, things had been as quiet as on the beach. Unlike the policeman, however, the men on the ship at least had something to do; they watched the radar to see if any vessel was approaching Krotonos.

Suddenly at 1:42 a.m. the radar beeped, and a blip appeared on the edge of the screen. The crewman on duty watching the radar screen called out to the lieutenant, "Skipper, there's a boat approaching Krotonos on a northeasterly course. Speed eighteen knots. If she maintains course and speed, she should reach the island in about an hour."

That's our man, Cosmatos thought, and walked over to take a look. "Keep tracking that boat," he said.

He addressed the chief petty officer, his second-in-command. "I think that our quarry is heading toward the island. I don't want to scare him off, so I'm going to wait here until he's anchored off the beach. He'll be here in about an hour. Once the men at the command post tell us that his anchor is down, we're going in at full speed. It should take us no more than seven minutes to sail around to the other side of the island. He'll see us only when we round that last headland, giving him no more than about thirty seconds to raise his anchor and flee. My guess is that they'll be so involved with the Zodiac that they won't even notice us until it's too late."

He picked up his cell phone and called Sergeant Kyrgiakos. "Sergeant, we've picked up a blip on the radar. From his course and his speed I reckon that's our target. We'll keep watching on the scope, of course. When he drops anchor, let me know, and we'll descend on him. That Muslim bastard won't know what hit him."

The man at the radar screen kept calling out the position, heading, and speed of the boat. The closer it got, the more certain Lieutenant Cosmatos became that this was his target. The man at the helm of the approaching boat was steering a course aimed directly at Argos Beach, making no attempt to disguise his intentions.

About an hour after the operator first spotted the boat, it came to a halt just off the beach. Sergeant Kyrgiakos phoned Cosmatos. "He's dropped anchor, and they're about to throw the inflatable overboard."

"Wonderful!" Cosmatos replied, and hung up, simultaneously shouting, "Full speed ahead to Argos Beach!"

The Coast Guard patrol boat rounded the final headland. There lay the cabin cruiser at anchor with the Zodiac tied to its side. As Lieutenant Cosmatos had foreseen, precious seconds went by while the crew continued to fetch boxes of weapons from the hold and stack them on the deck, preparatory to loading them into the Zodiac. By the time they realized that the patrol boat was approaching, it was too late. Lieutenant Cosmatos and his crew had armed themselves with M16A2 assault rifles. In addition, one of the crewmen was positioned behind the M60 machine gun mounted on top of the wheelhouse. All the guns were pointing at the men on the cabin cruiser.

The four Arabs could see that they did not stand a chance. There simply was no time to rush to the supply of weapons lying on the deck next to the Zodiac, open a crate of M4 carbines and unwrap four of them, open a box of magazines, insert a clip into each assault rifle and fire the M4s at the oncoming Coast Guard patrol boat. The two sailors had .357 Smith & Wesson magnums in their belts, popguns compared to the array of opposing weapons, and Mustapha and the captain were unarmed. Reluctantly they all faced the inevitable and raised their arms in surrender.

Lieutenant Cosmatos brought his patrol boat alongside the cabin cruiser. He gave an order, and a member of his Coast Guard crew put down his weapon, fastened a line from the stern of the cabin cruiser to the stern of the patrol boat, and picked up his M16A2 assault rifle again. Then a second member of his crew fastened another line to connect the bows of the two boats.

Now Cosmatos motioned to the first crewman on the cabin cruiser, indicating that he should slowly take his magnum from his belt and throw it over the rail into the sea. With three M16A2 assault rifles and the M60 machine gun aimed directly at him, the crewman had little choice but to comply. The second magnum followed soon after. With the four men unarmed, Lieutenant Cosmatos indicated to the captain of the cabin cruiser that he was to climb aboard the Coast Guard patrol boat. When he reached the deck, Cosmatos searched him carefully and then cuffed him with his hands behind his back. The two crewmen and Mustapha followed in turn.

The lieutenant ordered two men to search the cabin cruiser carefully and to bring any personal effects onto the patrol boat. They returned and reported that the cabin cruiser contained twelve assault rifles, two sniper rifles, ten hand guns, together with ammunition, all of which they had replaced in the hold. They gave Cosmatos the valise belonging to Mustapha and the three duffel bags that the crew had taken from the back of the truck.

The four Arab men from the cabin cruiser were standing on the deck of the Coast Guard vessel near the stern. Cosmatos turned to Mustapha. "I know you," he said in halting English. "You are Mustapha, the new owner of the house on Argos Beach."

Mustapha pretended that he did not understand English. Calmly the lieutenant raised his M16A2 assault rifle, aimed at the head of one of the crewmen of the cabin cruiser and fired a three-round burst. The man slumped to the deck.

"Mustapha, we both know you speak English. So I'm going to repeat my question. You are Mustapha, the new owner of the house on Argos Beach?"

"Yes."

"Why are you smuggling guns into Greece?"

Mustapha did not answer. The second crewman and the captain implored him in rapid Arabic to respond, but Mustapha kept silent. The lieutenant pointed his weapon at the second crewman and fired a second three-round burst. Mustapha just looked straight ahead.

"Mustapha, we saw you carrying Semtex into the house last night. What's the Semtex for?"

The captain begged Mustapha to answer, but Mustapha was obdurate. Cosmatos quickly realized that Mustapha wanted to die a martyr's death. Because there was no point in torturing him to try to extract information, Cosmatos obliged him by killing them both.

Cosmatos now picked up his cell phone and called Sergeant Kyrgiakos. "I don't know how much you and Heracles saw through your binoculars, but I've just finished off the three Arab men that Pantelis saw yesterday, as well as the captain of the cabin cruiser—yet another Muslim.

"And there's more good news," he added. "The Hellenic Spartan League is now the proud owner of a large cabin cruiser in excellent condition, a Zodiac, piles of weapons of all kinds with more than enough ammunition, some second-hand clothing, and a pile of signed documents written in Arabic. In addition, I've found a most interesting piece of paper that I need to discuss with you.

"My men," Cosmatos continued, "are about to use the Zodiac to transport the booty to the kitchen of the house. Yes, you heard me correctly. Tell your men to find four cinder blocks and carry them down to the water's edge. We'll bring them here to the patrol boat on the Zodiac's return trips—we need them to weight the four bodies before we throw them overboard in deep water. Don't worry, we've got plenty of rope aboard to do the job properly.

"Once we have the cinder blocks on board and the weapons are on shore, one of my crew will return the Zodiac to the beach and then he'll join you and your men. Then we're going to untie the cabin cruiser from our patrol boat and leave it moored offshore—we'll need it eventually to transport the shipment to the mainland. I'll take my patrol boat out to sea to dump the garbage and then we'll head back to the port. I'll join you at the house as soon as possible—stay there until I arrive. Out."

Sergeant Kyrgiakos thought about the calm, matter-of-fact way in which Cosmatos had stated that he had just killed the four men. Then he recalled the conversation they had had much earlier that day regarding Iphigenia Koteas. He shuddered.

***

The relationship between Lieutenant Cosmatos and Sergeant Kyrgiakos was complex and difficult. Even after working together for years in the Hellenic Spartan League, they were still not on first-name terms. Part of the problem was a chain-of-command issue. Cosmatos and his crew were based in Ermoupoli, on the island of Syros, some thirty miles from Krotonos. The area they patrolled included not just the Krotonos region but also the sea around several other islands lying to the west of Syros. So, the lieutenant's ties to Krotonos were somewhat tenuous. Kyrgiakos, on the other hand, was the head of the Krotonos branch of the League. As a commissioned officer, Lieutenant Cosmatos outranked Sergeant Kyrgiakos. Nevertheless, Kyrgiakos invariably fell back on his status as the local League leader and acted accordingly toward Cosmatos. The lieutenant was most unhappy with the situation, but he felt that there was nothing he could do about it. However, murdering the four Muslims in cold blood had emboldened Cosmatos to the point at which he would no longer tolerate Sergeant Kyrgiakos ordering him around. From that moment on, he started to treat Kyrgiakos as an underling. The sergeant, for his part, had instantly picked up on the radically changed relationship. However, he was a practical man, and he realized that there were worse things than Lieutenant Cosmatos ordering him around. The lieutenant shooting him dead in cold blood was one of them.

On seeing Lieutenant Cosmatos swagger into the Argos Beach house about an hour later, closely followed by the other five members of his crew, the sergeant's instinctive reaction was to say something like, "Okay, so what's this 'interesting piece of paper' you found? We both know you can't read Arabic. And why did you order the guns and ammunition to be brought here instead of the warehouse where we've stored the Semtex and the detonators?" Instead, he wisely said nothing.

Lieutenant Cosmatos also said nothing. He just handed the sergeant a small sheet of paper with a tear-edge all the way down the left side. The number 78 was printed in the top right-hand corner. Sergeant

Kyrgiakos looked at the numbers written on the paper in pencil, and handed it back to Cosmatos.

"Why are these numbers so interesting?" he asked as politely as he could. "I didn't know you played the lottery."

"We both know that lotteries are just a tax on the mathematically illiterate. And talking about mathematical illiteracy, it seems you have a problem with counting. There are exactly five numbers written there, but you need to pick six Lotto numbers." Lieutenant Cosmatos laughed unpleasantly before continuing. "Sergeant, I'll give you a clue. I found this piece of paper in Mustapha's valise, together with a pile of papers in Arabic. Now examine all the digits carefully—they're written the way we Greeks write numbers."

Kyrgiakos's face lit up. "It's the combination to the strongroom door, written by the locksmith who came here from Athens. He wrote the numbers on a page from a two-part notebook. He tore off the top copy, which he gave to Mustapha—that explains the left-hand edge of the paper. And presumably the locksmith has his copy, the other part of page 78 of his notebook. So, if Mustapha loses the code, the locksmith has it written down in his notebook. Hopefully, he's safely locked the notebook away somewhere. But wait a minute, a combination lock has a three-number code, not five numbers."

"Take a close look at the door—that isn't your usual three-cam lock. Anyhow, I'm going to try the combination." And Cosmatos started to walk down the stairs to the strong-room door. A half a minute later the steel door swung open.

"Sergeant, get in your jeep with your men, go to the warehouse, and bring the Semtex and the detonators back here. In the meantime, my men will load the weapons and ammunition into the strongroom. By the way, you left this box behind when you took the other stuff to the warehouse. I've just opened it. What's this?" And he held up a suicide vest.

Sergeant Kyrgiakos explained how the item of clothing is packed with explosives surrounded by shrapnel for maximizing casualties. The lieutenant laughed his nasty laugh again. "Yes, let's keep these. In the improbable event of any more Muslims daring to come here I won't shoot them, we'll just dress them in these suicide vests and I'll blow them up."

"Lieutenant, don't you think that more Muslims are going to come here?" Kyrgiakos asked. "When Mustapha fails to return to wherever he came from, won't they make inquiries? They'll come here and see their cabin cruiser—"

"*Our* cabin cruiser," Cosmatos interrupted angrily.

"*Our* cabin cruiser," the sergeant repeated obediently, "so they'll know that Mustapha arrived in Krotonos. If they climb aboard, they'll find that the secret hold is empty. What they won't know is whether Mustapha managed to unload the shipment into the strongroom here before he and the others disappeared. Won't they try to get their explosives and guns back?"

"Just how do you think they're going to get into the strongroom?" Cosmatos asked. "They don't have the combination for the lock, and even a Muslim isn't stupid enough to blast open the door to a room that he thinks contains Semtex."

There was a respectful pause. Then Sergeant Kyrgiakos asked, "But Lieutenant, how do you know that Mustapha didn't give the combination to anyone else?"

This time the pause was so that the lieutenant could reflect. "You may have a point there," Cosmatos reluctantly conceded. "We obviously can't bring a locksmith here to change the combination, because he'd see the weapons and explosives when he opens the door. You'll have to assign one of your men to watch this place 24/7. The spot just behind the ridge that you used as your command post will be ideal."

"Lieutenant, with all due respect, this is a small island. Everyone here knows everyone else's business. It won't take long before every single person on Krotonos is aware that we're watching the house and Argos Beach. And that would not be a good idea."

"So, what do you suggest we do?" Cosmatos asked aggressively. "You were the one who raised the issue. What's the answer?"

"Well, it's going to be a while before the Muslims realize that Mustapha has disappeared. Then they have to organize some sort of investigation. I suggest that we carry out an operation in Athens as soon as we possibly can and, while we're planning it, we try to find a location to store all the stuff, perhaps in Athens, possibly on another island. We know that everything fits into the hold of that cabin cruiser, so transportation won't be a problem. With all the men at our disposal, we can move everything to just about anywhere in Greece in hours."

"And what's our first operation going to be?"

Sergeant Kyrgiakos thought quickly. He now knew how much the lieutenant enjoyed killing, so he replied, "Let's do an assassination. We've got two sniper rifles and plenty of ammunition for them, and both Heracles and Pantelis are crack shots."

"Agreed. And who are we going to kill?"

Again the sergeant had to think quickly. "What about that imam who's so provocative when they interview him on TV? The one with the red hair who keeps saying that Muslims are all peaceful people who just want to live in harmony and friendship with their Greek neighbors. Do you know who I mean?"

"I can't think of the lying swine's name, but I know exactly who you mean. I'll contact our people in Athens and have them set this up right away. And in the meantime, we have to find a new hiding place for all the stuff. Including those suicide vests." And a sadistic smirk crossed his face.

CHAPTER FOURTEEN

Lagoneia, a small, uninhabited island on the outer edge of the Cyclades, is situated well out of sight of Krotonos and its incurably inquisitive inhabitants. Heracles Stavridis and Pantelis Papakostas lay prone at the top of the only hill on the islet. Below them, some two hundred and fifty yards away, stood a clump of pine trees. Resting on its bipod in front of each man was a rifle; more precisely, an Accuracy International AX338 sniper rifle fitted with a Schmidt & Bender 5-25×56 Police Marksman II LP telescopic sight. Between them lay a box of magazines each containing ten .338 Lapua Magnum cartridges. Behind the marksmen stood two men. One was Sergeant Kyrgiakos. The other man was a friend of his, a Hellenic Army marksmanship instructor from his military service days. Now a successful insurance salesman, the former instructor had agreed to train the two men in the use of the sniper equipment.

In any event, little training was needed. Both Heracles and Pantelis had shone at marksmanship during their military service. They had a deep understanding of key factors such as windage,

148

parallax compensation, elevation, and the like, so they almost immediately understood the workings of the Schmidt & Bender precision telescopic sights. Neither man had ever held a high-end sniper rifle before, so being permitted to handle them was a privilege for which they felt extremely grateful. Now they were about to fire their first rounds. The instructor had fastened eight-inch bullseye targets made of cardboard to two of the trees. Each man used the stadiametric rangefinding reticle in his telescopic sight to determine the distance to his own target. They estimated the wind speed by looking at a flag mounted near the pines. Having made all adjustments to the sights that they deemed necessary, they aimed their rifles and fired three shots about a minute apart.

The instructor walked down to the trees, removed the paper targets and examined them. He found that every one of Heracles's bullets had landed near the center of the bullseye zone. Pantelis, however, was somewhat less successful; all three of his bullets had hit just outside the bullseye, one to the left and two to the upper right. The instructor fastened fresh targets to two other trees, both slightly further away from the marksmen. The two men now exchanged rifles. They went through the standard preparatory procedure again and then fired three more bullets each. And again Heracles found the bullseye zone each time, whereas Pantelis was fractionally less accurate.

Sergeant Kyrgiakos spoke. "In my opinion, Heracles will do the shooting, with Pantelis as spotter and stand-by shooter. Do you all agree?" The other three men nodded. "Fine. Now I want you to fire at least another twenty rounds each, to be quite sure that you both become fully accustomed to using the rifles. Then we'll go back to Krotonos in the cabin cruiser. Tomorrow afternoon we'll come back here, and you'll practice again."

"What's the actual target?" Heracles asked. The sergeant ignored him. The insurance salesman, a senior member of the Hellenic Spartan League, turned his head away and looked out to sea.

***

During the sixteenth century, the Ottoman rulers of Greece built the exquisite Al Fazi Mosque in Athens; the square-domed prayer hall and the vaulted portico are of particular architectural interest. The current imam of the mosque, Azhar Khan, was a man who stood out in any crowd, for three reasons. He was unusually tall and extremely powerfully built, he had a shock of bright red curly hair that defied all attempts to control it, and he was exceedingly charismatic.

He never turned down a request for an interview of any kind. In particular, he encouraged reporters from all media to gather on Hadji Ali Square in front of his mosque every Friday afternoon after the *Jumu'ah* prayers and ask him any questions they wished. No matter how aggressive the questioner, Imam Khan would reply calmly and in detail. And the broad smile never disappeared from his freckled face.

Lately, however, the Friday afternoon interview sessions had become most unpleasant. A gang of adolescent youths started to gather on the square and harass worshippers as they left the mosque. On one occasion, a hooligan named Menelaus Tsolakoglou had thrown a stone the size of a golf ball at Imam Kahn. It missed the imam by more than a yard, but severely injured the right shoulder of a newspaper reporter who had written some days earlier that "half the police in Greece are members of the Hellenic Spartan League, and the other half are sympathizers." Needless to say, Menelaus was never arrested. But from then on, every Friday afternoon a squad of burly police officers was on duty at the square, and each week they warned the youths to restrict their protests to chanting and heckling—the throwing of projectiles was now forbidden.

The previous day Heracles Stavridis and Pantelis Papakostas had taken the early morning ferry from Krotonos to Syros, and then a high-speed ferry from there to Piraeus, the port of Athens. They took a Line One Metro train from the ferry port. A short stroll from a Metro station brought them to the insurance salesman's apartment. He woke them at three o'clock on Friday morning and gave them a quick breakfast of bread and coffee before their two-mile walk to a fourth-floor, one-bedroom apartment overlooking Hadji Ali Square and directly opposite the portico in front of the mosque. The owner had rented the apartment for many years to a wheelchair-bound pensioner who could not go outside without being carried down the stairs. Earlier that week, two men who said that they were social workers had visited the tenant, a childless widower, and told him that he was entitled to a week's vacation, at the government's expense, at a resort for handicapped people. The social workers had packed a suitcase for the lonely pensioner and then carried him downstairs and driven him to a hotel on the coast about forty miles from Athens. In his excitement and pleasure, the tenant never noticed that the social workers took his apartment key with them.

When Heracles and Pantelis unlocked the door of the apartment soon after four o'clock and walked in, they found one of the Accuracy International sniper rifles lying on the bed in its case. Next to it were two full magazines containing ten cartridges. Standard operating procedure was to equip both the sniper and the spotter each with his own rifle, but Lieutenant Cosmatos had decided to keep the other sniper rifle in reserve for a possible second assassination. After the shooting, if the clean-up team from the Hellenic Spartan League could not get to the apartment before the police arrived, both sniper rifles would fall into the hands of the authorities.

In the refrigerator in the kitchen they found a huge pile of sandwiches that would sustain them until the time of the assassination. They would drink tap water if they felt thirsty.

Heracles and Pantelis moved to the window of the bedroom, which Pantelis opened to its full extent. They set up the rifle with its bipod resting securely on the windowsill. Heracles sat on a chair and adjusted the telescopic sight, aiming at an imaginary man over six feet tall standing across the square some twenty-five yards in front of the portico. Satisfied, he removed the rifle before anyone saw it. Pantelis closed the window. The two friends now waited.

The *Jumu'ah* prayer is recited on Fridays just after the sun reaches its highest point in the sky that day. Clocks in Greece are set to Eastern European Time, so from April to October *Jumu'ah* in Athens starts around 1:20 p.m.

Soon after one o'clock the two assassins heard the *muezzin* intone the call to prayer. They observed worshippers entering the mosque, initially just a few and then in ever increasing numbers, and finally a few latecomers scuttled in.

At half past one, Heracles asked Pantelis to go down to the square to gauge the wind speed at the assassination site, while he observed the trees in the square and the clothing of the passersby to arrive at his own estimate. When Pantelis returned a few minutes later, they both agreed that the wind was blowing from the west at about five miles an hour. Heracles made the necessary minor adjustment to the windage knob on the telescopic sight.

Two television crews had arrived and set up their equipment for interviewing Imam Khan after the service. They had parked their vans in a street adjoining the square; only the two reporters and their cameramen stood waiting outside the mosque. Now about ten or twelve teenagers arrived, followed almost immediately by the Hellenic Police. Heracles commented to Pantelis that the constabulary had probably been relaxing around the corner, waiting for the youths to arrive; he thought that their orders would be to stay away from the square unless the members of the gang of youths decided to show up that week.

At two o'clock, the first worshippers started leaving the mosque. Pantelis re-opened the window. Heracles positioned the rifle on the windowsill and aimed it at the head of a tall man who was walking roughly where the sniper expected the imam to be a few minutes later. They both waited calmly. For the two islanders, this was no different to any of the military exercises in which they had participated.

The square started to fill with worshippers who had left the prayer hall. The television crews moved closer to the mosque. Imam Khan appeared, tall and strong. His red hair provided an irresistible target for Heracles, and he kept it at the intersection of the cross-wires of the reticle of his telescopic sight as the imam moved in the general direction of the center of the square. The teenagers, chanting "Muslims go home," now moved behind the imam, so that they would be photographed by the television cameramen and could see themselves on the news that night. Imam Khan walked toward the waiting television reporters. When his target was about twenty-five yards in front of the portico, Heracles gently squeezed the trigger.

***

As Imam Azhar Khan left the Al Fazi Mosque that Friday afternoon he was particularly pleased with his *khutbah* (sermon). He had taken "luck" as his topic, pointing out that superstition has no place in Islam. On the contrary, all fortune, both good and bad, is from Allah, the most gracious, the most merciful. The looks on the faces of the congregation made it clear to him that he was getting through to many of them. He decided that he would repeat this important message, in slightly different terms, in a month or so.

Imam Khan left the mosque to join the crowd of worshippers on the square. He noticed to his right a television reporter who usually took a sympathetic stance toward Islam, and he started to move in her direction. As he advanced, he saw out of the corner of his eye that another reporter was approaching him from the left, microphone outstretched. He knew that the second reporter worked for an extreme right-wing television station that was openly hostile to all non-Christian religions. Azhar Khan immediately turned his head and body to his left to acknowledge the second reporter. As he did so, a Lapua Scenar GB488 VLD bullet whizzed past his right ear and buried itself in the forehead of Menelaus Tsolakoglou who was standing behind him, bellowing "Muslims go home" and wishing that the police were elsewhere so that he could once again throw a stone at the imam.

CHAPTER FIFTEEN

Everything would have been so different if Heracles's shot had missed Menelaus Tsolakoglou and instead had struck one of the worn marble paving stones that covered Hadji Ali Square. Heracles would have calmly worked the bolt of his sniper rifle to eject the spent cartridge and load a new cartridge into the breech. He would then have made a second attempt to assassinate Imam Khan and, if necessary, a third. But as Heracles watched through his telescopic sight, he saw Menelaus Tsolakoglou dropping to the ground. The spurt of blood and tissue that shot up as the bullet entered Menelaus's brain was indelibly imprinted on Heracles's memory. He was paralyzed with horror. The Hellenic Spartan League had indoctrinated him to believe that killing a Muslim was not just permissible, but actually praiseworthy. But Heracles had a killed a Greek, a young teenager whose recent shouts had carried across the square and through the open window into the bedroom of the pensioner's apartment.

Pantelis, too, was in a state of shock. He had seen Imam Khan move to his left just as Heracles fired. Then he saw the lifeless body of Menelaus lying in the square and he immediately realized what had happened. Both men were temporarily unable to move.

Heracles recovered first. "Run, Pantelis, run!" he shouted, forgetting that the window was wide open. Fortunately for the two men, the uproar on the other side of the square drowned Heracles's voice.

"But what about the rifle?" Pantelis asked.

"That's the job of the clean-up crew," Heracles replied. "Now run!"

"No!" Pantelis responded. "Two men seen running from the scene of a murder are sure to get arrested. We'll walk at our normal pace."

They left the flat, forgetting to close the door, and started to descend the stairs.

"Where can we go?" Heracles asked. "Should we return to the insurance salesman's apartment?"

"Definitely not. They'll soon be conducting a house-to-house search of the neighborhood and then the whole of Athens. I think we'll be safest if we return to Krotonos. The Metro is the quickest way to the Piraeus Ferry Port."

***

Less than a minute after the two assassins had left the building, a man and a woman arrived at the apartment complex. They climbed the stairs to the fourth floor and entered the pensioner's one-bedroom apartment, closing the door behind them. First they put on the gloves they had brought with them. Then, one grabbed the rifle and put it back in its case, the other closed the window. The woman removed the remaining sandwiches from the refrigerator. Then they both methodically wiped down all surfaces that Pantelis or Heracles might have touched, including the door handle of the refrigerator. A final check of the apartment yielded the key that the two assassins had utilized to enter the flat. The two uniformed police officers left, the woman carrying the rifle case. They walked to the police van that they had parked around the corner and drove off. The Hellenic Spartan League clean-up crew had carried out its duties quickly and effectively.

***

During their train ride to Piraeus, both men were exceedingly nervous. They tried to appear calm, but the events of the afternoon had affected them to their very core. It would be wrong to say that they had undergone some sort of instantaneous conversion, like Paul on the road to Damascus—the realization that fascism is the epitome of evil came to them only much later. But they both now knew that they could no longer be blind followers of the philosophy of the Hellenic Spartan League. Saying "Death to all Muslims" was one thing; implementing the slogan was horribly different.

Strangely, it was Pantelis who was most affected, even though it was his friend who had pulled the trigger. In the train, Pantelis kept looking around for pursuers and for people who would publicly accuse him of murdering Menelaus Tsolakoglou. Heracles kept nudging him and whispering "Keep still" in his ear. But it was no use. Pantelis was racked by guilt.

Heracles managed to control himself all the way to the Piraeus Metro station. But as they alighted from the subway train at the end of the line he, too, started looking behind him. Eventually they boarded the fast ferry to Syros. They sat outside on deck during the entire two-and-half hour trip. Neither man spoke a word; they were totally alone with their thoughts and their utter remorse at what they had done.

The sun was setting as the ferry from Syros neared Krotonos. Pantelis started shivering uncontrollably. Heracles tried everything he could to assist his friend, but nothing helped. Fortunately for them, in the gathering darkness none of their fellow passengers seemed to notice that anything was wrong.

A worried-looking Sergeant Kyrgiakos met them at the dock and escorted them to the far side of the square in front of the port. He looked round to make sure that no one was within earshot. Then, in as kindly as manner as he could manage, he said, "I've seen both TV clips—I know it wasn't your fault." Neither man reacted, so he went on. "They keep playing the films over and over again. That Imam moved as you fired, but your shot was definitely dead on target."

The unfortunate way the sergeant ended his last sentence made matters much worse. Realizing what he had just said, he tried again. "It was simply bad luck. You know, kismet. We are all helpless against the unseen hand of fate," he said, not realizing that he was echoing the exact words of Abdul Rahman ibn Sultan just before Mahmoud ibn Laban murdered him. Again neither islander reacted, both deep in the grip of psychological shock. At no time had the Hellenic Spartan League prepared them for the possibility that anything might go wrong.

Sergeant Kyrgiakos walked them to their home, at one point having to support Pantelis to keep him from collapsing on the cobbled street. When they reached the house, he had to ask Heracles three times to give him the front door key. Once inside, he sat the two men down at their table. He knew not to give them any alcohol, but he thought that a cup of strong coffee might help. The three men sat in silence until the water containing the finely ground coffee beans came to a boil in the *briki*, a small copper pot placed on the stove.

The coffee helped a little; both men slowly became somewhat more responsive. The sergeant felt that it was time to tell them what was going to happen. "You men are heroes of the Hellenic Spartan League. But we have to get you out of Greece as soon as possible. Planning is now in full swing. A member of the League owns a restaurant in Glasgow. Because you both now speak such excellent English, he'll take you on as waiters until it's safe for you to return to Krotonos." This time the sergeant was careful to guard his tongue. He had no way of knowing how much the Athens police had learned about the killing. Accordingly, he feared the worst and assumed that the two friends would not be able to return to their beloved Greece without being arrested for murder until the Hellenic Spartan League came to power, an event that Sergeant Kyrgiakos was forced to admit to himself was an extremely unlikely future possibility.

Now he turned to the practical details of their escape from Greece. "The problem is that you cannot travel on any form of public transportation. Air, rail, even buses could be dangerous. We obviously have no way of telling if the authorities will ever find out what actually happened, but if they do, your photographs will be sent out via Europol or perhaps even Interpol. You could show your passports and then board a flight at Athens International Airport with no problems at all, and then find yourselves under arrest when you land in Britain. The same applies to the Channel Tunnel, and to all trains and ferries. And you can't rent a car either, for the same reason."

"So how do we get to Glasgow?" Pantelis asked. These were the first words he had spoken since they had boarded the Metro train several hours before. Kyrgiakos was pleased that the coffee had seemed to work, but he instinctively realized that both men were still under the greatest stress.

"Well," the sergeant said, "as you know we have sympathizers all over Europe, people like us who strongly oppose any form of multiculturalism. We've already found someone who lives in Bari, on the heel of Italy, who'll lend you his car. To get you there, we'll take you to Italy in our cabin cruiser. From Bari you'll drive to France. We still have to work out how to get the car back to Bari.

"We're also not yet sure where on the French coast you'll go," he continued. "We're still looking for someone with a boat to take you across the channel. And there'll be a car waiting on the other side for you to drive to Glasgow. So get a good night's sleep. There's nothing to worry about. The League is taking good care of you." Sergeant Kyrgiakos left the two men. There was nothing more that he could do.

After the sergeant had gone, Heracles and Pantelis went straight to bed. They lay awake hour after hour, reliving the horrors of the assassination attempt that had gone so terribly wrong. Toward dawn they dropped into an exhausted sleep, but their dreams were a repetition of their waking nightmares.

CHAPTER SIXTEEN

Early the next morning Lieutenant Cosmatos visited them at their home. He, too, greeted them as heroes and brushed aside their protestations that the assassination attempt had been a dreadful failure that had ended in tragedy. "Not at all," he averred. "As a consequence of your valiant exploits yesterday, every Muslim in Greece is today living in terror, not knowing when the next bullet will strike. Yes, the death of Menelaus was indeed a tragedy, but every revolution has its glorious martyrs."

He paused to see if his words were having any effect, but both men were staring at him blankly, so he tried a different tack. "The people at the headquarters of the League have successfully organized your trip to Glasgow. You'll leave here tomorrow morning before dawn in our cabin cruiser. We've arranged for two highly experienced sailors to take you to Bari. I think you'll enjoy their company—they've led really interesting lives. When you get to Bari the following night, you'll go ashore in the Zodiac. A man will be waiting for you on the beach. His name is Maurizio Farinelli. He'll take you to his apartment where you'll spend the night. The next morning you'll steal his car."

"What do you mean?" Heracles asked.

Delighted that at least one of his audience was actually listening to him, the lieutenant plunged on. "I'm only joking. He'll drive you to France in his car, of course. But you'll have to share the driving with him. We'd love to give you false passports, but there isn't time. At least we can get false driver's licenses for you from Ermoupoli. Someone will come here tonight on the Syros ferry to bring the new licenses to you."

"But what about the photographs on the licenses?" Heracles enquired.

"They're on file in Ermoupoli. Apparently there's some sort of bug in the current computer system, and it's really easy to print a genuine license with the correct photograph but a false name. The company that developed the software correctly pointed out that, when a woman marries, she'll probably want a new driver's license in her married name. However, there are no appropriate checks built into the system, so a clerk in the licensing office can reissue any license with any new name. Consequently, you two will be issued driver's licenses that will pass every check—"

"Except one," Heracles interrupted.

"What do you mean?"

"When the clerk makes up names for us, there won't be birth certificates for those names."

"Oh yes, there will," the lieutenant replied with a smirk. "We've thought of everything. In Ermoupoli they've found birth certificates for people born in the same year as you two but who died in early childhood. So, yes, there are birth certificates."

"But there are also death certificates for those names," was Heracles's next objection.

"Not any more," Cosmatos replied. "Our men have found a related flaw in the record-keeping system in the city hall in Ermoupoli. The geniuses who wrote the software also came up with another really clever idea. They reminded the members of the regional council that, even in the best-run bureaucracies, clerks sometimes make typing mistakes. Accordingly, the councilors agreed that their system has to offer the facility of changing any field in any record. That's fine. But again there are no appropriate checks in the system, so anyone can change any data item. Once our people have issued your new driver's licenses, the corresponding death certificates will be modified just enough to ensure that no one ever finds out that your new licenses are made out in the names of dead people. No, I've got that wrong. They have to change the death certificate first—the computer system doesn't allow you to issue a driver's license for someone who's no longer alive."

Heracles looked at Cosmatos in amazement. "Are you telling me that anyone who's authorized to use the births, marriages, divorces, and deaths computer system for the South Aegean region can change anything and no one will ever find out?"

"Essentially, yes. I understand that up to now there have been no problems because so few people know all the capabilities of the system, and those that do have meticulously refrained from misusing the computer system in any way. That's going to change today." He stopped talking and winked at Heracles. Heracles said nothing.

Lieutenant Cosmatos went on. "Consequently, you'll travel with driver's licenses that will pass muster, no matter what."

He paused again, but neither man said anything, so Cosmatos continued. "You'll drive from Bari to Saint-Malo in northern France. That should take you no more than twenty-four hours. The three of you will alternate the driving, stopping only for fuel and food. The toll roads in France and Italy have fully equipped service centers every twenty-five miles or so. When you get to Saint-Malo, you'll drive to the walled city. Farinelli will drop you off there, and then drive his car back by himself—it'll probably take him three days. On the way to Saint-Malo, he'll provide you with full instructions for making contact with Aristide du Chanel, your French contact, who has come up with an excellent way for you to cross the English Channel."

"Is that really his name?" Heracles asked. "It seems too much of a coincidence."

"Apparently it is. He's a highly respected and respectable dentist in Saint-Malo. I'm sure you can ask him to show you his consulting rooms, and you'll see his name on his certificates mounted on the wall there. Anyhow, Dr. du Chanel has arranged with a friend to take you across the Channel in his motor yacht, and he'll explain to you where you'll find the car that you'll drive to Glasgow. Just remember that the British drive on the wrong side of the road!

"One further item. We're going to provide you with a lot of money in cash, euros that you'll use in Italy and France. Obviously you can't take your ATM cards or credit cards with you—that would provide a trail that even a blind policeman could follow. What we don't have here on the island to give you are enough British pounds, the currency you'll need to pay for fuel and food on your drive to Glasgow."

"But surely we can change money in Britain? What do tourists do?"

"They use ATMs, which you cannot do. Or they use banks or money changing services, both of which require passports. And, as I pointed out, unfortunately it'll take too long to provide you with passports. But you don't need them, anyway. When you get to Saint-Malo, du Chanel will give you all the British pounds you'll need, and more.

But Heracles had come up with another objection. "But in order to travel in a foreign country, we need a passport, and you just said again that you can't provide us with passports."

"Yes and no. Yes, you need a passport to travel in a foreign country. But no, you don't need one to travel between European Union countries—all you need is a EU identity document. And we're also going to provide you with official Greek identity cards in your new names. So you don't need passports."

"Wait a minute," Heracles said, "you're talking about the Schengen Agreement, aren't you?"

The lieutenant nodded smugly.

"You're saying that if we're stopped between Bari and the French coast, we should show our driver's licenses. If they ask for proof of identity, our Greek identity cards are all that is needed."

"Correct," the lieutenant replied. "And that's why you mustn't drive via Switzerland, which isn't a member of the European Union. Farinelli will have maps that will show the route to Saint-Malo through Turin and Lyon, rather than Milan and Geneva."

"But that won't help us in the United Kingdom. We need a passport there. Britain isn't a signatory to the Schengen Agreement," Heracles insisted.

"Of course she is," replied the lieutenant brusquely. "Britain's in the EU, and it's an EU agreement."

"Yes, it's an EU agreement. But as far as I know, it doesn't apply in Ireland or Britain."

"You're still in a state of shock from yesterday," said Cosmatos in a kindly voice. "Just relax and take it easy, and I'll come back later with documentation to show you."

Two hours later he returned, only slightly chastened. "You were correct," he said. "You do need a passport for Britain. But it's all arranged. We'll send your new passports to Dr. du Chanel's house. If you get there before your passports do, you'll stay with him in Saint-Malo until the documents arrive. From then on you'll have Greek passports in your new names, in the unlikely event that someone in England or Scotland insists on seeing them. By the way, you can't take your cell phones with you, for obvious reasons—just your clothes. Please pack a small case each for the journey to Glasgow.

After Lieutenant Cosmatos had left, Pantelis spoke for only the second time since the murder of Menelaus Tsolakoglou. He turned to Heracles and said, "They didn't know that we need passports for Britain. What else don't they know?"

CHAPTER SEVENTEEN

The turquoise blue Aegean Sea surrounded the cabin cruiser as far as the eye could see. The men on board had last seen an island more than an hour before—the Cyclades lay below the horizon behind them. The two elderly seafarers who were taking Pantelis and Heracles to Bari wouldn't give their names, but they were quite open about their past. "We're retired smugglers. We've spent our entire working lives transporting goods all over the Mediterranean, evading the customs officers. The one thing we never knowingly carried was drugs. Alcohol, of course, especially to Muslim countries where it's officially forbidden. Duty-free cigarettes, all the time. Stolen goods, in abundance; if it fell off the back of a truck, it ended up in our boat. But never drugs."

The second seafarer chimed in, "We know every deserted beach from Gibraltar to Istanbul to Cairo, every abandoned port that the customs officers have forgotten about."

"Were you ever caught?" Heracles asked.

"Three times, but on two occasions they just confiscated the cargo and the boat, and they let us go."

"Why were they so lenient with you?"

"Customs officers are extremely badly paid, especially in North Africa. So, when they confiscated our cargo, they kept a considerable percentage for themselves. Now they couldn't turn us in, for fear we'd talk to the authorities in the hope of getting a lighter jail sentence. A few years ago, in southern Spain, we were unfortunate enough to encounter a totally honest customs officer. After that we sat for four years in a prison in Valencia. That was not a pleasant experience. While we were in that hellhole we lost our boat and we lost the goods we'd bought. So when they finally released us, we came back home to live on an island on our government pensions."

The four men stood in companionable silence as the cabin cruiser sped across the Aegean Sea toward the Ionian Sea and Italy. Then Pantelis asked cautiously, "How do you know Lieutenant Cosmatos?"

"The man who hired us?"

"Yes."

"We live on one of the islands that he patrols. We're regulars in the bar that he and his men frequent when their patrol boat is tied up at our port. We're always complaining about the rising cost of living, especially with the recent drastic cuts in our pensions. Two nights ago the barman called me to the phone. The lieutenant was on the line. He asked me if we wanted to earn some good money. He was quite cagey, he just told us to get to Krotonos right away with an overnight bag each. The ferry service in our part of the islands is as reliable as ever, so we got to Krotonos yesterday afternoon. When we arrived there was no sign of the lieutenant—apparently he was out on patrol somewhere. Instead, a police sergeant met us and explained the deal. He handed over half the money in advance, and we're going to get the other half when we return this cabin cruiser to Krotonos. By the way, he told us nothing about you, and we don't want to know anything. Especially not your names. Our only stipulation is that you're not involved with drugs, and the sergeant guaranteed that on your behalf. So here we are, and here you are. And tomorrow night we're going to put you on a beach about a hundred miles north of Bari. We've used the location in the past, with great success. We've given your people detailed directions for finding the beach—your contact had better be there to meet you."

"And if he's not there?" Pantelis asked.

"Our deal is to deposit you on the beach, preferably without you getting your feet wet. If your contact doesn't show up, you two are on your own. We take a photograph of you on dry land to show the sergeant, and after that it's *arrivederci*, as they say in Italy."

A few minutes later Pantelis motioned to his friend, and the two of them walked slowly into the saloon, leaving the two smugglers in the wheelhouse.

"What's Plan B?" Pantelis asked.

"You mean, what are we going to do if Maurizio Farinelli doesn't show up?"

"Precisely. The original arrangement was that we'd meet him on a beach just outside Bari, a location of his choosing. So presumably he knows how to get there. Now our smuggler friends have changed the pick-up point to one that they've used before, but that beach may be quite new to Farinelli. And do we know that they even informed him of the change of venue?"

"Now you're being ridiculous," Heracles said. "They couldn't possibly have let us leave for Italy without confirming the location of the beach with Farinelli."

"Couldn't they? This is the crowd who didn't even know that you need a passport for Britain. We've been out of Greece only once in our lives, for that week we spent on the beach in Majorca, and yet we knew all about the regulation."

"Okay, so they slipped up there," Heracles conceded. "But there's too much at stake for the League if we're caught. I think you're worrying unnecessarily. I've no doubt whatsoever that everyone in the Hellenic Spartan League from the top downward is pulling out all the stops to ensure that we arrive safe and sound in Glasgow."

"I hope you're correct. Now we'd better rejoin our smuggler friends. It would be highly inadvisable to make them suspicious in any way whatsoever. Especially if for some irrational reason they get it into their heads that we're smuggling drugs."

***

After midnight the following evening, the cabin cruiser anchored off a beach located within a fenced-off nature reserve. A notice board next to the main gate of the reserve stated that entrance was strictly forbidden between the hours of 6:00 p.m. and 8:00 a.m. In accordance with the notice, the gate to the reserve was chained shut. About a hundred yards away, an ancient white Fiat Punto was parked under a tree. The driver of the car, Maurizio Farinelli, had left his vehicle there at about eleven o'clock that night. He then climbed over the gate and walked two miles to the beach. He was extremely angry. He was a creature of habit who hated to deviate from his routine in any way. Furthermore, any change to a previously agreed arrangement was a source of particular irritation to him. All parties had agreed that he would meet the cabin cruiser at a small beach just outside Bari, a location that he visited on a regular basis precisely because it was almost always deserted even during the day, let alone in the middle of the night. But they had changed the arrangements behind his back, ordering him to go to a different location. Then he had discovered by looking at online maps that there were three beaches inside the perimeter of the nature reserve. The somewhat imprecise details of the location of the beach for the rendezvous that his Greek contact had given him could have referred to either of two beaches, situated about a kilometer apart. He had phoned Athens to ask for clarification but was told that the smugglers had already left for Italy and could not be reached.

Farinelli was a middle-aged bachelor, a tall, thin, bespectacled mathematics teacher at a Bari high school. His nickname among the students was

"Lom" because when he became agitated—which happened frequently—a pronounced tic started in his left eye, resembling the twitches that actor Herbert Lom created for his role as Chief Inspector Charles Dreyfus in the "Pink Panther" comedy films.

After he learned that the organizers in Athens had radically changed the pick-up point without even consulting him, Farinelli began twitching sporadically. But when he could not decide which of the two beaches in the nature reserve was the new venue, the tic became virtually permanent. In order to take sufficient time off during term time to drive the two Greek men to Saint-Malo and return home, he had intended to telephone the school and lie about his health. However, when the tic simply would not stop, he went to see his principal who, without being asked, immediately granted him a week's leave to recuperate. For some incomprehensible reason this infuriated Farinelli, and the tic reached grotesque proportions that even the late Herbert Lom would have had difficulty imitating.

He walked toward the beach that he had decided was the more likely candidate for the rendezvous. The path through the dense foliage ended and the coarse sand of the narrow beach began, and Farinelli immediately saw that he was in the wrong place; the waning crescent moon provided just enough light to reveal that all along the waterline there were rocks that had not appeared on Google Maps. Growing angrier by the minute, Farinelli backtracked and made for the other beach.

As he waited there, Farinelli dropped the torch he was to use to signal the boat, and had to scramble in the faint light of the sickle moon to find it in the soft sand. That was the last straw for him. He was about to leave in high dudgeon when he heard a boat approaching. It got closer and finally slowed to halt. He heard the sound of an anchor being lowered. Then he saw the flashes: two long, two short. He responded with three long flashes and two short ones. Soon he heard the Zodiac landing with a splash in the Adriatic Sea, the outboard motor started, and a dark shape headed for the beach. It came to rest on the soft white sand. Two men climbed out and stood for a moment on the beach as someone in the inflatable photographed them. Then they ran toward him.

"Are you Maurizio Farinelli?" Heracles asked in English.

"I am. Who are you?"

Heracles resisted the urge to reply, "You saw the sign and you gave the countersign. So who the heck do you think we are?" but instead introduced himself and Pantelis, using their cover names. Maurizio led the way to his car.

The three men climbed over the gate. When they reached the Punto, Farinelli informed the Greeks that the two of them would have to share the driving to Saint-Malo, because he had to drive the whole way back by himself. He then settled himself in the back seat. Heracles took the wheel, with Pantelis riding shotgun. Farinelli now announced that he would navigate.

"Aren't we going to use a GPS?" Pantelis asked.

"No GPS for safety," Farinelli replied. "I'll use maps. Much safer."

"Are you saying that they can track a GPS?"

Farinelli ignored him. "Continue straight here, and turn left at the end of this road," he instructed Heracles, speaking in a confident voice. For the next ninety minutes, the silence in the car was broken only by occasional terse but clear commands from the mathematics teacher. When they reached the A14 motorway, Farinelli made an announcement. "We're now on *Autostrada* A14, also called *Autostrada Adriatica* because it follows the coast of the Adriatic Sea. Stay on this road," he ordered. "Follow the signs to Bologna. It's about three hundred miles. I'm going to sleep." He folded his long body into the cramped back seat as best he could and closed his eyes.

During the remainder of the night, Heracles and Pantelis alternated as drivers. When one drove, the other tried to nap, with little success—both men were far too wound up to be able to sleep. They stopped every so often at service areas to change drivers and once to refuel the car. All this time Maurizio did not move. The sun rose and they changed drivers yet again. As they got out of the car, Heracles said softly to his friend, "Is he really sleeping or is he just trying to avoid conversation? Or is he trying to rest up for the twenty-four hours of driving back to Bari? After all, he probably hadn't slept at all before he picked us up."

"I've no idea, but we're getting close to Bologna, so we'd better wake him. We definitely don't want to find ourselves at a Swiss border post."

They returned to the car and Pantelis roused their navigator. He yawned. "Where are we?"

"We're near Bologna. You have the map. Where do we go now? And I suggest we stop for some breakfast when we next change drivers."

"I'm not hungry. Follow the signs for Turin. Take the A1—that's the *Autostrada del Sole* or Motorway of the Sun—and then at Piacenza take the A21. We call that one the *Autostrada dei Vini* or Motorway of the Wines." Farinelli was a compulsive teacher and he could not help himself from trying to instruct the two Greeks any more than he could control his tic. "You should be there in three to four hours. Then follow the signs for Lyons—the French border is only about half an hour's drive beyond Turin. I'm going back to sleep."

Maurizio slept and Pantelis and Heracles alternated the driving for the rest of the day. Eventually, just after midnight, Pantelis saw a sign that said "Saint-Malo 30."

Immediately he woke the mathematics teacher. "Maurizio, we're getting close to Saint-Malo. I need you to give me directions."

"Just follow the signs, like before."

"No, that's not good enough. We need to get to the walled city. You have to tell us exactly where to go."

Reluctantly, Farinelli straightened himself. He opened the hand luggage he had taken with him and took out a large-scale Michelin map. A series of concise commands followed, as laconic as the night before. Eventually they saw the walls of an old city in front of them, lit by floodlights. "Park here," Maurizio ordered tersely. "Now, do you see that archway on the left? Walk through there. You'll find yourself in Rue Cartier." He proceeded to spell both words slowly.

In order to forestall the inevitable explanation, Heracles quickly interposed, "Named after the jeweler, of course."

"Not at all," said Farinelli in a shocked voice. "Jacques Cartier was the French explorer who discovered Canada during the sixteenth century. He was born in Saint-Malo. So, walk up Rue Cartier and turn left at the third street. It's called Rue Fermat." And again he spelled both words.

This time it was Pantelis who tried to avoid the inescapable lecture. "Another explorer born in Saint-Malo?"

On hearing this, Farinelli became practically incapable of speech, but he somehow managed to blurt out, "Pierre de Fermat was one of the greatest mathematicians of all time. Haven't you heard of Fermat's Last Theorem, which was recently proved using a computer program?" The silence from the front seats confirmed Farinelli's worst suspicions.

Farinelli sniffed loudly, and then continued. "So, walk through the gate. That's Rue Cartier. Take the third street on the left, Rue Fermat. Dr. du Chanel lives at Number 29, the fourth door on the right side of the street."

"Shouldn't you phone him to tell him we're on the way?" asked Pantelis. "It's after midnight."

Maurizio's curt tone was the one he used when reprimanding errant students. "No GPS, no cell phones."

"Okay," replied Heracles, "we'll just ring the bell." The two men got out of the car and opened the trunk to take their suitcases. They shook hands with Maurizio Farinelli, thanked him for escorting them to Saint-Malo, and walked through the archway.

When they were out of earshot, Heracles said, "This morning we were complaining about his lack of conversation. But can you imagine what twenty-four hours of his treating us like ignorant schoolboys would've been like?" He shook his head slowly, and they walked on through ancient streets dimly lit by old-fashioned street lamps.

CHAPTER EIGHTEEN

Notwithstanding the many unflattering things that might be said about Maurizio Farinelli, at least the directions he gave were crystal clear. Accordingly, a three-minute walk brought Heracles and Pantelis to a door with two shiny brass plates. One plate informed passersby that this was Number 29, Rue Fermat. The other stated that the occupant was a dentist named Aristide du Chanel. On the right side of the door was a bell push, which Heracles utilized to alert the dentist that they had arrived.

They heard footsteps descending an uncarpeted wooden staircase. Then the door opened a few inches and a portion of a head appeared. Despite the poor light, three features struck Heracles: thick, unkempt white hair; thick glasses in wire frames; and a vast, thick white moustache under a bulbous nose. As for Pantelis, his first reaction was that he was looking at a caricature of Georges Clémenceau wearing trick spectacles and a huge white wig over his bald head.

The eyes behind the thick lenses glared. A voice barked out a question.

"I'm sorry, but we don't speak French," Pantelis answered in English.

"Who are you?" the voice asked in English, heavily overlaid with a French accent.

"We're from Greece," Pantelis replied.

"Yes, yes, and your names?"

"Pantelis and Heracles."

"No, no, your current names."

Surprisingly, Pantelis could not recall his new name, but Heracles was able to supply both. Satisfied, du Chanel opened the door wide and welcomed the men inside. "Come in, come in!" he said warmly. "Come upstairs. That's my surgery over there in front of you; we live on the second and third floors. You must be exhausted from your long drive. Your beds await you, but would you like something to eat? A glass of wine, perhaps? Or a digestif? Yes, a digestif! You're in Brittany now, so how about a glass of calvados? The best quality, of course, from Pays d'Auge. You don't know our apple brandy? Let me repair that omission! I'll bring you some right now." And Dr. du Chanel bustled out, returning with two small crystal glasses filled with a clear liquid.

Pantelis and Heracles were exhausted, and the only thing they wanted after nearly twenty-four hours of car travel was to go straight to sleep. But they had no choice. They looked at one another and then each took a cautious sip. Much to their surprise, it was utterly delicious, and they drank the rest in a few gulps. Their host immediately left the room, returned with the bottle of calvados and refilled their glasses, again almost to the rim. Both men slept soundly that night and well into the following morning, waking around noon.

Their third-floor bedroom was filled with daylight. On the dresser stood a vase of flowers and next to it they found a note. Dr. du Chanel's handwriting was excessively ornate, and the two men spent several minutes trying to decipher it. Their best guess was that Dr. du Chanel wanted them to know that he was going to be in his surgery until lunchtime; that his wife, Marie-Claude, would be delighted to help them in any way she could, including providing breakfast; and that it was vitally important that they were not to go outside under any circumstances whatsoever.

They bathed and dressed, and walked down one flight of stairs. They found themselves standing outside a sunny sitting room. Through the wide-open door they could see a plump gray-haired woman with rosy cheeks. Her glasses were as thick as her husband's and her hospitality was equally warm.

"Ah, you've woken up! I trust you slept well. Come in, sit down. My husband will be upstairs in a moment, unless he's encountered a tricky case this morning. If he's late for lunch, it usually means a wisdom tooth extraction. I've told Aristide time and time again, if a wisdom tooth has to come out, send the patient to the oral surgeons in Rennes—it's only an hour by car. But he's so old fashioned in many ways, and insists on doing everything himself. So we may have to wait for lunch. Can I bring you something to eat in the meantime? You must be starving."

Both men thanked her, but said that they would wait until their host returned for lunch. They sat in silence for no more than a minute. Then they heard footsteps on the wooden stairs, and the dentist entered the room with arms extended and a big smile on his face.

"Greetings and salutations to the noble heroes from Greece—your fame will redound unto the generations! We are honored to have you stay with us. I've no idea who you really are, but I do read the newspapers."

The dentist winked broadly before continuing. "I have to tell you that your passports haven't arrived, so we'll have the extreme pleasure of your company for a while yet. Let's repair to the dining room, where a sumptuous repast assuredly awaits us!"

Dr. du Chanel escorted them into the dining room and indicated where they should sit. Mrs. du Chanel went to the kitchen, returning with a tray laden with four bowls filled with steaming fish bisque, which she laid at each place. She sat down. And suddenly silence descended—the du Chanels had bowed their heads. The dentist intoned a lengthy grace in Latin. Neither of his visitors understood a word, but enthusiastically chimed in "Amen" at the end of the seemingly interminable prayer.

They ate the entire four-course meal without speaking a word. It was as if the du Chanels had taken a vow of silence that lasted until everyone had finished their coffee. At that point the dentist resumed his previous conversation exactly where he had suspended it. "As I told you, unfortunately your passports haven't arrived yet. It seems that there's been some sort of hitch, but no one seems to know quite what it is. But don't worry, it'll be our pleasure for you to stay here until the matter has been satisfactorily resolved."

Dr. du Chanel acknowledged their thanks with another broad smile. Then he continued, "In my note I asked you to remain indoors, for obvious reasons. But if you are to stay here for some days, I was wondering if you'd be prepared to take the risk of walking through the town. The chance of anyone recognizing either of you is remote, of course, but it's up to you to decide whether or not to venture outdoors."

Before either man could reply, the tall pendulum clock on the landing chimed. Dr. du Chanel took out his pocket watch and exclaimed, "I have to return to the surgery." He kissed his wife and went downstairs.

Pantelis stood up and said to Mrs. du Chanel. "Thank you so much for the delicious meal. Your husband was kind enough to suggest that we visit Saint-Malo. Where should we start and what should we see?"

"You have an opportunity to see one of the most beautiful ancient towns in France," their hostess replied. "I'm not going to give you a map. Start by getting lost in the old city. As you try to find your way back, you'll see the real Saint-Malo. We have dinner at eight. I'll see you then."

***

The voice coming from the secure smartphone said, "Speak."

"The sniper rifle that killed the Greek teenager was one of the two in the shipment to Krotonos," Sheikh Mansour said. "It has been destroyed. It can never be used as evidence."

"Message received and understood. Out."

***

Mahmoud ibn Laban was ushered into the Saudi banker's office.

"You are the acting head of the Islamic Front for Jihad and the Liberation of Palestine?"

"Yes," Mahmoud replied. "I'm in charge until Mustapha reappears."

"And what makes you think that there's the slightest chance that Mustapha is still alive?"

"The door to the strongroom is open."

"Meaning what exactly?" the banker asked.

"Mustapha told us that he'd arranged for a locksmith to come to Krotonos to reset the combination of the strongroom. He was quite emphatic that he'd locked the door before he left the island and he insisted that only he knew the combination. As I believe you are well aware, Mustapha and the three men he hired have all disappeared, and the empty cabin cruiser is once again moored opposite the house after an absence of a few days. But the fact that the door of that strongroom is open means that Mustapha must have arrived at the house with the shipment and unlocked the door so that the goods could be stored there."

"Could he have opened the storeroom door under duress?"

"Not Mustapha. He would sooner die under torture than obey the enemy."

"You say 'the enemy.' What makes you think that the Israelis are involved?" the banker asked.

"Who else could it be?"

"But do you have any evidence of any Mossad agents within a hundred miles of Krotonos?"

"Well, no."

"So why do you think the Israelis are involved?"

"Again, who else could it be?"

"There are dozens of organizations worldwide, perhaps hundreds, that would love to lay their hands on the Semtex and those weapons. So I ask you again: What proof do you have that the Israelis are involved?"

"None," Mahmoud ibn Laban replied.

"I see. Now, let's return to the door of the strongroom. You said that Mustapha declared unequivocally that he'd locked the door, and only he knew the combination. Correct?"

"Correct."

"What about the locksmith?"

"What do you mean? What does a locksmith have to do with this?"

"Mustapha didn't change the combination, the locksmith from Athens did. So, the locksmith must know the combination as well. Isn't it possible that the locksmith gave the combination to somebody else?"

"Why should he?"

"Possibly because that somebody else held a gun to the locksmith's head and told the locksmith that he'd blow his brains out unless the locksmith gave that somebody else the combination."

"Is that what happened?" Mahmoud ibn Laban asked.

"I've no idea. Didn't your people talk to the locksmith?"

"Well, no."

"Do you even know who the locksmith is?" the banker asked.

"We weren't able to find out."

The banker rose to his feet. "When Mustapha returns, tell him to come and see me at once. *Ma'a as-salaama* (goodbye)."

As soon as his visitor had left, the banker called in his confidential aide. "I've just had a visit from the acting head of the IFJLP. His name is Mahmoud ibn Laban, and he's in charge 'until Mustapha reappears.' Those clowns still don't realize that Mustapha isn't going to reappear. In addition to losing their incompetent leader, they've somehow managed to lose the shipment as well. And their new leader is even more inept than Mustapha. Regarding the strongroom, I have some fresh information to share with you.

"Salim's men," the banker continued, "located the locksmith and held a gun to his head to frighten him into giving them the combination. But some other group is apparently a lot more frightening than Salim's gang are, because the locksmith wouldn't say a word regarding the combination. Instead, he made it clear that there would be fierce retribution if anyone dared to lay a finger on him. They took no notice of his threat, tied him up and ransacked his shop. They found his two-part notebook hidden under a pile of empty boxes, but the second copy of page 78 was missing. Someone had extremely neatly excised it from the book—Salim said that, unless you were looking for it, you wouldn't notice that the page had gone. The usual trick is to lay a wet piece of string on the page and close the book. If you put the string right next to the binding, then it's easy to tear the page out leaving almost no trace. Anyhow, Salim's men decided to extract the information from the locksmith, and unfortunately they killed him in the process. I say 'unfortunately' because, as the locksmith had threatened, there have indeed been repercussions. I learned an hour ago that every single member of Salim's gang who was at the locksmith's shop that day has disappeared, including Salim himself, the men who were standing guard outside and the drivers of the two cars."

"Why would the Israelis do that?" the aide asked.

"What makes you think that the Israelis are responsible?" the banker replied.

"Who else could it be?" the aide asked.

The banker's head started to spin. This was déjà vu all over again. No way was he going to repeat every detail of the conversation he had just had with

Mahmoud ibn Laban. So he spoke somewhat more forcefully than usual. "I tell you that these latest killings have nothing to do with the Israelis. There are no Mossad agents anywhere near Krotonos. But there are numerous gangs all over the world who would love to get held of that Semtex. Including Greek gangs."

"Greek gangs?" asked the aide.

"Greek gangs who blow open bank safes with explosives. Greek gangs who try to overthrow their government with bombs and other acts of terror. And Greek gangs who try to assassinate imams with sniper rifles but murder teenagers instead," replied the banker.

"And you think that the shipment has fallen into Greek hands?"

"Yes, I do," the banker insisted.

"And how do you wish me to go about getting it back?"

"Contact the Islamic Front of Yemen. They've set up a new courier service that operates out of the Al-Mansoura district of Aden, so your message should reach Malik Ismali within a few hours. Inform him that we need to find out where the shipment is. By all means, tell him the location of the house on the island and let him know that they can use it as a highly effective base. But warn him what happened to Salim and all his associates. And there's something else. That perverted crook Ziyad bin Abu Dawud made his home in that house on Krotonos. Persons unknown murdered him, in all probability on the island. After the killing, Mustapha made it known that he now owned the house. Some group murdered Mustapha in turn, possibly the same people who killed Ziyad bin Abu Dawud, and probably again on Krotonos. It appears that Muslims are exceedingly unwelcome on Krotonos. So suggest to Malik Ismali that it would be advisable if the Islamic Front of Yemen paid a private investigator from Athens to investigate—an infidel investigator."

"After what happened to Salim, is Athens safe for Muslims?" the aide asked.

"Salim was a special case, I think. They didn't murder him and all his men because Salim and his gang were Muslims, they slaughtered our people because they killed the locksmith. But you've made a good point nevertheless. When you contact the Islamic Front of Yemen, warn Malik Ismali about what happened to Salim and his associates."

CHAPTER NINETEEN

On the third day they came back to the du Chanel house at lunchtime to find that their passports had at last arrived. Madame du Chanel opened the front door, a big smile on her face, and informed the two men that the UPS delivery woman had delivered the eagerly awaited travel documents an hour earlier.

The past three days had been extremely stressful for both Pantelis and Heracles. On the one hand, they had thoroughly enjoyed every aspect of Saint-Malo, both the old city and the large modern city beyond the walls. They had strolled all the way round the walled city on top of the ramparts, walked to the offshore islands at low tide, and made the most of the beautiful beaches. But all the time they were acutely aware of what they had done. Fear of retribution was not the thought that was uppermost in their minds. Instead, a constant feeling of guilt at having killed an innocent teenager gnawed into them. And they were just starting to comprehend that there could be no justification whatsoever for their attempted assassination of Imam Azhar Khan, no matter how much the Hellenic Spartan League tried to rationalize or validate what Pantelis and Heracles had done. They did not discuss the killing, but they knew one another well enough to be fully aware what the other was thinking.

As the two men started to follow Madame du Chanel up the stairs to the second floor, she turned round to them and said in a conspiratorial whisper that was loud enough to be heard back in Greece, "Commodore Milson is here."

Waiting in the sitting room was a tall Englishman in his sixties. His short gray hair was immaculately combed, as was his toothbrush moustache. He was wearing a tailored gray suit and old school tie. The two Greeks shook hands with the commodore, but before any of them could say anything, Madame du Chanel explained.

"Commodore Milson has houses in Dorset in Southern England and here in Saint-Malo, and he travels between them in his motor yacht. He'll be taking you across the channel. We phoned him as soon as the passports arrived, and he's already alerted his crew. So you'll sail straight after lunch in order to catch the tide."

The commodore nodded.

Madame du Chanel explained further. "Saint-Malo has one of the largest tidal variations in France. About forty feet at full moon, I think—is that right, Commodore?"

Milson nodded again as Madame du Chanel continued. "I do hope you'll have a smooth crossing. The English Channel, as you English insist on calling it, is so treacherous. Are you expecting good weather, Commodore?"

"No," the commodore replied succinctly.

"Let's eat the moment my husband comes upstairs, so you'll be able to leave soon. You positively have to catch the tide or your journey will be delayed by twelve hours. Ah, here's Aristide." Marie-Claude du Chanel swept the luncheon party into the dining room.

When the silent meal was over, Heracles and Pantelis went upstairs to pack and collect their bags. The warm farewell speeches from the du Chanels were far from brief. In the end, Commodore Milson had to all but drag them down the stairs, muttering, "The tide, the tide."

As they walked the short distance to the Saint-Malo yacht harbor, the Commodore spoke to them in a low voice so that passersby could not overhear. "Welcome to France and, let's hope soon, welcome to England! What you two did was a brave act, but what jolly bad luck you had. Don't worry, you're travelling under false names and no one told me what you've done. But I can put two and two together as well as the next man. And you can certainly trust me to keep my mouth shut.

"Talking about trust," he continued. "I'm not sure just how far I can trust my crew. They're all members of the Party, of course, but who knows these days? So, if they greet you or speak to you, just nod to them, please—they mustn't hear your accent under any circumstances. And when you go aboard, go straight to the saloon and stay there. There are two cabins if you want to nap, but it's only about a hundred and fifty miles as the crow flies, so we should there in no more than seven or eight hours—

the twin diesels can easily sustain twenty knots, even in bad weather.

"Oh, yes, before I forget," he went on. "Two things. First, I have some money to give you—you're certainly going to need plenty of pounds sterling in Britain. Second, there's been a minor change of plan. Instead of your driving to Glasgow, we've found someone to drive you there. With all due respect, the feeling was that you might forget where you are and drive on the wrong side of the road."

Both men nodded and Heracles smiled politely.

"One final point," the commodore concluded. "I hope that you're good sailors—it's going to be a rough crossing, I'm afraid."

The two islanders looked at one another but by common unspoken agreement said nothing in reply. It was obvious that the commodore had no idea that they had been fisherman for years before they became tour guides. As it turned out, however, their experiences with Mediterranean storms in no way equipped them for what they went through the rest of that day. When the boat finally docked around ten o'clock that night in the yacht harbor at Weymouth, both men were profoundly grateful to step once more on dry land.

A black Rolls Royce Phantom Extended Wheelbase drew up at the quayside. "Ah, here's my car," Commodore Milson said, clearly unaffected in any way by the crossing. "Get in. And again, not a word, please."

The two men climbed in, their bags on their laps. The commodore tapped on the glass partition that separated the driver's compartment from the passenger seating area and they set off. Soon they reached a major road, and the chauffeur sped up. But after about ten minutes, he turned off onto a series of side roads, ending up on a narrow street where they saw a sign reading "Lower Brent Caravan Park." The car drew to a halt behind a battered Mini Mark VII parked on the side of the road in front of the RV park. The Commodore took one look at the car in front, threw open the street-side passenger door, and stormed out of the limousine. He banged on the driver's window, which slowly opened. Neither man could see the driver inside the dark interior of the Mini, but through the open door of the Rolls Royce they could hear the commodore yelling, "I thought I told you to get that Party sticker off your back bumper."

The driver's response was inaudible, but the door of the Mini opened and a man of about twenty-two emerged. Illuminated by the interior light of his car, he looked like a skinhead who was trying extremely hard not to look like one. He could do nothing about his shaven scalp, but he appeared to have bought his attire at the local Salvation Army store. Furthermore, the style and condition of his garments suggested that a pensioner had donated them after wearing them for many years and then parted from them with the greatest reluctance.

The young man opened the trunk of his Mini, took out a box of tools and started working on the rear bumper. There were no streetlights, so Pantelis and Heracles could not clearly discern what he was doing, but presumably he was removing the offending bumper sticker under the watchful eye of Commodore Milson.

Eventually the commodore returned to the car. He signaled to the two islanders, who dutifully got out. "This," he said, "is Godfrey Clegg. Clegg will be driving you to Glasgow. I have informed him that he is to drive in such a way that he will not arouse the suspicions of the traffic police patrolling the motorways. He knows what will happen to him if he forgets and the police stop him, don't you, Clegg?"

The skinhead-in-mufti nodded unwillingly.

"Get in the car. You've got nearly five hundred miles of driving ahead of you."

Then Commodore Milson smiled for the first time and said, "Good luck and Godspeed!"

With a clash of gears, Godfrey Clegg started off. When they were once again on the major road, Clegg turned to Pantelis who was seated next to him, and asked, "What's your team?"

"Olympiakos. And yours?"

"Manchester United, of course." And turning round to face Heracles, he asked, "And yours?"

"Face the front!" Heracles yelled. After a while he added, in his normal speaking voice, "Panathinaikos."

During the rest of the lengthy drive, Clegg tried a few times to persuade his two passengers that their allegiance belonged to Manchester United rather than the two top Greek soccer teams. The islanders quickly realized that the best way to respond was to say nothing. Clegg, it seemed, loved to argue. But when his passengers simply sat calmly in silence, he was unable to continue the verbal battle and just drove on.

Unlike Maurizio Farinelli, Godfrey Clegg had no qualms about using a GPS or, as he called it, his satellite navigation system or satnav. As a result, he had no difficulty finding his way and deposited his passengers in front of a restaurant in Glasgow before noon. As instructed, he had taken pains not to attract the attention of the traffic police. Throughout the journey he had stayed well within the speed limit and had taken a short break from driving every hour or so.

The restaurant was not yet open for lunch. Pantelis repeatedly knocked on the door, and eventually a young man in a waiter's uniform opened it a crack. "We're not open," he said somewhat pointedly, indicating the sign that showed the hours during which meals was served.

"We need to see Mr. Anagnostopoulos, please," Pantelis said.

"I'll see if he's here," the waiter replied, and closed and locked the door again.

They waited for about five minutes. Eventually a stout elderly man wearing a blue suit and a harassed expression came to the door. "Yes, what is it?" he asked.

Speaking Greek, Pantelis said, "The Hellenic Spartan League sent us here."

The restaurant owner's face lit up like the rising sun. "Why didn't you say so? Welcome to Glasgow!"

***

Mr. Anagnostopoulos was a forgiving man, willing to overlook almost any minor fault in his employees. However, when a stream of piping hot soup cascaded onto the lap of a diner because Heracles carelessly tilted a bowl of avgolemono, the restaurant owner demoted him to busboy, restricting him to clearing empty plates. Two days later Pantelis tripped as he approached a table of diners, water jug in his hand. Within seconds he, too, was informed that his sole responsibility from now on was assisting his fellow busboy in his plate-removal duties. They realized that they were not cut out to be waiters, and carried out their menial tasks as best they could.

Each day, Pantelis became more and more depressed. Heracles first put it down to his friend's demotion to busboy. Next he thought it might be the weather—the contrast between the deep blue Aegean Sea that surrounded Krotonos and the intense blue skies over their island on the one hand, and the unending gray Glasgow weather on the other, was obvious. Finally Heracles thought it was just homesickness, and that it would soon pass. He was wrong.

One evening after the restaurant had closed for the night, Pantelis took Heracles aside.

"I feel so guilty about what happened to Menelaus Tsolakoglou."

"I know. I feel the same way. But I was the one who pulled the trigger, not you. Your role was just to sit next to me," Heracles reassured him.

"Rationally, you are correct. But I still feel guilty about the death of Menelaus, so guilty that I want to kill myself."

"Are you serious?"

"Yes."

"You know you mustn't joke about such things."

"I'm not joking."

"Shouldn't you see a psychiatrist or something?" Heracles asked.

"And what should I tell him?"

Heracles said nothing for a while, and then replied, "I see what you mean." He paused again and then he said, "We've got cell phones in our new names. I'm going to phone Sergeant Kyrgiakos."

"Are you crazy?"

"What else can I do? If I do nothing, you'll kill yourself."

"And if you phone Greece you'll end up in prison for the rest of your life."

"Why?" Heracles asked. "There's no way they could possibly be tapping this cell phone I bought two weeks ago. And if they're tapping the sergeant's cell phone, then it's only a question of time before they arrest both of us."

"I don't care—I'm going to kill myself anyway. If you want to phone home, do so. It's your funeral."

The next morning Heracles phoned Sergeant Kyrgiakos. "Hello, I'm calling from Glasgow," he said carefully in Greek.

"Don't say anything," the sergeant replied, immediately realizing who was phoning him. "Just listen carefully to me. They don't know anything, and they won't know anything. They'll never know anything. You can come home now. Take a train to Bari and then the ferry to Patras." And he hung up the phone.

Heracles repeated to Pantelis what Sergeant Kyrgiakos had said.

"But why did he say, 'Take a train to Bari, then the ferry to Patras'? If everything is really as hunky dory as he claims, then we could travel home any way we wish. Call him back and find out what's going on."

"There's no point in my doing that," Heracles replied. "He's clearly not going to say anything more over the phone. He disconnected immediately after he told us to come by train and then the ferry. One thing is for sure: We are going to need the help and co-operation of the Hellenic Spartan League for the rest of our lives. Disobeying orders is precisely the wrong thing to do. In any case, I think you're worrying unnecessarily. He didn't say that it was unsafe to travel any other way, he just told us to travel by train to Bari and then take the ferry to Patras, and that's what we're going to do."

"Just a minute. You did say 'Bari,' didn't you?"

"Yes, I said 'Bari' because that's what Sergeant Kyrgiakos said."

"Bari is where Maurizio Farinelli lives."

There was a long silence while both men tried to work out the implications of what Sergeant Kyrgiakos had said. Pantelis was the first to speak.

"Kyrgiakos has told us to travel from Scotland to Greece along a specific route. As far as I know, there are numerous alternatives. One is to fly from Glasgow to Athens. There probably isn't a direct flight, but we can change aircraft in London or Paris or somewhere. A second way would be to take the train overland via Vienna and Sofia. A third way would be to take the train to Venice, and the ferry from there to Patras. That would be my first choice, by the way—I've always wanted to see Venice. And there must be many other routes that combine trains and ferries. And then there are buses. We have to take a bus from Patras to Athens, and we certainly can take buses for other parts of the route. And we can always hire a car to drive from Glasgow to Athens, although a one-way rental is extremely expensive. With all those alternatives available and many more, Sergeant Kyrgiakos declares that we have no choice—we have to travel by train via Bari. Why?"

Heracles was considerably heartened by this speech. His friend had been depressed to the point of considering suicide, but now he was talking about wanting to visit Venice.

Heracles answered, "I told you word-for-word what Sergeant Kyrgiakos said, and I can state categorically that he made no mention of our good friend the Italian mathematics teacher." And after a pause he added, "Thank heavens!"

"Yes, that's excellent news," Pantelis replied. "But it makes the situation even more murky. What possible reason could he have for sending us via Bari?"

"I suggest we ask him when we return home. In the meantime we have to tell Mr. Anagnostopoulos that his two least favorite busboys are about to leave his employment. It was extremely kind of him to take us on and provide us with this room to stay in as well, but I think he'll be greatly relieved to hear that we're on our way. If nothing else, next month's bill for dropped plates will be a fraction of this month's."

Pantelis grinned broadly and then asked, "By the way, what reason are we going to give everyone on Krotonos for our month-long absence? We haven't contacted anyone since we've been here. Worse still, we didn't say goodbye, we just left. I'm sure our parents are worried out of their minds."

"No, I'm sure that Sergeant Kyrgiakos told them that we're fine. But what are we going to say to the islanders? Here's an idea: Do you remember those two gorgeous young women from England? We gave them the grand tour of the island, but sadly that's where it ended. How about we tell people that they invited us to stay with them in London for a month?"

CHAPTER TWENTY

The Saudi banker called in his confidential aide. "What news from the Islamic Front of Yemen regarding the shipment to Krotonos?" he asked.

"They sent a man named Hidayatullah ibn Saleh to Greece to find out what happened. He met with various contacts that we have in Athens and asked them to suggest a private investigator. He then hired one of the two detectives that they'd highly recommended. He instructed the man to go to Krotonos, look around and ask a few questions. The private eye apparently arrived on Krotonos and checked into the only hotel on the island. He was seen an hour later having coffee with one of the local inhabitants in a café overlooking the fishing harbor. A few minutes later the investigator checked out of the hotel and took the next ferry out of Krotonos. It appears he didn't even ask where the ferry was headed—his sole concern was to get off the island right away. Then, after he returned to Athens he refused to have any more business dealings with Hidayatullah ibn Saleh. He phoned his client and simply said that he didn't wish to proceed with the case, and that there would be no charge for his services to date or for his expenses."

"Interesting. Presumably the same people who scared the locksmith also frightened off the private detective. And it seems from what you said that at least one member of the group lives on Krotonos. Is there any way you can find out who the person was who had coffee with the investigator in the café? I assume that Hidayatullah ibn Saleh found another investigator to delve into that angle."

"Not exactly," the confidential aide said.

"Meaning what?" asked the banker softly.

"Meaning that Hidayatullah ibn Saleh has also disappeared."

"What!" the banker shouted.

"I'm afraid so," his aide replied. "As far as I can tell, Ziyad bin Abu Dawud, Mustapha, and the three Lebanese men from the cabin cruiser all disappeared from Krotonos. But it seems that Hidayatullah ibn Saleh never left Athens."

The banker looked at his aide in horror. "When Mustapha came to see me," the banker said, "he explained precisely why he chose Krotonos for the base for the IFJLP. One reason was that Ziyad bin Abu Dawud was well liked there. Now it seems that there is a group on Krotonos that doesn't merely dislike Muslims, it has apparently killed no fewer than five members of our faith there. And they have done so in such a way that their bodies have disappeared. Yes, Krotonos is an island, but bodies thrown into the sea have a mysterious way of reappearing at inconvenient times in unexpected places. However, no one has seen the slightest trace of any of the five missing men. So whatever group was responsible is highly competent.

"And now we turn to Athens," he continued. "You just told me that Hidayatullah ibn Saleh disappeared from Athens. But so did Salim and the seven other men in his group who were involved in killing the locksmith, including even the two drivers who waited outside. And no one has found the slightest trace of any of them, either. I think you were correct when you suggested that they killed Salim and his gang at least partly because they were Muslims. That means nine Muslims have disappeared from Athens, also presumed dead.

"So," the banker went on, "who's behind all this killing of Muslims in Greece? The Greeks know that we Qutbist jihadis believe that we have to wage Holy War and reconquer all territory formerly ruled by Muslims. And that includes Greece. Now it seems that there's a group of Greeks who are fighting back. But who are they? And what's the importance of the small and insignificant island of Krotonos?"

"There's a factor that perhaps we haven't considered," the aide said. "The key to the whole situation is undoubtedly Ziyad bin Abu Dawud. After Ziyad disappeared, Mustapha acquired the house, and then he and his three sailors were killed. Before that, Mustapha summoned the locksmith from Athens—that eventually led to the murder of Salim and his team of seven in Athens. And further investigations on the part of Hidayatullah ibn Saleh resulted in his death. That makes a total of fourteen Muslims. Had it not been for the killing of Ziyad bin

Abu Dawud, none of this would have happened. But Ziyad bin Abu Dawud was certainly not one of us. He totally ignored all Five Pillars of Islam. In addition, he took malicious pleasure in being seen in public drinking alcohol and eating forbidden foods. And as for the Sixth Pillar, jihad, he considered it a joke, a throwback to the seventh century—the fact that the word is found forty-one times in the Holy Koran meant nothing at all to him. So, if there is a anti-jihadi movement in Greece, Ziyad bin Abu Dawud would be the last person that they would kill."

"You're quite right," the banker said. "And there's something else. I'm certain that the people who killed all fourteen Muslims were also responsible for the attempted assassination of Imam Azhar Khan, a man who consistently condemns violent jihad both publicly and in private and, therefore, a man who is an enemy to our cause. So, why did they kill Ziyad bin Abu Dawud and why did they try to murder Imam Azhar Khan? It just makes no sense at all."

"And what about the sailors? I've discovered that none of them had the slightest political outlook. They were just doing what sailors do—why were they killed?"

"Maybe they saw something they weren't supposed to see?" the banker suggested.

"Such as?"

"The murder of Mustapha."

"Yes, that's possible. And if you're right, all the other murders were carried out for the same reason.

There's a problem with that explanation, though," the aide said.

"And that is?"

"It doesn't explain why Ziyad bin Abu Dawud was killed. If we knew why they murdered him, we might know why they killed the others."

"But what's more important," the banker said, "is who did the killings. Find out for me who murdered our people so that I can take revenge."

CHAPTER TWENTY-ONE

It took three days for Pantelis and Heracles to get from Glasgow to Krotonos. They travelled by train to Bari and from there by ferry to Patras, and then by bus and ferry to Krotonos, where they arrived just after sunset. The news of their return spread like wildfire; the reason that they gave for their absence spread even faster. Consequently, most of the men greeted them with a broad wink, and the majority of the unmarried younger women flashed them a sultry come-hither look. Almost everyone on the island came out that evening to welcome them home.

One person who was conspicuously absent from the cheering crowd was Iphigenia Koteas. Another individual who chose not to join the throng of well-wishers was Sergeant Kyrgiakos, in his case because he thought that the two men would want to talk to him privately. He was right—as soon as they could eventually get away, they walked to the Kyrgiakos home. When they arrived, he shooed his wife and daughters out of the house and poured the men a glass of Metaxa.

"First and foremost, welcome home! A toast to the heroes of Krotonos!"

After he had refilled their glasses with the spiced brandy, he sat back and said, "Next, before we say or do anything else, let me have your new passports, identity cards, driver's licenses and cell phones. They need to be locked away securely. It's most important that nobody finds them lying around, for obvious reasons." The two men handed over the sets of documentation they had received, as well as the telephones they had bought in Glasgow.

Then Sergeant Kyrgiakos asked, "Now, what do you want to know?"

Pantelis looked at Heracles, who shrugged and said, "Fine, I'll go first. Why did you send us via Bari? It took us three long days to get here, what with all the trains and the ferries and that bus. We could've flown to Athens, we could've taken the train all the way from Glasgow to Athens, but you insisted that we go via Bari. Why?"

Sergeant Kyrgiakos smiled. "You couldn't have travelled by rail from Glasgow to Athens, because the train no longer runs from Sofia to Thessalonica—in 2011 Greece put a stop to all trains crossing its borders as part of its austerity program, though I've no idea at all why stopping international train travel saves the government any money. And the reason that I suggested that you travel via Bari is that it's the cheapest route—it's five or six euros less than the air fare."

"For the past three long days we've done nothing but try to work out why you sent us via Bari. And that was the reason—to save us a few euros? And think of all the money we had to spend on food."

211

Pantelis said in a shocked voice. "If we'd flown home, it would have taken us half a day. We're leaving. Right now."

"Don't you want to know what's been happening?" the incredulous sergeant asked.

"That can wait until tomorrow," Heracles replied. "We'll talk to you then."

"Where are you going?" the sergeant asked, as the two men got up and headed for the door.

"Home," Pantelis growled, "to sleep."

"And how do you propose to unlock the front door?" the sergeant asked. "Remember, you left here with only your clothes." And he walked to the mantelpiece, picked up a key and handed it to Pantelis. This action somewhat mollified the two men, but they nevertheless walked to the front door. Heracles shouted "Good night" as they left; his friend said nothing at all.

The next morning they returned to the Kyrgiakos home. The sergeant welcomed them as if there had been no unpleasantness of any kind the night before. "So, you've come to hear the facts now? Excellent! Sit down, I'll make us some coffee, and we can talk."

When they were seated around the table, Sergeant Kyrgiakos said, "The news is all good—despite the fact that the forensics team has positively identified the apartment from which the shot was fired."

"How can they be so sure?" Pantelis asked.

"First, the ballistics experts analyzed the two TV films independently. Both yielded the same trajectory for the bullet, starting at that apartment. Second, there were no fingerprints whatsoever in the apartment, not even of the tenant. Third, there were marks on the windowsill of the bedroom that in all probability were made by the bipod of an Accuracy International AX338 sniper rifle. Fourth, what the tenant told the police makes it certain that he was tricked into leaving his apartment. Is that enough for you yet? If not, there's more."

"What about the rifle? Have they found it yet?" Pantelis asked.

"No, and they're not going to be able to find it, either. It no longer exists. Well, the atoms and molecules that used to be part of the rifle still exist, but little more than that. More to the point, as I just told you, they didn't find a single fingerprint anywhere in the apartment. They sent in three different teams, all with the same negative result. So they don't have any clues as to the identity of the shooters."

Heracles had a different concern. "But wasn't the tenant able to identify the two men who were masquerading as social workers?"

"Yes, and the police found them within an hour."

"And?"

"And they're both social workers. They work in a small branch office near Hadji Ali Square. A cleverly worded letter fooled them completely. The letter purported to come from their supervisor's supervisor, quite a senior manager in Athens, who happened to be in hospital at the time, recovering from a serious operation."

"But we heard afterward that the social workers took the key of the apartment from the tenant," Heracles said.

"The letter was quite explicit on that point. It stated that there was a legitimate concern that the elderly pensioner might absentmindedly lose his key while out of his familiar surroundings, so the social workers were to take his apartment key, keep it in their office while he was on vacation, and take it with them when they went to bring him home from the resort. The letter stated precisely where the key was to be kept for security. Needless to say, it quickly disappeared from there."

"So what happened afterward?" Heracles asked.

"What with the ongoing investigation, another flat had to be found for the tenant. He's happy in his nice new apartment. Also, the two social workers feel really stupid that they fell for the letter, but that's about it. No one has attached any blame to them—the letter was clever enough to fool almost anybody."

"Have the police closed the file yet?"

"Murder files are never, ever closed. On the other hand, everyone concerned, including the Public Prosecutor, is absolutely convinced that this wasn't a case of murder with Menelaus Tsolakoglou as the victim, but rather an attempted assassination of Imam Khan that went wrong. But in the total absence of any clues at all, they've had to put the case into abeyance. And I see no reason why it shouldn't stay that way forever."

"So what happens now?"

"You just get on with your lives. You have a home, you have a business, and you apparently have a large number of local admirers who all want to prove to you that they are far superior in bed than your English former clients. After all, Aphrodite, the Goddess of Love, was Greek, not British."

Heracles had no trouble following the sergeant's advice, and almost immediately returned to his old life as if nothing had happened. With Pantelis it was different. After the initial euphoria at his return to his beloved island of Krotonos had worn off, he became even more depressed than he had been in Glasgow. He spoke almost every day about suicide. Try as he might, Heracles could not find a way to help his friend. Heracles went to Sergeant Kyrgiakos for advice, but he, too, was unable to see how to assist.

And then Lieutenant Cosmatos received an urgent letter regarding the Cyprus Memorandum. In response, the Hellenic Spartan League drew up a plan to detonate a Semtex bomb on the platform at Waterloo Underground station. In both senses of the word, the Cyprus Memorandum proved to be explosive.

CHAPTER TWENTY-TWO

One day, Lieutenant Cosmatos returned to his quarters at Ermoupoli to find an express letter waiting. Written in Greek, it read as follows:

PRIVATE AND CONFIDENTIAL

My dear Cousin,

My name is Lukas Cosmatos. Your father may have told you about me. His late father (your grandfather) and my late father were brothers. I moved to Britain in 1970 and decided, for reasons that are no longer important, to give up my Greek heritage, my Greek culture, even my Greek name. I also, regrettably, cut myself off from my family. At that time in my life, the only important thing for me was to become totally British. I took elocution lessons to hide my Greek accent. I became a British citizen and changed my name to Luke Cosworth. And I turned my back on the situation in Cyprus.

I was well aware that about three-quarters of the people living on Cyprus are of Greek descent; less than a fifth of the population have Turkish ancestry. I knew that, in 1974, a group of Greek Cypriots attempted to gain control of Cyprus and make it part of Greece. Turkey retaliated by invading the northern part of the island. Cyprus was partitioned into two pieces: the Republic of Cyprus on the southern part of the island, and the Turkish Republic of Northern Cyprus. The only country that recognized the Turkish Republic of Northern Cyprus was Turkey; all other countries considered that part of the island to be occupied territory of the Republic of Cyprus. Feelings were running exceedingly high in Greece. But I considered the Cyprus situation to be a Greek problem, whereas I was now British.

Soon after I arrived in London I found employment as a cleaner, labouring all night in a large building that housed thousands of civil servants. Like most Greeks I am hard working and most ambitious, and within nine months I had started my own business cleaning offices. After a few years, my company specialized in providing janitorial services for government buildings, especially those that require a security clearance to enter. In particular, we have the contract for cleaning the Prime Minister's Office, which occupies more than a hundred rooms at Number Ten, Downing Street, including the Cabinet Room.

Last week, the senior manager who supervises the cleaning of the Prime Minister's Office suddenly fell ill, and I decided to inspect our cleaners' work myself. I arrived at the back entrance at about four o'clock in the morning. As all cleaners entering the premises have to do, I handed over my cell phone to the security staff on duty and they let me in. I checked what my employees had done. They seemed to have performed everything to our usual high standard. Then I entered the Cabinet Room.

In order for you to understand what happened next, I need to tell you more about that room. In the center is the huge Cabinet table, surrounded by twenty-three chairs. Each Cabinet Minister has a reserved seat at the table. A leather-backed blotter inscribed with the Cabinet Minister's title marks each minister's place. (In case you are too young to remember, we used blotting paper to absorb excess ink from paper in the days when we still wrote with a fountain pen and ink.)

I was wondering whether my crew had polished the entire table to my satisfaction, so I lifted one of the leather-backed blotters. To my surprise, underneath the blotter I found a sheet of paper that had attached itself to the leather.

I suspect that part of the paper had become damp, perhaps as a consequence of a spill from a glass of water. It seemed to me that someone had accidentally shifted the blotter on top of the paper and, when the moist patch dried, the paper stuck to the leather.

I peeled the paper off the blotter and read it. It was part of memorandum describing a possible new initiative by the British Government for settling the Cyprus conflict. I cannot stress too highly that this is not yet policy, but is still merely a proposal that someone in the Foreign and Commonwealth Office has put forward. But the central pillar of the plan hit me like a ton of bricks: After more than forty years of partition, Britain will begin a new peace initiative by recognizing Turkish sovereignty over Northern Cyprus. And then the British government will persuade other countries, especially the members of the United Nations Security Council, to do the same.

I thought that I was a true-blue Englishman until I read that memorandum or, more precisely, the single page of the peace plan that I had seen. At that instant I became a loyal Greek again. My blood boiled and I was about to explode, as any Greek would on reading such a suggestion. But then I realized that anger would not achieve anything. On the contrary, it would be totally counterproductive.

Furthermore, I would lose my security clearance and, with it, the opportunity to learn anything more about this reprehensible idea.

Accordingly, I immediately remoistened the page and put it back under the blotter the way I had found it. The security people keep a meticulous count of copies of documents, so I dared not remove it from the Cabinet Room. They also monitor the various photocopiers in the Prime Minister's Office like hawks, so I could not make a copy. In any case, I do not have the code to use their machines. And the security people still had my cell phone, so I could not photograph the Cyprus Memorandum.

Then it suddenly hit me. This was not a piece of paper that some Cabinet Minister had accidentally mislaid; this was a trap that British Intelligence had set to test my loyalty. In reality, my senior manager was perfectly well. His emergency midnight call was just a ruse to get me to check on the cleaners at Number Ten. After all, everyone knows that I am fanatical if not obsessive compulsive when it comes to cleaning. There was no question that, if my senior manager fell ill, I would come in person to Number Ten to make sure that my cleaners had done everything to my highest standards. And I undoubtedly would lift one of the blotters to check that the cleaners had polished the entire table, not just the visible areas. But then another thought struck me: How could the British have known in advance which blotter I would lift? The answer was obvious—they must have put a piece of paper under every blotter. So I checked underneath the other twenty-two leather-backed blotters. There was no other paper. Next I looked to see which Cabinet Minister's blotter I had picked at random, and found it belonged to the Secretary of State for Culture, Olympics, Media and Sport. Now, if I were a spy looking for Cabinet secrets, the last place I would look would be the Department of Culture, Olympics, Media and Sport. The conclusion was obvious: This was not a trap. And then I remembered that, for obvious reasons, there are no surveillance cameras or recording devices in the Cabinet Room itself, so if British Intelligence had decided to test me, they would not have set the trap in that room.

I left for home at once, somehow remembering to pick up my cell phone at the guardhouse on my way out. My mind was in a whirl as I tried to decide what would be the right thing to do about the Cyprus Memorandum. My initial idea was to contact the Greek Embassy, but that would lead nowhere. The British would obviously deny everything—after all, I had no written evidence of any kind. Then I wondered if there was someone in Greece I should inform, but I have cut myself off from my homeland for the past forty years or so. Then it came to me: The members of my family would know what to do. I used Google to find out as much as I could about my relatives. As far as I could determine, you are the only appropriate person. As a lieutenant in the Coast Guard, you have the necessary contacts, as well as the discretion to keep my name out of this situation. I do not mind going to jail or even giving up my life for the sake of our beloved Greece, but if there is a way to keep me out of it, I would greatly appreciate it.

Long live Greece! Long live freedom!

Your cousin,

Lukas Cosmatos (Luke Cosworth)

CHAPTER TWENTY-THREE

On the Wednesday evening after he had read the letter regarding the Cyprus Memorandum, Lieutenant Cosmatos's patrol boat was tied up at the quay on Krotonos. Accordingly, that night's meeting was held aboard the vessel. The lieutenant spent most of the session talking about the document his cousin had found. In order to protect his source, Cosmatos was circumspect, but his message was clear: There was a distinct possibility that the British Government might soon recognize the Turkish Republic of Northern Cyprus.

During their seemingly interminable trip home, Heracles and Pantelis had decided that they should distance themselves from the Hellenic Spartan League. But then they realized that this would be impossible; their future freedom depended on the League. Accordingly, they reluctantly continued to attend the Wednesday meetings. That night, Pantelis was as depressed as ever, but suddenly he perked up near the end of the lieutenant's remarks.

"We have to warn the British not to proceed with their so-called peace plan," Pantelis declared. "You have that Semtex you took from the Islamist terrorists. I don't know where you've hidden it, but

I'm sure you can lay your hands on some of it at short notice. We need to stage a bombing at the busiest Underground station in London. We certainly don't want anybody to get hurt, so the explosion has to take place when there's no one on the platform. We simply want to send a message to the British to drop this insane plan forthwith."

This suggestion received unconstrained enthusiasm. Once the shouting had died down, one of the Coast Guard crew asked the obvious question: "How are we going to set off the bomb?"

"Easy!" Pantelis replied. "I'm going to travel to London with the Semtex, a detonator, and a suicide vest. And I'll wait until the platform is clear and then detonate the bomb."

There was total, shocked silence for nearly a minute. Then the chief petty officer spoke up. "I thought you just said that you didn't want anybody to get hurt," he said pointedly.

"What I meant," Pantelis said, "is that I don't want any innocent parties to get hurt."

Once again there was a long silence. Then Lieutenant Cosmatos shouted out, "Meeting adjourned!"

During the next few days, the members of the Hellenic Spartan League participated in innumerable tense meetings held at the home of the two tourist guides. The purpose of the sessions was to try to convince Pantelis that his idea of exploding a bomb in an Underground station on an empty platform was an excellent one, but a suicide bomb was totally out of the question. Pantelis repeatedly countered that he was going to kill himself anyway to atone for the death of Menelaus Tsolakoglou, and he wanted his act of suicide to be meaningful. His fellow members of the League understood why Pantelis wanted to commit suicide, but they were unable to come up with a strategy that would dissuade him from self-destruction. Eventually he wore them down, so much so that the topic of the meetings slowly changed to planning for the forthcoming suicide bombing. All through these gatherings Heracles said nothing. The more he heard, the more helpless he felt, and the more he was tormented by guilt for what he had done to Pantelis as a consequence of the assassination attempt.

Once everyone except Heracles had tacitly agreed that the suicide bombing would proceed, the main issue was to determine how to get Pantelis and the Semtex to London. Public transportation of any kind was obviously out of the question. Hiring a car and then driving from Athens to London was the next suggestion, but every suggested route crossed several international boundaries before entering the European Union; the risk of border guards or customs officers finding the Semtex was too great. Finally Lieutenant Cosmatos pointed out that, because Britain had opted out of the Schengen Agreement, there was no way of entering that country legally without passing through customs and immigration, with the concomitant risk.

Eventually Pantelis came up with a solution. He would travel to London the same way that he and his friend had travelled to Glasgow, only this time

Heracles would not accompany him. Also, on this second trip he would have his new passport with him from the start, so there would be no wait in Saint-Malo. In fact, he would go straight from Bari to Commodore Milson's motor yacht—there was no need to involve the du Chanels at all. And this time Godfrey Clegg would not drive him to Glasgow but rather to a hotel near Waterloo station. From there he could walk to the Underground station and detonate the suicide bomb on a deserted platform.

Lieutenant Cosmatos put this plan to League headquarters. The Secretary-General immediately came back with an objection: Surely the two elderly smugglers, Maurizio Farinelli, Commodore Milson and Godfrey Clegg would all object to transporting Semtex?

Sergeant Kyrgiakos was quick to come up with a good solution to this problem. They would securely wrap the flat Semtex bricks, each of them the correct size for inserting into a compartment of the suicide vest, in multiple layers of colored plastic to hide both the distinctive odor of bitter almonds and the orange color, and then replace them in their metal ammunition boxes. The League would try to come up with wording that they would stencil on the boxes that would ensure that they would be handled respectfully, but would not have anything like the same effect as a label that read "Semtex." They would place the Frishman detonator and the suicide vest in a separate ammunition box. They would then tape all three boxes tightly shut. This solution satisfied the powers that be, and they proceeded to organize Pantelis's trip. A member of the Hellenic Spartan League came to the island and spent an afternoon explaining to Pantelis how to assemble the suicide bomb and how to detonate it.

Pantelis left the island three days later. Other than being haunted by a sense of déjà vu, the first leg of the new trip went smoothly for him. As before, the two smugglers asked no questions. They came aboard and, finding the ammunition boxes in the saloon, tied them down to ensure that they would not move about in the event of rough seas. Then they ignored them for the rest of the trip. When the cabin cruiser was finally at anchor off the beach in the nature reserve, the smuggler who brought Pantelis to shore on the Zodiac helped him carry the boxes to where Farinelli was waiting—with a woman.

"This is Lisa," he said by way of introduction. "She's going to help us with the driving."

Farinelli helped Pantelis by carrying one of the boxes the two miles from the beach to the locked gate. Lisa helped them lift the boxes over the gate, but played no other role in the proceedings. The two men loaded the boxes into the trunk of the Fiat Punto and then joined Lisa in the car.

Lisa turned out to be one of Maurizio's neighbors. Pantelis never quite managed to determine what she did for a living, if anything. Her conversation was almost exclusively limited to invectives against Muslims, all of them laughable. For example, she kept referring to Tallahassee, the capital of the State of Florida. Her complaint was that the second through sixth letters of the name "Tallahassee" spell "Allah" and that this was part of an Islamist plot to take over the United States, a conspiracy that she repeatedly described in detail. The first time she trotted out this nonsense, Pantelis tried to reason with her, but it was useless. Lisa had made up her mind, and that was that. The second and third times she raised the issue, Pantelis said nothing. That approach did not work either. Lisa simply repeated, almost verbatim, everything she had already said about the Islamist plot. It was obvious that she was obsessed with this threatened take-over of America, and nothing and no one could deflect her from airing her delusions over and over again. To the surprise of Pantelis, Maurizio Farinelli encouraged her. Whenever she flagged for a moment, he would prompt her to continue. Not surprisingly, Lisa's repeated diatribes depressed Pantelis even further. Their arrival at the Saint-Malo yacht harbor around midnight came as a welcome relief.

Commodore Milson greeted them at the gangway, and motioned to two of his crewmen to bring the ammunition boxes. They carried them onto the motor yacht and deposited them in the saloon. From the casual way that they handled the three boxes, Pantelis assumed that they were well aware that empty metal ammunition boxes are widely utilized for storing or transporting a variety of different items. Again the boxes were tied down, this time for the Channel crossing. The tide was right, so they set sail almost at once.

Commodore Milson joined Pantelis and assured him that on this occasion the trip from France to England would be smooth. As it happened, Lisa's incessant diatribes had kept Pantelis awake for the past twenty-four hours, so the exhausted islander slept all through the voyage and did not notice that the commodore's prediction proved accurate. Half an hour before they were due to arrive, Milson woke Pantelis so that he could have breakfast in the saloon.

When the boat docked at half past seven, the large black car was on the quay to meet them. The two crew members who had carried the three boxes onto the boat now fetched them and loaded them into the cavernous trunk of the Rolls Royce. As on the previous occasion, the chauffeur drove to the RV park. And as before, Godfrey Clegg was waiting in his Mini. Only two boxes could fit in the tiny trunk, so the chauffeur helped them to load the third box into the back seat of the small car. Godfrey and Pantelis got into the front seats, and they set off for London.

Everything went well until two miles after they joined morning rush-hour traffic on the M3 motorway. Suddenly the car started swerving from side to side. "We've got a flat tire!" Pantelis shouted.

Godfrey wasn't in the least disconcerted. He pulled off the motorway onto the hard shoulder and turned on his hazard warning lights. Both men got out. Godfrey opened the trunk and took out the two ammunition boxes, placing them on the edge of the road behind the car. He opened the compartment beneath the floor of the trunk and took out the spare tire, jack, and lug wrench. Godfrey now started changing the tire. Pantelis was surprised to see how adept Godfrey was.

Within ten minutes the flat tire was lying on the road and Godfrey was starting to tighten the lug nuts on the spare tire when a police car drew up with blue lights flashing. The driver opened the door of the patrol car, clambered out and walked toward the Mini.

"May I be of assistance?" a deep voice said, as the policeman cast a professional eye over the tire Godfrey was changing so competently.

"I think everything's under control, officer," said Godfrey, with justifiable pride in his voice.

But the second policeman in the patrol car had noticed the two ammunition boxes on the side of the road. He opened the passenger door, climbed out somewhat stiffly and approached Clegg. "Excuse me, sir, but do you have an Firearms Certificate for transporting that ammunition?"

Godfrey answered in a forthright manner. "That's not ammunition, officer. That's a used ammunition box that my friend here is using to transport his clothes."

"I see, sir," replied the second police officer. He turned to Pantelis and asked, "May I please see inside those used ammunition boxes?"

Pantelis saw the two large police officers and realized that there was nothing he could do. "Yes," he replied, his voice quavering.

"Would you please remove the tape from that box?" the second officer asked, pointing to the box that was closer to him. Pantelis had no choice but to comply.

"Now open it, please, sir."

Pantelis slowly raised the lid.

"Those aren't clothes, sir, like your friend said. What's in that box, sir?"

Pantelis was unable to speak.

The second police officer took one of the packages out of the box and carried it over to the patrol car, placing it on the hood. While he did so, his colleague watched Pantelis and Godfrey. Godfrey calmly finished tightening the lug nuts; Pantelis stood paralyzed with fear. The second policeman took a penknife out of his pocket, opened the blade, picked up the package in his left hand and started slicing away the layers of wrapping. He simultaneously smelled bitter almonds and saw the orange color. Holding tightly onto the package with his left hand, he dropped the knife, grabbed his Airwave personal radio and yelled, "Emergency, Semtex!"

CHAPTER TWENTY-FOUR

"Albert, thank you for coming to see me so promptly," Sir William Hartsford-Knipe, the Director General of MI5, said to his deputy. "We need to resolve the thorny issue that's arisen in this suicide bomber case. If the news about the Semtex gets out we're going to have a major problem on our hands, so there's no way that the word 'Semtex' can be mentioned in open court. On the other hand, we obviously can't just let this Greek terrorist go free. Orpheus Koutoufides—if that's his real name—came to Britain with the intention of blowing himself up and no doubt taking hundreds of innocent people with him."

"The Director of Public Prosecutions is unwilling to hold a secret trial of any sort," Admiral Albert Marsdon said, "so it seems that there's no way we can charge Koutoufides with anything at all if we can't mention that word."

"And what about that skinhead, Clegg?" Sir William continued. "As far as I'm concerned, he's innocent. He had no idea what his passenger was carrying. But he heard the police officer shouting the word 'Semtex' into his radio. What are we going to do with him?"

"I have an idea," Admiral Marsdon answered. "The third box contained the suicide vest and a detonator. Why don't we charge Koutoufides with carrying a detonator without an explosives license?"

"Now that's a good suggestion. We'll have a word with the magistrate and ensure that Koutoufides receives the maximum term of imprisonment. And while he's serving his sentence, I'm sure we can find some way to resolve this bothersome Semtex problem."

"Certainly."

"And as for Clegg, I see no alternative to releasing him right away," Sir William continued. "He's not involved with this suicide bomber in any way. After all, he calmly went on tightening wheel nuts while the police were unwrapping the package. No one facing life in prison for terrorism could possible stay that cool. And his answers to the police when they stopped to help him change the tire were equally innocent. No, we're just going to have to release him."

"Now what about the role played by Commodore Milson?" Marsdon asked. "We haven't been able to get a single word out of the Greek terrorist from the time we arrested him, and Clegg has stayed silent, too. However, someone spotted Milson's car in front of the Lower Brent Caravan Park that morning. We interviewed Milson and he admitted quite freely that he brought Koutoufides from Saint-Malo to Weymouth in his motor yacht and then gave him a lift in his car to Lower Brent. But he declared that he knew nothing about the contents of the sealed ammunition boxes, and there's no way to prove that he did. So, what crime did Commodore Milson commit?"

"Bringing an illegal immigrant into Britain?" Sir William suggested.

"Not at all—the Greek fellow has a valid passport and is here perfectly legally. The fact that there were no immigration officials on duty at Weymouth before nine o'clock in the morning to stamp his passport isn't Milson's fault. No, the only person we can charge in this affair is Orpheus Koutoufides, the suicide bomber. And we can't even charge him with attempted suicide—that hasn't been a crime here since 1961."

"And how does the Commodore explain his transporting Koutoufides from Saint-Malo to the caravan park?" Sir William enquired.

"He says that a friend—whom he won't name— asked him to do the Greek fellow a favor. That's not a crime either, and Commodore Milson knows it."

"Isn't it possible that this is all part of some vast international extreme right-wing conspiracy, with the suicide bomber brought from Greece to England by a series of co-conspirators, including Commodore Milson and Godfrey Clegg?" Sir William asked, raising one eyebrow interrogatively.

"As far as I'm concerned, Milson and Clegg are far right-wing fanatics who want to overthrow our democratic system and replace it with fascist rule, but Milson isn't crazy enough to sail across the Channel knowingly carrying high explosives and a detonator in his motor yacht, let alone drive with them in his car," Marsden replied. "And Clegg may be the ultimate Manchester United supporter, but he's not so certifiably insane that he's prepared to wittingly drive along the M3 motorway in a Mini filled with Semtex. Yes, there probably is some sort of 'vast international extreme right-wing conspiracy' involved here, but the conspirators probably don't include Commodore Milson or Godfrey Clegg. The only person with a death wish in this case is Koutoufides, who knowingly and willingly travelled with two ammunition boxes packed with you-know-what. And he's the least likely suicide bomber I've ever encountered. There's absolutely no reason for him to want to become a martyr for a cause. The psychiatrists have a problem because he won't say a word to them, but despite that they all confidently declare that he suffers from what they call 'endogenous depression,' that is, there was no specific external event that triggered it. In other words, he's just naturally depressed. One day he became depressed for no reason at all, and that's it. When I asked the various shrinks if people with endogenous depression make good suicide bombers they tended to change the subject quickly. And when I enquired whether any other suicide bomber in history has ever suffered from endogenous depression, they changed the subject even more quickly. But that's their diagnosis, and they're sticking to it."

"Albert," Sir William said, "we probably need to keep a close watch on Commodore Milson because he may be dangerous to the safety of the realm.

Godfrey Clegg is a simple-minded football supporter who's fallen for Milson's fascist ravings. However, after what's happened to him, I doubt that he'll be the least bit interested in any sort of politics in the future, right wing, left wing, or even center forward."

"Do we bring the Greek government into this, or at least the Greek National Intelligence Service?"

"Yes, of course," Sir William replied, "but not until we've cleared up the Semtex problem. In the meantime, the only information that our police have managed to obtain from their Greek counterparts via the usual channels is that Orpheus Koutoufides has no police record and has somehow evaded his military service."

"Maybe they found him to be too depressed to allow him to handle a firearm," Marsdon suggested.

"Possibly. But in that case you'd expect that there's a piece of paper somewhere indicating a discharge for psychiatric reasons. But there are no military records at all for him."

"Yes, I admit that's a bit odd," Admiral Marsdon replied. "In fact, the total lack of any record at all other than his birth certificate, driver's license, identity card and passport application is quite surprising."

"I've heard that some of the smaller Greek records offices are totally chaotic. It's possible that on one occasion some clerk entered the name 'Koutoufides' with a wrong letter, and all his subsequent records are under that misspelled name."

"Except for his driver's license, identity card, and passport, where they got it right again? Unlikely.

Anyhow, the easiest explanation is that this is all part of some vast international extreme right-wing conspiracy. Let's stick to that until we discover what actually happened. Agreed?"

"Agreed," Sir William replied.

***

"Speak," said the familiar voice emitted by the encryption device built into the secure smartphone.

Sheikh Mansour replied, "Police in England have arrested a man from Krotonos in possession of some of the shipment to that island."

"Message received and understood. Out."

***

The expression on the face of the Saudi banker as he spoke to his confidential aide was one of deep concern.

"Two weeks ago I heard a rumor from a contact in London. It seemed that the police had arrested someone in Britain in possession of a supply of Semtex. I employed a confidential agent in London, one whom I've used before with great success. I gave him strict orders not to leave that city under any circumstances, but rather to use his police contacts to uncover the facts."

His aide nodded.

"From those contacts he learned that the police had in fact arrested two men in Southern England for possession of Semtex. One man was English.

The other was a Greek national named Orpheus Koutoufides. MI5 quickly took the case out of the hands of the police and handled it themselves. Unfortunately, my man in London has no informants in MI5."

His aide nodded again as the banker continued.

"The authorities subsequently charged Orpheus Koutoufides with the minor offence of illegally transporting a detonator; it seems he should've had an explosives license. The confidential agent sent an employee to the Magistrate's Court in Southampton to observe the case. This was contrary to my orders and could've been exceedingly counterproductive— the police might have investigated anyone who showed even the slightest interest in the legal proceedings. The Greek pleaded guilty and the magistrate sentenced him to six months in jail, a surprisingly heavy sentence. My agent told me that usually there's just a small fine, if that; most people seem to get off with just a warning. In view of the guilty plea, the prosecutor offered no detailed evidence. In particular, there was no mention in court regarding the type of detonator.

"I asked my agent to obtain all the information he could about this Orpheus Koutoufides. All my man could find was a birth certificate, an identity card, a driver's license and a passport application. No baptismal certificate, no school records, no medical records, no military service records. Nothing else at all. The agent sent me copies of the four documents he located. Here are the translations from Greek into Arabic. Do you see anything interesting?"

The aide started looking through the documents and then said excitedly, "He lives on Krotonos."

"Precisely. He lives on Krotonos. Now, there's no doubt whatsoever that Mustapha chose Krotonos for the many positive reasons we've discussed so often. Nevertheless, we know that someone murdered five Muslims on Krotonos, although no one has found their bodies yet. And now it seems that some of the Semtex that Mustapha bought with my money and took to Krotonos was discovered in England in the possession of a man from that island."

"What did he intend to do with the Semtex?" the aide asked.

"I haven't been able to find that out. It seems that, since his arrest, he hasn't said a single word. But there's something else you need to know. They quickly released the man whom they arrested with Orpheus Koutoufides. The Englishman has no Islamic ties. On the contrary, he's a paid up member of a racist and xenophobic extreme right-wing party. What I'm saying is that two terrorists were driving in a car loaded with Semtex and the police understandably arrested both men. But then they released the driver—they brought no charges against him at any time. They charged the passenger for illegal possession of a detonator, presumably a Frishman detonator, although we don't know this for a fact. But they never charged either the driver or the passenger with possession of Semtex. Does any of this make sense to you?"

The aide thought deeply for a few minutes. Then he spoke. "I thought I understood why MI5 is handling this case—the police force has many Muslim informants. So, when the authorities suspect that jihadis are involved, they give the case to MI5 and they keep the police out of the loop. In this instance, however, that explanation makes no sense whatsoever. The British terrorist who was arrested is incontrovertibly an avowed anti-Muslim racist. As for the Greek terrorist, we don't know much about him, but one thing we do know: There's no way that the British terrorist would knowingly have collaborated with anyone with the slightest Muslim ties. So, there's absolutely no reason for this case to be handled by MI5."

"But isn't it true that the Zionists also have their police informants? Maybe MI5 intervened in this case because of an Israeli connection," the banker suggested.

"The English terrorist hates Jews as much as he hates Muslims," the aide said. "If he even suspected a Jewish connection of any kind he wouldn't have got involved in any way at all."

"So," the banker said, "you're telling me that there's no conceivable reason for the case to be handled by MI5."

The confidential aide nodded and then continued. "The second issue is even more mysterious. The English police arrested two terrorists for possession of Semtex. The penalties in

Britain for terrorism are draconian. Yet they released one without any charges, they brought the other terrorist before the court on a far lesser offence, and he received a much more severe sentence than anyone might have anticipated. This makes no sense either."

"Could the two men have been ignorant of what they were carrying?" the banker asked. "After all, in Britain they can't charge you just for being stupid and not checking the contents of your car."

"Well, that's possible," his aide replied. "But they charged the Greek terrorist with possession of a detonator, so he must have known about that. What this means is that only one of the two terrorists knew that they were carrying a detonator, and neither knew anything about the Semtex. Again, with all due respect, that makes no sense at all."

"I agree, and that is why I'm so worried. But there's more. What about the fact that the Greek terrorist comes from Krotonos? And what about the lack of a paper trail—did nothing at all happen to Orpheus Koutoufides between his birth on Krotonos and his obtaining an identity card, a driver's license, and then a passport?"

The aide looked steadily at the banker and then asked, "And what about the remaining Semtex—is that hidden on Krotonos, too?"

CHAPTER TWENTY-FIVE

The air conditioning unit in the room above the spice shop in the Souq Khan el-Zayit in East Jerusalem was out of order. The heat and the humidity were stifling when Mahmoud ibn Laban, the acting head of the Islamic Front for Jihad and the Liberation of Palestine, called the meeting of the executive committee to order.

"We have a major problem," he began. "We're rapidly running out of funds. The Saudi banker has cut all ties with us, and our other major donors are asking for proven results before they're prepared to even think about giving us any more money. Does anyone have any suggestions?"

"What about the house on Krotonos?" Hashim bin Baba asked. "Selling it should bring in quite a bit of money."

"Unfortunately, we don't own it," Mahmoud replied. "The Saudi banker insisted that we register the title deed in the name of one of his many subsidiary companies."

"What about the cabin cruiser? Who owns that?" the same questioner asked.

"We do."

"Can you prove it?"

"Presumably we can," replied Mahmoud ibn Laban. "Mustapha bought it through Sheikh Mansour ibn Aziz Arabiya. So there must be a signed contract. We can ask the sheikh and—"

"Just a minute," Hashim bin Baba interrupted. "I know where the Semtex is hidden."

There were shouts of "Where, where?" Mouths dropped open. Mahmoud ibn Laban just stared at Hashim, who slowly rose to his feet.

"Let's put ourselves in the shoes of the gang of Greek infidels who stole our Semtex," said Hashim. "Where's it safe for them to hide it? The obvious place is the strongroom in the house. But they don't own the house. As a result, there's always the danger that the real owner will suddenly arrive some day and take occupancy before they have a chance to remove the shipment.

"Could they have stored it somewhere else on Krotonos, or another island or even in Athens?" he continued. "Yes, that's certainly possible, but what about the smell of the Semtex? So, there's only one place where they could possibly be storing the Semtex, together with the weapons and the rest of the shipment—on our cabin cruiser."

An uproar broke out. Mahmoud ibn Laban didn't even try to quell the cheering. In fact, he was largely responsible for leading it. Eventually the members of the executive committee quietened down.

Then Mahmoud rose to his feet. "There's just one problem. Given that we now know that the shipment is on our boat, how do we get it back? I'm sure that the Greeks who stole our Semtex are watching the cabin cruiser night and day from the shore and there must be heavily armed guards living on board the vessel. So, how do we get back our Semtex? We don't have a navy, so we can't capture the cabin cruiser. We don't have an army or an air force, so we can't stage a paratrooper drop on the shore. Any suggestions? None? Meeting adjourned!"

***

"I'm sorry to bother you," the confidential aide said, "but I think I know where the Semtex is stored."

"Where?" the banker asked.

"In the strongroom under the house on Argos Beach."

"What makes you say that?"

"They've been doing everything they can to keep our people away from Krotonos," said the aide, "including killing Mustapha and the three sailors. They also frightened off that private detective in Athens whom Hidayatullah ibn Saleh hired to come to the island and investigate, and then they killed Hidayatullah himself. So I think it's on the island."

"I agree," the banker said.

"Good. Now, where on the island can they have hidden it? If they stored the Semtex in, say, a warehouse or someone's back room, the odor would be a dead giveaway and security would be a huge problem. The only possible place, as far as I can see, is the strongroom."

"That makes sense," said the banker. "But I don't want the Semtex. What I want is revenge. I want to know who killed our people, and I want every one of them to be killed slowly and painfully, *Inshallah.*"

"May I suggest a way of achieving that?" the confidential aide asked.

"Of course! Go right ahead."

"To find the assassins, you need information about Krotonos. The problem you've encountered is that there's a gang on Krotonos that doesn't like detectives and doesn't like Arabs. You have a trump card, however—you own a huge swatch of land on the island, and most of it is totally undeveloped. So, first you transfer the title deed to one of your American subsidiaries. Then you hire a firm of Greek architects to design an exclusive resort to be built on your beach property. The key thing is to convince every man, woman and child on Krotonos that an American company wants to invest billions to build a luxury resort on Krotonos that will have a positive impact on island life. Of course, the Greek architects are going to need to hire teams of consultants."

"Why?" the banker asked.

"Because the architects that you choose will have had little or no experience in building resorts. And your contract with them will include a list of the consultants that they are to use. And some of those consultants will include specialists, but not in architecture."

"I'm beginning to get your drift," the banker interrupted. "If I send a private detective to Krotonos, they'll almost certainly kill him. But if I send in a large team of consultants, some of whom just happen to be private detectives, we'll get the fullest co-operation."

"Yes, indeed, and you'll have Ziyad bin Abu Dawud to thank for that. By now the economy of the island must be badly missing his almost limitless flow of money. The arrival of Greek architects who are working for an American company that wants to invest billions in Krotonos will seem like their Arab benefactor Ziyad all over again, but without all the problems.

"And another suggestion," the aide added. "You might want to start the process by hiring local island people to demolish Ziyad's monstrosity of a house. I think that your American company should pay them significantly more than the going rate. That should prime the pump very nicely."

"And once the gang of Greek terrorists sees the demolition starting," the banker added, "they're going to have to find a new hiding place, inevitably a far less secure one. This is starting to look quite interesting …"

**

"Speak," the encrypted voice said.

Sheikh Mansour pronounced his words slowly and clearly. "In the light of the impending demolition of the house on the beach, the remainder of the shipment is currently being stored on the Coast Guard patrol boat that Lieutenant Cosmatos commands."

"Message received and understood. Out."

***

The people of Krotonos squeezed into the municipal auditorium that Ziyad bin Abu Dawud had built. There were no empty seats in the body of the hall, islanders occupied all the folding chairs laid out at the back of the room, and men and women stood in the aisles. The council had called the meeting for eight o'clock, but the building was crammed to capacity by a quarter to eight, and many disappointed residents had to stand outside in the cool evening air.

The mayor opened the proceedings on time, a first in the centuries-long history of Krotonos. He then called on the music teacher at the local high school to lead the singing of the national anthem, the *Hymn to Liberty*. The entire audience joined in lustily, their enthusiasm and eagerness to raise their voices exceeding by far their ability to sing on key. At the end of the anthem, everyone lucky enough to have a chair sat down. The mayor then introduced the lead architect, the senior partner in a well-known Greek firm.

"Our client is a major American corporation," the architect began, "that would like to build a luxury resort on Argos Beach. The reason that I am here tonight is that our client is absolutely insistent that the critical aspects of the resort must conform to the wishes of the residents of Krotonos. If we cannot achieve a broad consensus, then the resort will not be built. A particular concern of my client is to ensure that the traditional way of life here on Krotonos is changed as little as possible.

"Our client," he continued, "wants to know how every resident of the island aged fourteen and older feels about the project. On our client's behalf, we have retained a firm of skilled interviewers. Ideally, each of you will meet one-on-one with an interviewer. Of course, there's no obligation whatsoever to take part. And if you would prefer to meet with an interviewer together with your spouse, or in the company of a small group of friends, that would be fine, too. It's entirely up to you. The sole object of the exercise is to find out what sort of development the people of Krotonos want. Are there any questions at this point?"

An elderly man stood up. "Are you saying that if the majority of us don't want anything at all built on Argos Beach, the Americans will respect our wishes?"

"Absolutely. In fact, they won't go ahead even if a sizeable minority is opposed. And if you don't believe me, may I remind you of what happened on Megalo Megati and on Kalysara when developers built vast hotels against the wishes of the islanders? My clients are in the business of making money, and they know that if the local inhabitants are opposed to a development project, it has a good chance of failing. Other questions?"

A mother of four stood up. "What questions are they going to ask us? And are they going to ask our teenagers the same questions?"

"Two good questions. First let me talk about the teenagers. Everyone is this room knows that young people are leaving the islands and moving to the large cities. Our islands are becoming underpopulated and our cities are already overpopulated, especially Athens and Thessalonica. It's not good for the islands, it's not good for the cities, and, most importantly, it's not good for Greece. We propose to ask your teenagers what sort of facilities we need to include in the resort that would encourage them to stay on Krotonos."

This reply was met with a buzz of approval. Then the elderly man rose again. "And if the rest of us don't want godless nightclubs and discotheques on our island, what's going to happen?"

This question was met with a loud chorus of boos and catcalls. It seemed that almost all the people of Krotonos were strongly in favor of the resort, and would probably go along with just about anything that the developers cared to propose.

The architect resumed speaking. "Now let me tell you about the questions to be put to the adults. We need to know whether you want the resort to be walled off in order to separate it from the town, or whether you want it to be an extension of the town. Then—"

But before he could continue, a voice from the back boomed, "No walls. We've had enough with high walls on Argos Beach." The crowd whistled and applauded.

The architect tried to regain control of the meeting. "I assure you that each and every one of you will have your opportunity to have your views heard, and at length, when you meet with an interviewer. I was just giving you an idea of one of the questions that you'll probably be asked, to give you a chance to think about the issue in advance. Let me give you another example."

He thought for a second or two, and then said, "Like most islands in the Cyclades, the population of Krotonos is relatively homogenous. Just about everyone in this hall was born here, everyone speaks Greek, you were all educated in Greek schools, all the houses of worship on the island are Greek Orthodox, and so on. The resort will attract people from a wide variety of different countries, languages, religions and cultures. They'll—"

But before he could continue, someone standing near the front on the right shouted, "No more Muslims on Krotonos!"

A tiny handful of participants echoed this sentiment. Then a woman screamed out, "Don't be so stupid!"

At this point the meeting dissolved into chaos. The mayor stood up and tried to calm the incipient riot, but to no avail. Everyone seemed to be shouting at once, and two men seated on the folding chairs at the back came to blows. The music teacher started singing the national anthem again, but this time she found herself singing alone, so she stopped at the end of the first line, "I recognize you by the fearsome sharpness of your sword," which somehow seemed highly appropriate for the no-holds-barred battle that was now taking place in the body of the hall.

***

"The architects have withdrawn from the project," the confidential aide said.

"And I can't say I blame them," the banker responded. "That town meeting degenerated into nothing less than open civil war. And in view of the fact that they've cancelled the construction project, the mayor has withdrawn the demolition permit, so that eyesore of a walled-in house on Argos Beach that the bank owns is still standing."

"Well, there's been one good outcome of that chaotic debacle," the aide said.

"And what's that?" the banker asked skeptically.

"When the mayor called on the police to quell the riot, nothing happened, because the police were too busy fighting. There seems to be a relatively widespread belief that the instigators of the fracas were the local police officers, led by their sergeant. By the way, they also say that he's the one who shouted 'No more Muslims on Krotonos!' that set everything off. News of what happened spread quickly to Ermoupoli. Here was an opportunity for a huge foreign investment on the island that would attract myriads of rich tourists to Greece from all over the world, and the racist police officers ruined everything. I hear that, if it turns out that the four policemen were indeed responsible for the riot, the authorities will transfer them from Krotonos, hopefully to some godforsaken island.

"As a matter of interest," the aide continued, "did you actually intend to build the resort?"

"Not exactly. As you know, my sole motive was revenge. And as soon as I'd achieved that, I was going sell my holding on Argos Beach, hopefully at a huge profit."

***

Three days later, the aide returned to the banker's private office.

"I have two ideas that I'd like to share with you," he said.

"Go on."

"First, we now know definitively that the four policemen were active participants on the anti-Muslim side of the Krotonos riot, and that the inflammatory cry of their sergeant sparked off the whole thing. Do you think that the police were involved in the five murders on Krotonos?"

"Probably. That would explain why the police never found the perpetrators and why they haven't found the victims' bodies either. Is there a way we could find out for certain?"

"Well, that leads to my second idea. After what happened at that meeting, the locals are extremely upset for many reasons. The newspapers and TV stations are claiming that the people of Krotonos are all racist xenophobes. Yes, a handful of people on the island are like that, and the four policemen were probably the worst of them. But most of the islanders definitely aren't anti-Muslim, and they're justifiably upset that the media have publicly lumped them together with the few bad eggs. Also, as you well know, Greece is currently in the midst of an utterly crippling financial crisis. Here was an opportunity for a huge foreign investment and numerous new jobs, initially in construction and then in the hospitality industry, but the people of Krotonos threw it all away. Of course, that's not quite what happened. Only a few bigoted individuals objected, and you never had any intention of building the resort anyway, but that's the way the press is portraying the incident. So, if a group of rich American tourists were to come on holiday to Krotonos and stay in your house, they'd receive a warm welcome, wouldn't they?"

"Yes, they would. But no rich tourist, American or otherwise, is going to stay in an empty walled-in house, even on one of the most beautiful beaches in the Greek Islands," the banker replied.

"But what if the 'rich American tourists' were actually private investigators whom you've paid to research the situation on Krotonos and discover what happened to the five men?" the aide asked, smiling slightly.

"No. There's no way that would work. The locals know all about the house and would quickly see through the scheme. Nice suggestion, though."

The banker paused, and then continued, "But you've given me an idea. What if the mayor and leading citizens were to write a letter to the

American corporation apologizing profusely for what happened, and asking them to reconsider their cancellation of the project? The American corporation might respond by sending a team of executives to Krotonos on a fact-finding mission. They'd obviously stay at the house, which we'd have to furnish only minimally. They'd meet with the local citizens, all of whom would bend over backward to be helpful. Of course, we'd have to find someone to suggest to the mayor that he writes the letter, but that shouldn't be a problem."

"I agree. But where are you going to find American private investigators who can masquerade as your executives and can speak fluent Greek?" the aide asked.

"Good point. The American corporation would have to have a Greek subsidiary. In fact, it might even be better if a Greek corporation owned the resort. So we'll send in some American executives who'll talk to the few locals who can speak English fluently, and Greek executives to interact with the islanders who would be more comfortable speaking Greek. And all the executives would be private detectives, of course."

"Yes, that might well do the trick," the aide said. "I'll get my contacts to approach the mayor. The letter should be in the works shortly. By the way, it probably wouldn't be a good idea to arrange the killings of those four policemen yet. We need to have the islanders concentrating on the previous set of murders for now, so that we can find out the names of everyone involved, without exception."

254

CHAPTER TWENTY-SIX

Following the transfer of Sergeant Kyrgiakos and his three colleagues away from the island and with Pantelis in jail in England, Heracles Stavridis was the sole remaining resident member of the Krotonos branch of the Hellenic Spartan League, and an unwilling member at that. Meetings of the League were now held on only those Wednesday nights when Lieutenant Cosmatos and his crew were in port. Despite the lieutenant's repeated attempts to modify his patrol schedule, during the previous month there had been only one gathering.

At that meeting, held on board the Coast Guard patrol boat, the lieutenant stressed the importance of proceeding with the terror campaign in London. At the end of his rousing speech he looked meaningfully at Heracles. And Heracles simply looked back at him. It was unclear to Lieutenant Cosmatos whether Heracles was still in a state of shock from the shooting of Menelaus Tsolakoglou, or whether he just did not want to participate actively in the campaign to combat the Cyprus Memorandum.

At the end of the meeting, Heracles went up to Cosmatos and asked him, "Sergeant Kyrgiakos kept my new identity papers, including my passport. Do you know where they are now?"

"I've no idea, but I know how to contact Sergeant Kyrgiakos. I'll let you know."

Four weeks later, at the end of the next meeting of the League, Cosmatos took Heracles aside. "The sergeant mailed your passport and your other papers to me. I can let you have them if you want to go to England. Do you?"

"I'm not sure. Yes, I want to stop this insane British peace plan. As a loyal Greek, I have to do everything in my power to prevent the British from recognizing the Turkish Republic of Northern Cyprus. But under no circumstances whatsoever am I prepared to kill any more people. And I am definitely *not* a suicide bomber."

"I understand. Let me talk to party headquarters in Athens and get back to you."

Four days later, Cosmatos's patrol boat docked in Krotonos Harbor at ten in the morning. The Lieutenant walked over to Heracles's house and was pleased to find him at home. "Are you still working as a tour guide?" he asked.

"Yes, certainly. But no tourists arrived on the ferry this morning, so I just went back to the house. What can I do for you?"

"I contacted headquarters as I promised you I would. They made a suggestion that I'd like to discuss with you."

"Go ahead."

"First I need to talk to you about Frishman detonators. As you know, a detonator is just a device to trigger an explosion. You embed the detonator in the explosive, Semtex in your case. The standard Frishman model is manual. Two wires connect the detonator to the controller. When you press the red button on the controller, an electric current is sent down a wire to the detonator, which then triggers the explosion. Obviously you want to be far away from the explosive when you press that red button, so you use really long wires to connect the detonator to the controller—unless you're a suicide bomber, that is. Suicide bombers keep their controllers right next to their suicide vests for equally obvious reasons.

"Now," he continued, "the Secretary-General of the League told me that there's a second kind of Frishman controller, a timer controller. You set the electronic timer on the controller to, say, 150 minutes, and press the red button. You then leave. Exactly 150 minutes later, the detonator triggers the explosion. They're getting a Frishman timer controller for you. When you leave your hotel in London, you'll set the timer to 150 minutes. When you get to the platform at Waterloo on the last train of the day, you place your bomb on the platform and, as you do so, you press the red button. Then you calmly go up the escalator to the street and safety. Two and a half hours later the Semtex explodes on the deserted platform destroying the Underground station, but no one gets hurt in the process. After all, the last train will deposit you on the platform shortly after midnight, and the first train of the morning is at about five, so there's no question that the platform will be deserted at about half past two when the bomb goes off. Does that sound reasonable to you?"

"Yes, except that there's one problem: London Underground trains run all night."

"No, that's not going to happen before September 2015. Currently they stop running for about five hours in the early hours of the morning."

"Are you sure about that?"

"Positive. I've looked it up on the Internet. And you can check for yourself if you don't believe me," Cosmatos replied.

"Now," he continued, "while they're waiting for the Frishman timer controller to arrive, the people at headquarters will find the best way to transport you and the Semtex to Britain. I somehow doubt that either Commodore Milson or Godfrey Clegg is likely to help us this time."

"And the du Chanels are also most unlikely to participate," Heracles added. "They've probably learned what happened from their good friend Commodore Milson. And from what I've heard, I'd like to avoid Maurizio and his paranoid lady friend if at all possible. She's probably found out about the city of Walla Walla in the State of Washington by now, and wants to add the eighth letter of the English alphabet at the end of each 'Walla' to warn people about the impending Muslim takeover there. And anyone who's unfortunate enough to be named Callahan is sure to be a target, too."

"No problem. We'll work on a totally new route."

Three days later Heracles received a phone call. A gruff voice spoke.

"No names. The lieutenant gave me your telephone number."

"I understand," Heracles replied.

"Can we meet tomorrow afternoon?"

"I have two Australian couples coming for a walking tour of the island. Can we set it up for six o'clock or later?" Heracles asked.

"We'll meet at your house at six promptly," replied the gruff voice, and terminated the call.

***

The four Australian tourists proved to be most congenial and hospitable, and it was hard for Heracles to find a polite way of turning down their friendly offer of drinks after the tour. When he used his usual excuse of army reserve duty, one of the husbands offered to phone Heracles's commanding officer and explain that the promotion of friendly relations between Australia and Greece was far more important than any military activities planned for that evening. Eventually, however, Heracles managed to get away without insulting the Australians. He ran back to his house, arriving just after six. Standing outside were a man and a woman, both in dark, wraparound sunglasses. Heracles rushed up to them apologetically and opened the door as quickly as he could.

He ushered them into the house. The man was middle-aged, his hair starting to thin and turn gray at the sideburns. His face was heavily wrinkled, perhaps from overexposure to the elements. Heracles guessed that the woman was about twenty-five years old. Her black business suit was more formal than the clothing that most people wore on Krotonos; Heracles wondered if she was a lawyer or perhaps an accountant. Her fashionably short haircut accentuated the roundness of her attractive face.

He invited them to sit down and offered them a drink. Both asked for retsina, and Heracles joined them. After the obligatory "Death to all Muslims" toast, the woman got straight down to business.

"Names don't matter. We know who you are, and you know why we're here."

Heracles nodded.

"We also know what you've done for our beloved Greece, and we're extremely proud of you and most grateful to you."

Heracles just nodded again; he could not think of anything suitable to say in response.

"We hear that you want to do something about this unspeakable Cyprus Memorandum," she continued. "We're most appreciative of your willingness to act once more to save Greece. Our people have informed us that you've stipulated that you don't want anyone to get hurt in the proposed London bombing, including yourself."

Heracles finally found his tongue and responded, "That's correct."

"Of course, we'll scrupulously carry out your wishes. To this end, we've managed to obtain a Frishman timer controller for you. We'll give it you in Athens on your way to London. You'll bring with you ten flat bricks of Semtex in a rucksack—the lieutenant will supply them. As you know, Semtex emits a distinctive smell, so you'll have to wrap the bricks securely in multiple layers of plastic. Semtex also has a distinctive color, so you're going to have to use colored plastic. We'll show you how to assemble and dismantle the time bomb that you'll transport in the rucksack."

"Why would I want to dismantle the bomb?" Heracles asked.

"Because transporting an assembled bomb is extremely dangerous—you'll have to take the components separately and then re-assemble the bomb when you arrive in London."

"I see," Heracles replied. "And how am I to travel to London?"

The woman took a sip of retsina and then answered him. "One of our leading members is a bus driver for a tour company. He pointed out that customs officers rarely if ever stop young people on bus tours for an inspection. In a week's time he'll be driving a busload of people aged between eighteen and thirty on a three-week long trip from Athens to London and back. It'll take him nine days to drive to London, via Rome, Paris and Amsterdam. Of course, you'll leave the tour when it gets to London. The key point is that, instead of travelling through the Channel Tunnel, which is subject to close inspection, the tour party goes by ferry from the Hook of Holland to Harwich. According to the driver, the officers at the customs post in Harwich hardly ever stop anyone at all, let alone busloads of young people, most of whom don't have enough money to have anything to smuggle other than a small quantity of drugs, and have drunk so much duty-free alcohol on the ferry that they're far too intoxicated to care about anything."

"So what's the route?" Heracles asked.

"You'll travel by bus from Athens to Igoumenitsa and by ferry from there to Brindisi in Italy—it's a ten-hour crossing. Then you'll board a second bus in Brindisi for travel to Rome, Paris and Amsterdam, and on to the Hook of Holland where you'll travel on the ferry that I mentioned before. The crossing to Harwich takes only about seven hours. A third bus will take you from Harwich to London where you'll leave the tour."

"That sounds fine to me. But I see one possible problem. I assume that we'll be sleeping two to a room. But I'm going to have the pieces of the disassembled bomb with me. Of course, when I'm out of the room, my rucksack will be securely padlocked. But I'll have to unlock it to change my clothes. Won't my roommate notice anything?"

"I'm impressed that you picked up on that point," the woman said with a smile. "But the solution is easy. You'll be sharing a room with your girlfriend."

"But I don't have a steady girlfriend," Heracles protested. "I much prefer to play the field."

The woman laughed. "The League will supply a young woman to play the role of your girlfriend. She'll obviously have to know that she'll be sleeping in a room that contains a dismantled bomb. You'll share a room with her, and the two of you will ensure that no one else on the tour comes into that room at any time. Also, you'll keep alcohol consumption to a bare minimum, and you will not, of course, take any drugs of any kind whatsoever. You and your girlfriend will indulge in public displays of affection, so much so that when the two of you leave bars and nightclubs early or if you decline to join the partying activities of the other members of the tour, your fellow travelers will assume that the reason for your apparent unfriendliness is that you're returning to your room for more pleasurable activities."

"And are we at least allowed to make love?" Heracles asked.

"I'm afraid not," the man said in a gruff voice, taking part in the conversation for the first time. Then he continued, "I hope that you appreciate that the directives we've given you are to protect your mission. You'll have in your luggage Semtex and the other components of your bomb. You'll be travelling with forty or so young people. People of that age are inquisitive, and you'll have to ensure that no one becomes so curious about you that they feel obliged to snoop in your luggage. However, if they think that the two of you are continuously engaged in sexual activities, they'll understand your desire for privacy and leave you alone."

"I understand, at least I think I do," Heracles replied.

"Look," the woman said. "You're on this trip for one purpose and one purpose only: to prevent the British recognizing the so-called Turkish Republic of North Cyprus. You'll achieve this by taking the components of a time bomb to London, assembling it there and setting it off on a deserted platform of Waterloo station. The British will be told that, unless the Cyprus Memorandum is permanently withdrawn, the next bomb won't just paralyze the London transportation system by destroying a key Underground station. Remember, you'll be on a mission for Greece. So you need to put out of your mind all activities that might hamper your mission. And that means staying celibate for nine days. When you return to Greece as a hero, there'll be no shortage of beautiful women competing for your attention."

"But will I be able to return to Greece?" Heracles asked.

"Why not?"

"Well, my first concern is: How will I get out of Britain?"

"We'll provide you with an air ticket back to Greece and plenty of British money. When you reach the station exit, you'll take a taxi to Heathrow Airport. The Waterloo station complex, consisting of the Underground station and the adjoining mainline railway station, is the busiest in London. So there'll be a long line of taxis outside, even just after midnight. There's a plane from London to Athens that leaves at 2:35 a.m. that you'll make with plenty of time to spare."

"But won't they shut down all airports after the explosion?" Heracles enquired.

"They may do that eventually, but certainly not within five minutes of the bomb going off," the woman replied.

Then she added, "Do you have any other concerns?"

"Yes. I've read that the streets of central London have more security cameras than any other city in the world, and I'm sure that Waterloo station has plenty of its own on every platform. Within minutes of the explosion, my picture will be plastered all over the world. In the unlikely event of the Heathrow personnel allowing me to fly to Athens, I'm sure that the police will arrest me on my arrival there, and they'll deport me back to London to face trial and probably life imprisonment. If I have to give up my life for Greece, so be it, but this doesn't seem like a very good plan."

"When you leave the tour in London," the woman replied, "you'll go to a hotel within easy walking distance of Waterloo. You'll have with you everything that you'll need for disguising your appearance when you place the bomb on the platform: a false beard; a large Afro wig; heavy horn-rimmed spectacles—with clear glass, of course; and so on. Your girlfriend will accompany you to the hotel. When it's time for you to go to the station, she'll help you with your disguise, as well as with the assembly of the bomb."

"But what about my clothes? Won't the security cameras record them? Police at airports all over the world, including in Athens, will be looking for a passenger from London wearing my clothes."

"When you leave the hotel near the station, you'll be wearing one of those Aloha shirts, and—"

"What's an Aloha shirt?" Heracles interrupted.

"Haven't you've seen American tourists on Krotonos wearing those brightly patterned cotton shirts from Hawaii? They're printed in garish colors, and they usually have a large floral motif of some kind."

"Oh, you mean a Hawaiian shirt. You want me to wear one of those in London in the middle of the night?"

"Of course. The few people you'll encounter will notice your hair, your beard, your old-fashioned Woody Allen-style glasses, and, above all, they'll notice your brightly colored Hawaiian shirt. But they won't notice you."

"But when I arrive back in Athens, the shirt will be a dead give-away."

The woman rolled her eyes. "You won't be wearing the Hawaiian shirt by then. In addition to your rucksack, when you leave the hotel you'll be carrying a duffel bag—airline security personnel get extremely suspicious when they see a passenger with no luggage. Among other items, inside the duffel bag there'll be a pale blue dress shirt and a brown paper bag from a take-away restaurant. When you get to the airport, you'll go the nearest men's room. Inside a cubicle you'll take off your Hawaiian shirt and your disguise, and put everything inside the brown paper bag. You'll put on the blue shirt, leave the men's room and walk over to the food court. There you'll deposit the brown paper bag in one of the waste receptacles. After eating at a fast-food restaurant, most people dump the paper wrapping and any uneaten food in the nearest trashcan. So, no one will be in the least bit surprised when you take your brown paper food bag and drop it in."

"And what about my girlfriend?" Heracles asked, somewhat protectively. "How will she get back?"

"Don't you worry about her—she knows what she has to do and how to do it. But because you asked the question, I'll tell you: There's a flight on a different airline from yours leaving for Athens at about 11:30 p.m. She'll be on that plane."

CHAPTER TWENTY-SEVEN

Heracles was most impressed when he discovered that the location of the headquarters of the Hellenic Spartan League was a luxurious high-rise office building a few blocks from Syntagma Square in downtown Athens. He entered the lobby and approached the bank of elevators. He first thought that there were six elevators, three on each side. Then he noticed that there were only two elevators on the left. In place of the third set of elevators doors there was a solid sheet of metal made of the same material as the doors.

As previously instructed, he took an elevator to the third floor. There he found a large office containing armed security guards, an x-ray machine, and a metal detector. As he entered, he was asked for his Greek identity card. The guard carefully compared the name on the card with each one listed on his clipboard until he found the match. Then he returned the card and allowed Heracles to proceed to the next security guard, who asked Heracles if they could check his rucksack. Heracles readily agreed, and handed his rucksack to the guard to be x-rayed. The rucksack stayed inside the machine for a considerable length of time while three of the guards conferred. Then they again asked Heracles for his identity card. Finally, the conveyer belt of the x-ray machine disgorged his backpack, one of the guards returned his identity card to him, and yet another armed guard asked Heracles to walk through the metal detector.

Having satisfied the security personnel, Heracles was escorted to an elevator that took him straight to the twenty-ninth floor. Now he understood why the sixth elevator was missing in the lobby. Engineers had configured that elevator to run in nonstop mode from the third floor to the twenty-ninth floor and back, and the other five elevators were prevented from stopping at the twenty-ninth floor. This gave the League an additional layer of security. Heracles wondered why all these precautions were necessary.

As the elevator doors opened, two more armed security guards walked up to him. One escorted him to an unmarked wooden door. The guard knocked. On hearing the command "Enter!" he opened the door and motioned to Heracles to go in. Behind the desk he saw the woman who had visited his home in Krotonos. She stood as he entered. As before, she was formally dressed in a black business suit. The guard closed the door behind him.

"Welcome to Athens!" she said. "Did you have a good trip? And more importantly, did you bring the ten bricks of Semtex with you?"

"Yes, to both questions," Heracles replied.

"Good. Give me the Semtex."

Heracles took the ten flat bricks, each of them tightly wrapped in layers of blue plastic, out of his rucksack and placed them on her desk. She went over to a large safe in the corner of the office, unlocked it and carefully placed all ten bricks inside. Then she closed the safe door firmly and spun the dial of the combination lock.

She turned to Heracles. "And did you also bring your false identity documents?"

"I have an identity card, a driver's license, and a passport in the name of Diomedes Economou."

"How very appropriate. As I'm sure you know, Diomedes in Greek Mythology was King of Argos, and Economou is a Cypriot name."

Heracles said nothing.

"And from now on," the woman continued, "I will call you Diomedes and you must call me Evgenia—the name in my false passport is Evgenia Hatzis."

"Do you also have a false passport?" asked Heracles. "Why?"

"I thought you'd have guessed by now. I'm your girlfriend, at least for the purpose of the trip to London."

Heracles's mouth dropped open.

"And just so that you don't get the wrong idea," she continued, "as I told you, we will repeatedly indulge in *public* displays of affection. But when the two of us are alone, if you come anywhere close to me, I will repeatedly kick you extremely hard where it really hurts. Do you understand me?"

Heracles's mouth was still open, so he just nodded.

"You and I are playing roles. In public we play the role of a besotted couple. We are so desperately in love that we are physically inseparable, so obsessed with each other that we take every opportunity to go to our hotel room to make passionate love. In private, however, we are two members of the Hellenic Spartan League engaged in a desperate struggle to prevent Britain from recognizing the so-called Turkish Republic of Northern Cyprus. In our room, we act professionally at all times. Do you understand what I'm saying?"

Heracles thought for a moment. Then he said, "I assume that we're not going to be staying in five-star luxury hotels."

"Regrettably not. On this sort of tour, the hotels are little better than badly run youth hostels. Descriptive terms like 'fleabag' and 'dump' spring to mind. Also 'flophouse.' Why do you ask?"

"Well, the walls of cheap hotels are paper-thin. Aren't the other members of the tour group going to be just the tiniest bit suspicious when all they hear coming from our love-nest night after night is total silence?"

Evgenia did not respond to this question for a long time. Heracles thought that he had overplayed his hand and feared that he was in deep trouble. But finally she smiled. "You win," she said. "I just hope that you're not going to let the League down by sleeping at night when you should be making passionate love to me, hour after hour. You can sleep on the bus."

Heracles smiled back at Evgenia. For the first time he was really looking forward to the bus tour.

"Now to business," she said. "You're going to have to learn how to assemble and dismantle a bomb. The Semtex stays locked up in this safe in the corner of my office—we're not taking any chances here. I've made a good supply of play dough from flour, salt, water and oil, and I've managed to color it a sort of browny-orange. I've even added some almond essence. The smell is reasonably close to that of the real product, but I couldn't get the color right, I'm afraid. Here in Athens you'll use the play dough—the Semtex is for London."

"Fine," Heracles replied.

"Let's go into the office kitchen. There's a table I can use to teach you bomb making."

Three hours later Heracles felt confident that he could assemble or disassemble a bomb in his sleep. "Evgenia, don't you think we've done enough for today?" Heracles pleaded. "It's well after seven o'clock. Can't we get something to eat and do some more of this tomorrow?"

"Okay, let's call it a day. You're staying in my apartment, and I'll cook some dinner for us. I hope you like moussaka—it's the only thing I can make that's vaguely edible. More precisely, it's just barely palatable provided it's washed down with gallons of red wine.

"By the way," she continued, "you'll be most disappointed to learn that I live in an old building, and the walls are really thick. In any event, there's no need to impress my elderly neighbors. You'll sleep on the couch in the living room, and I think you know exactly what's going to happen to you if you try any nonsense."

Heracles wasn't sure if she was serious or if this was her way of seducing him. He finally decided to play it safe.

***

Four days into the trip, Heracles was utterly exhausted. For the past three nights Evgenia had insisted that they engage in hours of lovemaking. Heracles had enjoyed the company of many different women, but even a novice would quickly have realized that Evgenia's primary objective in bed was to put on a highly audible show for the benefit of the tour members trying to sleep in the rooms on either side of theirs. As soon as she heard someone opening the door of an adjoining room, Evgenia would prod Heracles into action. Then she would grunt and groan loudly like the star of a pornographic movie, thereby ensuring that their unfortunate neighbors were all but active participants. Unlike Evgenia, Heracles did not enjoy their amorous activities. As teenagers, he and Pantelis had wondered what it would be like to make love to an insatiable nymphomaniac. Now, forced to perform for much of the night in a loudly creaking hotel bed, he had some idea. Evgenia had to repeatedly whisper in his ear to be a more active participant, and kept urging him to moan convincingly in an erotic ecstasy that he certainly wasn't experiencing.

After an hour or two of sleep that night, they had breakfast with the group. The two of them sat, as always, with their limbs intertwined. Heracles was tired beyond belief. After the meal, he took Evgenia aside and escorted her to an empty corner of the hotel dining room.

"I can't go on like this much longer," he whispered. "You've made me stay awake for three nights in a row. I need a good night's sleep."

"So sleep on the bus, like I told you in Athens. That's what I do."

"But that guide keeps waking me to go and see some stupid Roman ruin. Yesterday I couldn't nap for more than fifteen minutes at a time. I told her that I'm not interested in piles of old rocks, but she took no notice. She seems to think that because I paid for this tour I have to see everything. I don't know how you managed to persuade her to leave you alone and let you sleep."

"Diomedes," said Evgenia, "when an Englishwoman marries, her mother gives her 'The Talk' the night before her wedding. She tells her daughter as follows: 'When your husband wants to make love, you should lie back, close your eyes and think of England.' In your case, you need to think of Greece. Closing your eyes is optional. But making appropriate loud noises that can be clearly heard in the next room is absolutely required. Where's your patriotism? Do you want perfidious Albion to recognize that unspeakable country? We have to get the bomb to London without it being discovered. And to do that we need to convince our fellow tourists of our unending ardor so that they'll keep out of our room."

"Don't you realize that your endless groaning, moaning, panting, and grunting keeps everyone awake for much of the night? How about letting our poor neighbors get a good night's sleep just once?" Heracles begged.

***

The ferry slid into the dock at Harwich. The efficient dockworkers tied up the vessel and made sure that the gangway was safely secured. The tour members stumbled off the boat and joined the line of passengers heading for the sign bearing the St. Edward's Crown inside a circle and the wording "HM Revenue and Customs." Since leaving the Hook of Holland, the members of the group, with the exception of Heracles and Evgenia, had been steadily drinking large quantities of Polish vodka. Furthermore, the previous day they had visited an Amsterdam coffee shop where they each had bought five grams of marijuana, the maximum permitted, and on the ferry they had smoked the remainder of their purchase. The combination of cannabis and alcohol proved too much for some participants of the bus tour, and they had to be helped off the ship by their companions. Because all the members of the group kept together, this meant that they were among the last to leave the vessel.

Much to the surprise of Heracles and Evgenia, they found that the customs post was staffed by more than forty uniformed men and women. The inspectors had set up a line of zinc-topped tables, and the 1,200 passengers started to form separate queues, one in front of each customs officer. Six uniformed police constables and a sergeant stood a few yards behind the inspection tables. Each traveler was forced to open every piece of his or her luggage, which was carefully searched by a customs officer.

Evgenia whispered, "They must have received some sort of tip-off. They're obviously looking for something specific."

"Such as Semtex?" Heracles replied in a worried low voice.

"How could they possibly know anything about that?" she responded.

"I've no idea. But our bus driver told us again last night that the customs officers here hardly ever stop anyone. They don't care about small quantities of marijuana from The Netherlands, so they let busloads of young people go through unchecked."

"Well, despite what he said, they're not letting anyone through this afternoon," Evgenia replied.

"What do I do when they ask me to open the rucksack?" Heracles asked her.

"I've no idea."

"And what do I say when they ask me about the ten bricks of Semtex?"

"Tell them it's play dough," Evgenia answered.

"Orange-colored play dough with the smell of bitter almonds?"

By way of reply, Evgenia swore fiercely under her breath.

There was a long silence while they both tried desperately to think of a solution. Finally Heracles spoke, still keeping his voice to an undertone.

"Can we make a run for it?"

"No. The gates behind us are shut, so we can't go back on board the ferry, and there are seven policemen standing in front of us," Evgenia replied.

Even though Her Majesty's Revenue and Customs had seconded numerous officers to Harwich to augment the customs staff who were permanently based there, the methodical search proceeded slowly. It took nearly an hour before the first members of the tour group reached the inspection point. Soon it was Heracles's turn.

"Would you please open that rucksack?" the customs officer asked. He was a short man, with long hair carefully combed over his scalp to hide an obvious bald area. Like his hair, his moustache was dyed jet black.

"Certainly," Heracles replied, trying to talk with a confidence that he indubitably did not feel at that moment.

As he opened his rucksack, there was a sudden shout, "Here, police!"

Two of the policemen who up to now had been passively watching the proceedings suddenly swooped on a ferry passenger standing at the front of a queue three away from where the customs officer was inspecting Heracles's luggage. Evgenia, who was standing behind Heracles, saw the man being led away in handcuffs—her partner was too concerned about what was about to happen to him to notice anything at all.

The police sergeant spoke loudly to the few remaining passengers. "Thank you for your co-operation, ladies and gentlemen. That concludes the customs inspection for today. I apologize for the delay."

One of the members of the bus tour, still under the influence of both vodka and marijuana, staggered up to the sergeant. "Offisher," he said in Greek-accented English, "why didja arresht that man?"

"Because he stole the Klopman diamond. Move along now, please."

Evgenia turned to Heracles and marveled, "Can you imagine a Greek policeman making a joke to a tourist who's drunk and high?"

They walked together, arms over each other's shoulders, past the customs post. They could see the passenger whom the police had arrested seated in the back of a police vehicle. From his white crocheted skullcap, beard, and robe it was obvious that the man was a Muslim. Evgenia whispered in Heracles's ear: "It's one thing to say 'Death to all Muslims,' but this one saved you from life imprisonment for terrorism."

Heracles just nodded. It would be some time before he recovered from the sheer blind fear of waiting for the customs officer to inspect the contents of his rucksack item-by-item, and having to come up with an explanation for those ten orange bricks wrapped in blue plastic film. He and Evgenia entered the waiting bus and settled down for the two-hour ride to London. When the bus pulled up at a sleazy hotel in Camberwell, they alighted, took their luggage from the stack of suitcases and rucksacks piled up on the sidewalk, and walked to the other side of the bus. Without saying goodbye to anyone in the group, they hailed a passing taxi. Fifteen minutes later they were at Waterloo station.

"Where's the hotel they booked for us?" Heracles asked.

"Supposedly a ten-minute walk from here. They told me that it's the nicest of the hotels in the vicinity of Waterloo station. That should be a change from the kind of place we've been staying at for the past week or so.

"By the way," Evgenia added, "you're going to sneak out of the hotel close to midnight tomorrow night. So, the Hellenic Spartan League has paid for the two-night hotel stay in advance. Also, we're taking all our meals in the hotel restaurant, and we'll pay cash there. The League doesn't want any problems afterward."

"Why are we eating all our meals at the hotel? When we visit the sights of London tomorrow we'll eat as we go. There must be cafés near Westminster Abbey and Big Ben and—"

"Forget it, we're not going anywhere tomorrow," Evgenia said.

"What? We have just one day in London, so let's do as much as we can. I want to see the changing of the guard at Buckingham Palace. Remember, I was a member of the *Evzones*, the Greek Presidential

Guard, and I'll bet that the soldiers in the Queen's Guard aren't one tenth as impressive as we were. Stay in the hotel—are you crazy?

"No, you're the one who's crazy. When we met in your house on Krotonos, it was you who mentioned that there are security cameras all over London. Do you really want to leave your likeness on record at every major tourist site in this city? No, we're staying in the hotel until it's time to leave. You can relax, take it easy, catch up on your sleep, eat to your heart's content and recover from what nearly happened at Harwich. But no way are we going to play tourist tomorrow. And there's another reason why we're staying put. If we leave the hotel room, the cleaning staff may snoop and find the Semtex. So, we're remaining in our room. We'll put up the 'Do Not Disturb' sign and we'll leave the room for one reason only: to eat in the hotel restaurant."

Late the following afternoon, they went downstairs for an early dinner in the restaurant. They ate in a spirit of quiet companionship, both knowing that this would probably be the last time that they would share a meal. Then they went straight back to their room. Evgenia watched intensely as Heracles carefully re-assembled the bomb. Then he emptied the contents of his rucksack onto the bed and placed the bomb inside. Evgenia swept half the items from the bed into the empty duffel that she had brought with her. She packed the rest into her suitcase in the space left by the items she removed for Heracles to use to complete his mission.

They checked meticulously to make sure that they had left nothing behind. Then Evgenia helped Heracles put on his disguise: the Aloha shirt, the Afro wig, the beard and the horn-rimmed spectacles with clear glass. When she was satisfied with his appearance, she kissed Heracles goodbye and then left for the airport en route to Athens. Heracles spent the next few hours casually flipping between TV channels, the same way he had spent the rest of the day.

Near midnight he checked the bomb once more and made sure yet again that neither he nor Evgenia had left anything in the room. Then, carrying his duffel and with his rucksack on his back, he left the hotel and walked to Waterloo Underground station. The Hellenic Spartan League had provided him with a new Oyster Card, which he used to pass through the gates. He followed the signs to the Bakerloo line.

He stepped onto the platform and waited for the last southbound train of the night to arrive. It drew into the station and came to a halt. Thirty-three passengers alighted. Almost all of them looked tired; a few appeared to be totally exhausted. Their shoulders were stooped and they tended to drag their feet as they walked. As the train left the platform and entered the tunnel heading for Lambeth North station, Heracles walked away from the tracks. When he reached the platform wall, he placed his duffel on the ground and stooped to tie his shoelace. And as he did so, his rucksack tumbled off his back. He carefully caught it and placed it gently on the platform. Before they left Athens,

Evgenia had made Heracles practice that maneuver repeatedly until the fall of the rucksack seemed a natural consequence of his bending down and moving his hands forward to adjust the laces of his well-worn boots.

He methodically untied and retied both of his laces in turn as he watched the last of the weary passengers leave the platform and walk slowly toward the escalator. Heracles looked around—he was totally alone. He ripped open his rucksack and plunged his hand inside. He checked yet again that the "150" was showing on the electronic timer. Then he firmly pressed the red button.

To his surprise he heard an explosive sound. He quickly withdrew his hand and watched in amazement as his rucksack started to burn. Part of his brain told him to rush to the escalator and try to get out while there was still time before the inevitable explosion, but Heracles just stood there mesmerized by what was happening. As the flames took hold, a gap appeared in the fabric of the rucksack. Through the black-edged hole, he noticed an orange-colored circle, rimmed by fire, on the surface of one of the ten flat bricks. He could now see the layers of the blue plastic wrapping that covered the brick curling and melting.

He knew with absolute certainty what was about to happen but, try as he might, he simply could not move. His brain said one thing, his feet said the opposite. Flames soon appeared on the surface of the other bricks. Heracles watched stupefied as the bomb quickly incinerated in front of him, leaving behind only the smoldering ruins of the rucksack and a few pieces of unburned plastic film. There was no trace of the orange substance. He staggered to the escalator. When he reached the top, he asked the sole uniformed transport worker still on duty there to direct him to the nearest police station. As he made his way to Holmes Terrace, he tore off the beard, wig and sunglasses, and dropped them onto the sidewalk.

***

"Speak," the voice said, coming from the secure smartphone with the built-in digital encryption device.

"The Semtex lookalike that was detonated at Waterloo came from the Krotonos shipment."

"Message received and understood. Out."

CHAPTER TWENTY-EIGHT

Sir William Hartsford-Knipe held his glass to the light. "What's the matter with this claret? It tastes like cat's urine."

Admiral Marsdon was equally unenthusiastic about the wine that the waiter had poured for them in the private dining room of MI5. "It's probably part of these new cost-cutting measures," he suggested. "Next thing we know, instead of filet mignon medium-rare with sauce *Béarnaise* we'll be getting sandwiches made with Spam Lite on stale sliced bread."

Sir William rolled his eyes in horror.

"Well, Albert," he finally replied, "at least we've got some answers regarding the Greeks and the Semtex. I've heard quite a bit of it, but please tell me everything from the beginning, so that I have the full picture."

"The news is definitely better than this wine. Let's start with the first incident. The police arrested Orpheus Koutoufides on the M3 outside Southampton in possession of ten bricks of Semtex lookalike, a Frishman detonator and a suicide vest. We wanted to charge him with conspiring to commit terrorism—after all, he had no idea that he was carrying the Israeli inert substitute rather than actual Semtex. However, the Director of Public Prosecutions pointed out that Koutoufides wasn't in possession of an explosive, and therefore there was no evidence that he ever intended to detonate any sort of bomb. But he didn't know that, and even the hint of international terrorism charges is enough to terrify anyone.

"He refused to say anything, as is his right under British law, but even without his testimony it now seems certain that neither Commodore Milson nor Godfrey Clegg knew anything about Koutoufides's plans. So we did the best we could under the circumstances. In order to prevent the detailed facts coming out in court, we convinced him that if he pleaded guilty to the unlicensed detonator charge, we'd agree not to prosecute him for terrorism. Then we leaned on the magistrate to give him the six months maximum in the clink."

"Correct," D replied. "The problem was we couldn't use the word 'Semtex' in court because he wasn't carrying Semtex. And if we'd made any mention of the lookalike, the Greek terrorist organization would've realized that they'd acquired a cache of an inert substance and gone out to buy the explosive instead."

"Which is the last thing we wanted," Marsdon said. "I, for one, strongly encourage terrorists to set off non-explosive bombs, if you'll allow the oxymoron. We arrest them for terrorism, jail them and throw away the key, and no harm is done to life or limb."

"I felt that Koutoufides had in fact contravened the Terrorism Act 2006," Sir William said. "But I couldn't convince the Director of Public Prosecutions."

"Don't you have even the slightest bit of a bad conscience about the way we tricked him?" the Deputy Director General asked. "We told him that if he pleaded guilty he'd get no more than six months imprisonment. The fact of the matter is that, if he'd fought the charges, he might have gotten off entirely, or at worst come away with a fine. And then he might have gone to the newspapers with his story."

"I never have even an iota of a bad conscience when it comes to terrorists," replied Sir William primly.

"Which brings us to the second Greek terrorist," the admiral said. "Unlike Koutoufides, this one actually detonated a bomb in the Underground. He's facing life imprisonment, and he's singing like a proverbial canary."

"Good," Sir William said. "Again, I've heard lots of what he's said, much of it from you. But I need to have the complete story."

"Of course. To begin, the second Greek has given us his actual name, Heracles Stavridis, and also the actual name of the other terrorist."

"But the Greek police gave us the man's birth certificate and those other documents," D objected.

"The real Orpheus Koutoufides died soon after he was born. The spelling of the baby's name on his death certificate was slightly tweaked on the appropriate Greek computer. Because the software system now decided that Orpheus Koutoufides was still alive, it had no problem in issuing him with a driver's license, an identity document, and then a passport."

"Does the Greek government know about this problem?" D asked.

"Yes, but with their current financial difficulties, they don't have the funds to fix it. We're going to have to treat all documentation from Greece extremely carefully in future."

"Even that cloud has a silver lining. Now that we know his real name and how he obtained his passport, we can keep Orpheus Koutoufides—or whatever his actual name is—in prison much longer by charging him with entering the United Kingdom with false papers. Unfortunately, we still can't do much about those two far right-wing scoundrels, Milson and Clegg, because obviously they had no idea that they were accessories to a crime of terrorism."

"Pity," General Marsdon said. "But maybe we can find something else to charge them with."

"Please look into that, if you would. In the meantime, returning to the second Greek terrorist, Heracles, what else did he say?" Sir William asked.

"Another piece of useful information he gave us," Albert replied, "is that the organization behind all this is the Hellenic Spartan League or, more precisely, a clique within the League. Most of the members of the Hellenic Spartan League are your run-of-the-mill neo-Nazis, but a small faction within the League has crossed the line from racism and fascism into terrorism."

"But as you well know, Albert, we've suspected that for a long time. That's why we organized that letter from Luke Cosworth to the Coast Guard lieutenant."

"Yes, I meant to ask you about that. Wasn't it a bit risky to include the claim that Luke Cosworth was Lieutenant Cosmatos's first cousin once removed?"

"Not really," Sir William said. "When the Greek National Intelligence Service approached us and asked us to work with them in their plot to expose the terrorist faction within the Hellenic Spartan League, they assured us that Lieutenant Cosmatos and the members of his family weren't on speaking terms—his relatives are apparently fine, upstanding people who've had nothing to do with him for years. At family gatherings he came out with such outrageous utterances that some time ago they all decided that he was *persona non grata*. The only person who could've told the lieutenant that Lukas Cosmatos wasn't related to him was the lieutenant's father, and there was no way that that was ever going to happen—his father would never communicate with him via any means whatsoever."

"But how did you manage to find Luke Cosworth?"

Sir William Hartsford-Knipe smiled from ear to ear. "My dear fellow, there's no such person. He's entirely a product of the imagination of one of our more gifted MI5 officers. The Greek National

Intelligence Service suspected that Lieutenant Cosmatos was behind the killings on Krotonos, but they couldn't prove a thing. The fact that the League as a whole has been protecting the members of this terrorist inner clique, without knowing what they've been up to, hasn't helped matters at all. When the Greek National Intelligence Service approached us, they mentioned that Cosmatos is a relatively common Greek family name. So someone suggested that the League might believe a letter from a person with that name claiming to be a relation.

"Anyhow, returning to the Cyprus Memorandum, I for one was most surprised that the terrorists in the League fell for it. In my opinion, and I told the Director General of the Greek National Intelligence Service this more than once, the whole idea was ridiculous—no sensible person would believe a word of what 'Luke Cosworth' wrote. However, my Greek counterpart assured me that his people all knew that it was a truly stupid letter, but that even the thought of recognizing the Turkish Republic of North Cyprus would be enough to encourage the terrorists to strike at Britain. Or, as he put it, when you wave a red rag in front of a bull, the animal doesn't care if the rag is made of genuine cloth or is just a piece of red paper."

"But weren't you taking an awful risk?" the admiral asked. "For all you knew the Greek terrorists might have had Semtex."

The director just sat there and smiled again.

"In fact, just how did you know that they had the lookalike?" the admiral enquired.

Sir William laughed. "There's a Lebanese arms dealer in Beirut. He calls himself Sheikh Mansour ibn Aziz Arabiya, though he's no more a sheikh than you or me. The Lebanese don't care what he does, just as long as he pays his taxes. The Israelis could easily bomb him out of business anytime they wish, so he has to co-operate with them."

"Meaning what, exactly?"

"If he sells arms to certain people, he has to tell the Israelis about it. And if he supplies Semtex to groups operating in the West Bank or Gaza, he has to substitute the inert lookalike."

"It's a wonder that he's still alive," Admiral Marsdon said.

"Yes, indeed. So far he's been able to keep the practice a secret, but I suspect that it's only a matter of time until one of the terrorist groups catches on or an enterprising reporter puts two and two together. Still, we might as well use him as an asset while he lasts."

"But what does that have to do with the Greek affair?" Admiral Marsdon asked. "Sheikh Mansour didn't supply them."

"How do you know that?" asked Sir William.

"Well, it's obvious. The Hellenic Spartan League hates Muslims, so they wouldn't even approach Mansour, let alone travel to Lebanon to buy Semtex. And Mansour knows that the League's primary objective is to kill Muslims, so he would never ever supply them with anything."

"Actually, my dear Albert, he did supply the Semtex. Here's how. The Islamic Front for Jihad and the Liberation of Palestine bought the Semtex from Sheikh Mansour. They operate on the West Bank, so Mansour substituted the Semtex lookalike and told the Israelis about it."

"How? There's no communication between Lebanon and Israel."

"No official communication, but the Israelis have given Mansour a smartphone with a built-in digital encryption device. When the Semtex—or rather, the lookalike—left his warehouse, he told the Israelis. Then he learned via his worldwide network of informants that Lieutenant Cosmatos had hijacked the shipment off Krotonos and killed the four Arab men aboard the cabin cruiser in cold blood, and he informed the Mossad about that, too."

Admiral Marsdon nodded.

Sir William continued, "I'd heard that from the Israelis but, as far as they were concerned, it was no more than an unsupported rumor, so I didn't bother to share the information with anyone. Also, whether it was true or not, it didn't concern Britain or MI5 in any way. Even after we'd arrested the first terrorist, Orpheus Koutoufides or whatever his actual name is, I still didn't put two and two together. Stupid of me, I know. Only when the second Greek told his interrogators that the way the Hellenic Spartan League had acquired the Semtex was by killing the men on the cabin cruiser did I realize what was going on. At that time I decided that the sensible thing to do was to share all the information we had with the Israelis, so I invited Ambassador Ze'ev

Yaroq and his Second Secretary, Gabriella Lapid, to meet with me."

"The ambassador I can understand, but why the Second Secretary? Oh, yes, I've got it! Sorry for the interruption, William, please continue."

"As I said, I decided to tell them everything, starting with the bombing on the Bakerloo line organized by the IFJLP. I even told them about the computer problem we had with that high-energy cosmic ray."

"Why?"

"I certainly didn't want the Israelis to come to the wrong conclusion as to why we'd allowed the bomber, Suleiman Haroun, to get as far as Waterloo. I felt it was important to tell them what really happened, otherwise they might start to imagine that there's a top-level pro-Islamist mole in MI5 who ordered our officers to ignore the CIA warning."

"Good thinking," the admiral said.

"Interestingly enough, when I told them the facts about the malfunctioning of our computer in Cheltenham and its consequences, a meaningful look passed from the Ambassador to the head of the Mossad in London and an equally meaningful look went back in the opposite direction. Most unusual for Israeli diplomats."

"No doubt they wanted you to see both those looks, but I've no idea why they should. Let me think about it for a moment. Ah, I've had an idea. Is it possible that their analysts had already concluded that there's a mole in our organization, and that the diplomats wanted you to know that you'd satisfactorily cleared the matter up?"

"Yes, I think you're quite right," Sir William replied.

"Now," he continued, "let's return to Sheikh Mansour ibn Aziz Arabiya. The Semtex lookalike was part of the consignment he'd sold to the IFJLP, so he felt obligated to keep informing the Israelis about the whereabouts of the Semtex and the other components of the shipment, even though it was now in the hands of the Greek terrorists. One of the things he told the Mossad was that the Semtex that Orpheus Koutoufides brought to Britain was part of the goods that Mansour had sold to the IFJLP. As far as the Israelis were concerned, it was only an unconfirmed rumor, so they didn't pass it on to us. Also, it made no sense to them—why would the Hellenic Spartan League want to set off a bomb in Britain?"

"But didn't you tell the Israelis about the Cyprus Memorandum?" Admiral Marsdon asked.

"At that time I didn't realize that an Israeli connection even existed, so the answer is no. Anyhow, please get back to the second terrorist, Heracles."

"Certainly. Well, one of the reasons that he's telling us everything he knows is because of what the Hellenic Spartan League did to him. It seems that he volunteered to go to London to set off a bomb at Waterloo station after the last train for the night had left. He'd made it unambiguously clear to them that no one was to be hurt, including himself—he stressed repeatedly that he wasn't a suicide bomber. So they told him about the other kind of Frishman detonator, the one with a timer. Do you know what I'm talking about?"

"Quite frankly, no," Sir William said. "As far as I'm aware, Amir Frishman makes one kind of detonator and one kind only."

"You're absolutely correct. But the terrorist clique inside the Hellenic Spartan League wanted to be sure that Heracles died in the blast, for reasons I'll come to in a minute. So they took a standard Frishman detonator and attached some sort of electronic timer to the front. They added a couple of wires, and that was the 'timer detonator' that they gave to Heracles. When he pushed the red button it didn't start the timer counting down. Instead, it did what every Frishman controller does—it sent an electric current to the detonator, which triggered the explosion."

"Except that, in this case, there was no explosion, because there was no explosive, just the Semtex lookalike."

"Exactly," the admiral said with a grin. "The detonator merely set the Semtex lookalike on fire. The flames then burnt the material of the backpack. And that was the end of the terrorist bombing on the Bakerloo line. Heracles had no idea why the bomb had failed to explode, but he was fully aware that the Hellenic Spartan League had tried to kill him. And he also knew that, if he returned to Greece, they would finish the job. So he made for the exit, asked someone how to get to the nearest police station and turned himself in. He told the sergeant on duty that he'd exploded a bomb on the Underground. The sergeant naturally didn't believe him. So the terrorist told the sergeant to phone Waterloo Underground station and tell them to look next to the wall of the southbound platform of the Bakerloo line. After a long pause, the person who answered the phone came back and reported that there had been a fire. Now the sergeant suddenly became very interested indeed. In short, he called us in, and the rest you know."

"Not everything, though. You haven't explained why the Hellenic Spartan League wanted Heracles to be destroyed by his bomb," Sir William said.

"The League wanted a martyr, someone to die for the cause."

"But they had a martyr, that teenager who was shot and killed in Athens during the failed assassination attempt on Imam Khan. The Greek authorities still don't know who did that, by the way. And they probably never will."

"There's a difference," Marsdon said. "The teenager, I think his name was Menelaus Tsolakoglou, wasn't a member of the League. Yes, he certainly was a racist—a number of TV videos prove that beyond all doubt, including one that shows him yelling 'Muslims go home!' and then throwing a stone at Imam Khan, missing him, and instead hitting a newspaper reporter on the shoulder. But the xenophobic activities of a teenager are not the same as the actions of a paid-up member of the Hellenic Spartan League, a former soldier in the

Greek Presidential Guard. The League wanted to show that one of their members cared so much about the Cyprus Memorandum that he was willing to die for it."

"And I assume that they've arrested Lieutenant Cosmatos and charged him with four murders?"

"Far from it," the admiral replied. "He denies in a sworn statement that anything like that ever happened, and his five crewmen back him up fully in their affidavits. His lawyer says that the accusation comes from a self-confessed terrorist who'll say anything to have his sentence reduced."

"And the other terrorist?"

"He's continuing to say nothing. But even if he were to affirm every detail of Heracles's accusations, it would still be the word of two confessed terrorists against fine, upstanding members of the Greek Coast Guard who all just happen to be members of the Hellenic Spartan League."

"Have they searched the Coast Guard patrol boat?" Sir William asked.

"Yes. They found a tiny trace of blood on the main deck. That proves nothing—people cut themselves all the time. And the DNA doesn't match that of anyone involved in the case."

"I suspect that the blood comes from one of the sailors who Cosmatos shot," Sir William suggested.

"You're probably right," the admiral answered. "But unless they find the bodies, which now seems increasingly unlikely, we'll never know. Anyhow, they also found microscopic traces of that taggant that they now embed in Semtex, I think they call it something like DMDNB."

"Or 2,3-dimethyl-2,3-dinitrobutane for short," Sir William added helpfully.

Admiral Marsdon grinned knowingly and continued. "But it's well known on Krotonos that, on some Wednesday nights, the League held its weekly gathering on the Coast Guard patrol boat. So the six members of the Coast Guard claim that the source of the taggant was one or both of the terrorists. And there's absolutely no way to prove how it got there."

"So what have they done about the lieutenant and his crew?" Sir William asked.

"They've transferred them from Krotonos. More than that, they've assigned the six men to six different Coast Guard patrol boats, none of which patrol within a hundred miles of Krotonos—they're all stationed in different parts of the Ionian Sea, on the west side of Greece."

"And the police sergeant and his three men?"

"They authorities have done the same thing with them. They've transferred them to four different mainland locations, far from one another and far from Krotonos," Marsdon replied.

"I'd heard that they demoted the sergeant—the authorities claim that he was responsible for starting the riot in the municipal auditorium."

"He deserves to be drummed out of the police," Sir William said. "Maybe he will be, when they obtain more evidence. This case isn't over by a long shot."

"And neither is the case of this ghastly claret," Admiral Albert Marsdon moaned.

CHAPTER TWENTY-NINE

"What a waste of money!" the Saudi banker said to his confidential aide. "I've been paying a fortune to that firm of private detectives in London but in *The Times* this morning there's a story that tells me everything I wanted to know about the developments on Krotonos, and a whole lot more besides. I've no idea how British newspapers get their scoops, but next time I need information of any kind, I'll just hire a British reporter."

"What's in the newspaper that you didn't know already?"

"The key point is that it's now safe for us Muslims to go to Krotonos. They've transferred the policemen to four different police stations on the Greek mainland, and they've assigned the Coast Guard lieutenant and the members of his crew to six different ships on the other side of the Greek peninsula. Also, the two bombers are safely in British jails, and they're going to stay there for a long time. So, there are no more members of the Hellenic Spartan League left on Krotonos, *Alhamdulillah* (praise be to Allah)," the banker said.

"Are you sure about that?"

"Well, it says so in *The Times*, and that's good enough for me."

"And what would you like me to do now?" the aide asked.

"First and foremost, I want you to arrange to have those four policemen and six sailors killed. Ideally, I would like them to be killed as slowly and painfully as possible, and the world needs to know why and how they were killed. In practice, that may be difficult. For example, once our jihadis have tortured two or three of them to death, the others may try to hide. But we need to hunt down all ten and kill them like the dogs they are."

"Of course."

"In addition," said the banker, "If those two Greek bombers ever get out of jail, I want them killed, too. My guess is that I'll be dead and buried long before the British release them, but you never know with the British Home and Commonwealth Office."

"I understand."

"Also, we need to do something about that eyesore of a house on Argos Beach. What do you think about the idea of telling the Islamic Front of Yemen that they can use it as a base for jihad against Greece?" the Saudi banker asked.

"In my opinion, there's a serious difficulty: How will they get the explosives that they need for jihad into the storeroom? And that's where the difficulty lies. In my opinion, the Greek Coast Guard is going to be extra vigilant from now on. After all, the whole story is now public. The Hellenic Spartan League has made fools of the Greek authorities, and the Greeks are justifiably an extremely proud people. My guess would be that the Greek islands would *not* be a good location for a base for conducting jihad for a long while. And using Krotonos would probably be especially unwise," the aide advised.

"I think you're quite right," the banker replied. "Sell the Argos Beach property."

***

Hashim bin Baba, the new rector of the agricultural college, phoned Mahmoud ibn Laban in some excitement.

"Mahmoud, come here at once. Drop everything. I can't explain over the phone."

An hour later, Hashim welcomed the current leader of the Islamic Front for Jihad and the Liberation of Palestine into his office.

"Hashim, this had better be really important. What's the problem?" Mahmoud asked.

"No problem at all, only a wonderful opportunity. Read this."

"I can speak English, but you know I don't read English letters too well," Mahmoud said. "Tell me about it."

"We've just had a two-day visit from a professor at the Queen Victoria College of Agriculture in Tricester. He stayed overnight in one of the guest rooms upstairs and, when he left, we found this newspaper in his room. It's yesterday's *The Times*, the most authoritative and respected newspaper in Britain."

"And?" Mahmoud asked.

"And there's a two-page article on the happenings on Krotonos."

For the first time, Mahmoud showed some interest. "Really?"

"Yes. The saga is long and complicated, and you know most of it anyway, so I'll get straight to the point. They've transferred all the policemen and the Coast Guard sailors who were on Krotonos to different locations elsewhere in Greece, and the two Greek bombers are going to be sitting in jail in England for a long, long time."

Mahmoud caught on at once. "So who's guarding the cabin cruiser with our shipment?"

"Precisely!" Hashim bin Baba answered.

"Just a minute. It's not that simple."

"How so?"

"I agree that there are no more members of the Hellenic Spartan League left on the island, but we still have the problem of repossessing our boat," Mahmoud ibn Laban replied.

"That's easy. As you just said, it's *our* boat—we own it. So you go to Krotonos, together with three sailors. You walk to Argos Beach. You use the Zodiac to get from the shore to the boat. And then you sail our boat back to Lebanon."

"As I said, it's not that easy," Mahmoud insisted.

"Yes, it is. All you have to do is to fly to Athens, go to a maritime recruitment agency in Piraeus, and hire a captain and two sailors. In every port there are always out-of-work seamen looking for a job. It won't cost too much—three or four day's wages plus air tickets to fly them back to Athens or wherever else they want to go. What's the problem?"

"How would I prove that I own the cabin cruiser?"

"What do you mean?" Hashim asked.

"If I were to go to a recruitment agency, they're going to demand proof that I own the boat. No reputable firm is going to work with me unless they know that everything is above board. For all they know, I may be looking for crewmen to steal a boat and take it to Lebanon, and they certainly won't want to be involved in anything like that. So they're going to ask me for some form of written proof that I own the boat, or a letter from the owner stating that he's hired me to transfer the boat from Krotonos to Beirut."

"But we don't have any documents like that," Hashim replied.

"Precisely. And that's why I can't go to a maritime recruitment agency in Piraeus or, for that matter, anywhere else."

"So what's the solution? Do you have any ideas?"

"You can always find out-of-work seamen in those bars located just outside the gates of every port," Mahmoud ibn Laban replied.

"How can you suggest such a thing? Like you, I'm a pious Muslim—I don't drink alcohol."

"I didn't suggest that you should actually consume spirituous liquor. All you have to do is walk into a bar in Piraeus and engage a group of seamen in conversation. If they're not looking for a job, they'll shout across to the next table, and soon you'll have your captain and crew lined up. When can you leave for Athens?"

"Why me? I run this agricultural school," bin Baba objected.

"I know you do. And you do a fine job. But you'll do an even finer job when you fly to Athens, recruit a crew in Piraeus, and sail our cabin cruiser from Krotonos to Lebanon."

"And why Lebanon?"

"Because we have something to settle with Sheikh Mansour ibn Aziz Arabiya. We paid him for genuine Semtex manufactured in the Czech Republic. Instead we received boxes of that Israeli Semtex lookalike."

"Are you quite sure that he didn't sell Mustapha the real thing?"

"I'm certain. This article in *The Times* says that the Greeks acquired fake Semtex, and that's the reason why the bomb in Waterloo Station failed to explode. The paper doesn't mention that the phony explosive came from Sheikh Mansour's warehouse—if the reporter had written that, that crooked arms dealer would be dead by now—but you and I both know how the Greeks obtained their Semtex. So, you need to go to Beirut and make Mansour exchange that orange-colored, almond-smelling camel dung for the genuine Czech-made explosive. Next, you unload the cargo and sell the boat—we won't be needing it any more. Then we use the money we receive from the sale of the cabin cruiser to wage jihad against the

Israelis, using the real Semtex that Sheikh Mansour will give you, as well as the guns from our boat, to drive the Jews into the sea, *Inshallah*."

"But how am I going to convince Sheikh Mansour that the Semtex he sold us isn't the real thing?" Hashim asked. "If I show him that newspaper article, he'll just laugh."

"That's simple, too. You have extensive knowledge of bomb making. So, construct a rucksack bomb, just like the one that the second Greek terrorist tried to explode in London, and take it along with you when you go to Mansour's warehouse. If he agrees to supply us with the same amount of Semtex as before at no charge, but this time the genuine stuff, then fine. If not, then you 'explode' the 'bomb' in his office. When he sees the lookalike burning harmlessly on the floor, he'll realize that he hasn't a leg to stand on, that's for sure."

CHAPTER THIRTY

Carrying his briefcase and with a rucksack containing his clothes on his back, Hashim bin Baba carefully navigated the badly worn old stone steps that led down into the subterranean Piraeus bar. There was no handrail. Hashim paused halfway down and looked around the centuries-old room. It seemed to him that the last time the cellar had received a fresh coat of whitewash was well before the Ottomans conquered the city in 1456. The wall in front of him was lined with three layers of large wooden wine casks. On his left was the wooden bar counter, dark-brown with age. The proprietor and his assistant stood behind the counter; Hashim noted eight men in front of it, all seamen as far as he could tell. Smaller groups of sailors were seated at the four wooden tables that dominated the center of the vault-like room. None of the twenty or so chairs seemed to match any other.

When he reached the uneven stone floor, Hashim walked up to the three men seated at the table nearest the staircase. Their clothes were stained and scruffy; their calloused hands were those of working men. All three men had tattoos, one on his neck, the other two on their hands. They stopped talking as he approached and looked at him somewhat suspiciously. No one said anything.

Hashim spoke first, in his heavily accented English. "I'm looking for a captain and two crew to take a boat from the Cyclades to Beirut. The trip should take three days, four at the very most."

This remark was met with silence. Then one of the men replied, speaking English with a thick accent that sounded vaguely Balkan to Hashim. "How much?"

"Five hundred euros," Hashim replied. "Each."

"Not enough," the man growled.

"Seven hundred, then," Hashim bin Baba countered.

"Cash?"

"Cash," Hashim confirmed.

"And airfare to get back?"

"Another three hundred."

The second man said, "Half up front, half on completion."

"Half the wages up front, the rest of the wages plus airfare on completion," was Hashim's counteroffer.

The first two men nodded.

The third man then spoke. "Double for me, I'm the captain," he said, in the same accent as the first man. "That's double the wages and double the airfare."

Double wages was reasonable, but double airfare was not. Nevertheless, Hashim agreed. As far as he was concerned, it was essential to get the cabin cruiser to Beirut, and if it took an additional three hundred euros, so be it.

"Sit and have a drink with us," the second man said, fully aware of the fact that Hashim would have to refuse for religious reasons.

"Thank you, but we need to leave right away for Krotonos."

"What's Krotonos?"

"The island in the Cyclades where the boat is moored. We take a ferry from here to Syros and from there to Krotonos."

The three men looked at one another for a while without speaking. They communicated wordlessly with one another, the way old friends do. Then the captain rose to his feet, followed by the other two men. "Pay us half now."

Hashim put his briefcase down on the table, took a thick pile of euro banknotes out of his right hip pocket and slowly counted out each man's advance. He put the rest back in his pocket, took his briefcase and walked up the stairs. The three men picked up their duffel bags and followed Hashim. They strolled to the Piraeus Ferry Port.

The three men ignored Hashim on the fast ferry to Syros. While they waited there for the Krotonos ferry, they stood in a tight circle facing one another, making it abundantly clear to Hashim that he was an outsider in every sense. And they ignored him again on the ferry from Syros to Krotonos.

Finally they arrived on Krotonos. Even though it was his first time on the island, Hashim knew the way to Argos Beach—he had carefully studied and memorized Google maps of the island. He led the way from the harbor to the beach, the three men staying some five or ten yards behind him the whole time.

They finally reached Argos Beach. It was the late afternoon. Hashim proudly pointed to the Zodiac on the sand and the cabin cruiser in the intense turquoise blue water beyond it. The beach was deserted.

The captain turned to Hashim bin Baba. "I want to see the papers for the boat."

"What?"

"The boat's papers. Show me the papers."

Hashim was nonplussed. "Why do you want to see them?"

"We're sailors, not thieves. We have to be sure that you haven't stolen the boat and want us to take it to Lebanon. So, show me the papers."

"I haven't got them with me," Hashim said.

"Impossible," said the captain. "No one sails a boat without papers."

"The man who had the papers was killed, and we're still trying to get hold of the papers," Hashim bin Baba replied.

The captain ignored what Hashim had said and joined his two friends. The three men again stood in a tight circle. They spoke in low voices for a minute or two. Then the captain rejoined bin Baba.

"We'll take you to Beirut if you pay us double, the entire amount up front, including airfare. And if you don't agree, we'll take you to that police station that we passed on our walk through the town and lay charges against you of bribing us to help you steal that boat."

There was nothing Hashim could do. With a heavy heart he took his remaining money out and paid off each of the men. They counted the money slowly and put in their pockets. Then the captain spoke again. "Come with us to the police station."

"But you said that if I paid you double you'd sail my boat to Lebanon."

Again it was as if Hashim hadn't spoken. The three men moved aggressively toward Hashim, and pointed in the direction of the town. Once more he had no choice. He slowly walked in the direction of the police station with one of the crewmen on either side of him and the captain right behind.

When they reached the police station, one crewman opened the door, and the other shoved Hashim inside, nearly causing him to lose his balance and fall. The captain marched to the counter. Sergeant Devetzi, who had replaced Sergeant Kyrgiakos, came out of the inner office.

"Can I help you, sir?" he asked in Greek.

Speaking English, the captain replied, "This man has tried to bribe us to steal a boat and take it to Lebanon."

Switching to flawless English, the sergeant asked Hashim, "Is this true, sir?"

"No, it is not. We own the boat on Argos Beach."

"Oh yes, sir," replied the sergeant. "I know about that boat. Our people in Athens have translated all the papers that Lieutenant Cosmatos found on board from Arabic into Greek as part of the police inquiry. Let me see where they are."

And the sergeant disappeared into the inner office for five minutes, returning with a thick file of papers. "Yes, here's the translation of the deed of sale of the cabin cruiser. The New Palestinian Agricultural School purchased it from a company in Lebanon. Are you from that agricultural school, sir?" he asked Hashim, who nodded.

"Yes, I certainly am. First, let me identify myself," and he showed his passport to the sergeant. Then, he took out his wallet and extracted a business card, which he gave to the sergeant. "As you can see, I am the rector of the agricultural school. Also, in my briefcase I have correspondence addressed to me as rector. Some of it is in Arabic, of course, but let me show you two letters in English sent to me from the Queen Victoria College of Agriculture in Tricester, United Kingdom." Hashim rummaged through his papers and finally produced the correspondence, which he showed to Sergeant Devetzi.

The sergeant asked the captain if he was satisfied. Embarrassed, he had to agree that everything seemed legal. Hashim now turned to the sergeant. "I think these men owe me some money."

Now the three men who had blackmailed Hashim found themselves in a difficult situation. They weren't sure what he could prove, but they could not discuss the matter with the police sergeant standing there. And there was no way that they could even exchange meaningful glances. So the seamen had no choice. As one, they put their hands into their pockets and then shamefacedly handed the extra money back to Hashim. The sergeant was no fool, and immediately understood what had happened.

He addressed the three men courteously but firmly. "Gentlemen, as you can see if you look up, this police station is equipped with video cameras. They have recorded you from the time you walked in here. I would strongly suggest that you sail this gentlemen straight to his destination in Lebanon."

Turning to Hashim, he said, "Sir, here is my card. I would like you to phone me when you arrive safe and sound in Lebanon. If I'm not here please leave a message for me with whoever answers the phone. In view of the impending development of Argos Beach by an American corporation, the Lieutenant General of the Hellenic Police Force has issued a directive that everyone who works in this police station has to be fluent in English, so you should have no language problem when you call the number on my card. I wish you all a pleasant trip. *Kalo taksidi!* That's 'bon voyage' in Greek." And with a cheery wave, the sergeant retreated into his inner sanctum.

Hashim bin Baba walked back to Argos Beach doing his utmost to keep a poker face. Behind him trailed three dejected seamen. They used the Zodiac to reach the cabin cruiser, carrying out the transfer from shore to boat in total silence. Once aboard, the three sailors checked the boat and then the captain met with Hashim in the saloon.

"Two of the fuel tanks are bone dry," the captain said, "and the third one is almost empty. Is diesel available at the port? If not, how do you suggest that we fill the tanks?"

"Is there enough fuel to get to the fishing harbor? It's not that far."

"I'm not sure. We can give it a try. The other problem is that there's almost no food aboard—we found two cans without labels, and that's it. The good news is that the water tank is almost full, but we obviously don't know how old it is. So if you absolutely insist on drinking water, boil it first."

"Okay. Now let's go to the port."

The captain started the engine and raised the anchor. The cabin cruiser slowly moved in the direction of the fishing harbor. As they neared the entrance to the port, the engine died. Momentum carried the boat forward for a while, but soon even that was not enough. The three men started rocking the boat from side to side to try to coax the last few drops of diesel into the engine. Eventually the motor coughed into life, and the captain was able to reach the fuel pump.

While the tanks were being filled to capacity, the captain told Hashim to give two hundred euros to the crewmen to buy food. It seemed a reasonable sum to feed four people for three days, so Hashim handed over the money. The two crewmen left and walked toward the shops in the town. Half an hour later they returned. One man was carrying three supermarket carrier bags—Hashim could see a packet of sliced bread protruding from one of the containers. The other man was heavily laden with cases of beer. It was abundantly clear where the two crewmen had spent the bulk of his money. Hashim sighed, realizing that for the next three days he would probably have to subsist on bread and tea—if the sailors had bothered to buy tea bags.

The sun was setting as they left the harbor. The sky was filled with shades of red, pink, orange and purple, all reflected in the calm sea. But Hashim saw none of this. His mind was focused on reaching Beirut and acquiring the Semtex that his organization so desperately needed to spread terror and death. Three hours later Hashim suddenly realized that he was hungry and extremely tired. He went to the galley where he made himself a sandwich. Then he threw himself on the bunk in the nearest cabin.

He woke in the middle of the night. Something was terribly wrong—but what was it? He could hear the hum of the engine and the small waves striking against the hull, so the boat was still under way.

He looked outside. It was dark. The moon had not yet risen, and the stars were glittering in the cloudless sky. There was no sound of wind. So it wasn't a weather issue.

He put on his shoes and walked around the cabin cruiser. One of the crewmen was at the wheel. There was no sign of the captain or the other crewman. Hashim assumed that they were sleeping in the second cabin. Hashim looked around the saloon. Everything seemed to be in its proper place. He took another quick look at the helmsman, but nothing had changed in the wheelhouse.

Then he suddenly realized what was bothering him—he could not smell Semtex. In fact, he did not recall smelling bitter almonds at any time since boarding the cabin cruiser. On the one hand, this was good. The odor might bother the sailors and they would search the boat from stem to stern to find the source of the smell and discover the secret hold under the carpet in the saloon. And if they found the weapons there, the consequences for the IFJLP might be grave. The three men might turn the boat around, sail back to Krotonos, and tell the sergeant that Hashim was a gun smuggler. Or they might disregard the police sergeant's warning, overpower Hashim, take the guns and sell them. But if they thought that the orange material was Semtex, who knew what might happen? They might dump the Semtex lookalike overboard, which would considerably weaken his case with Sheikh Mansour. Or they might dump Hashim overboard and try to sell the blocks of what they thought was Semtex. So the fact that he could not detect an odor was a definite plus.

On the other hand, the absence of the smell of bitter almonds might mean that, contrary to his insistence at the meeting of the executive committee of the IFJLP, the Semtex lookalike might not be aboard the cabin cruiser. And if the substance was still in the strongroom in the house on Argos Beach, then so were the weapons and ammunition. And if that were the case, the members of the IFJLP would in all probability decide to deal with his failure the way that they had dealt with the failures of Abdul Rahman ibn Sultan.

Shivering with fear, Hashim realized that the only way he could settle the matter would be to roll back the carpet in the saloon, open the hatch, and see what was inside the hold. But the man at the helm would turn round when he heard noises coming from behind him, with potentially catastrophic consequences.

Hashim bin Baba had no choice. He would have to wait until the crew had tied up the cabin cruiser in the Beirut small boat harbor, he had paid them off and they had left the vicinity of the vessel. Then, and only then, could he find out whether the Semtex lookalike and the weapons were aboard. For the rest of the voyage, Hashim was in a state of high anxiety. He wasn't hungry in the least, but if he ate nothing, the crew might become suspicious. For the same reason, at night he lay on the bunk in his cabin, even though he was unable to sleep for more than an hour or two as a consequence of the worry and the tension. Hashim's anguish finally came to an end when the cabin cruiser arrived in Beirut early in the morning of the fourth day.

As soon as he had paid off the three men and was alone on the boat, Hashim went to his cabin. He dumped the contents of his rucksack onto the bunk. Ignoring the clothes, he picked out three innocent-looking items from the pile and carried them to the saloon, together with the now empty rucksack. Next he carefully closed the curtains of the saloon and opened the secret hold. It was full of containers of various sizes. But was the Semtex there? He pulled out one of the smaller ammunition boxes. Inside were five bricks, each tightly wrapped in blue plastic film. Hashim held a brick right against his nose but could smell nothing. He fetched a sharp knife from the galley and hacked off the plastic as quickly as he could. As the last piece fell to the ground, he saw the orange color and smelled bitter almonds—the Semtex lookalike! Immense relief flooded through his body. He placed all five bricks on the table in the saloon.

Now he took another box out of the hold. It contained the Frishman detonators. He took one out, together with its controller. Next he found a second box of Semtex, extracted the five bricks and put them on the table with the others. Then he replaced the two empty Semtex boxes and the detonator box in the hold, threw the discarded blue plastic in and closed the hatch.

Hashim was about to put the carpet back in its previous position when he suddenly realized that he could not take the first Semtex brick with him. Stripped of its plastic wrapping, it emitted a strong odor of bitter almonds that would immediately arouse suspicion. He regretfully reopened the hatch and placed the brick in one of the empty boxes.

With his expertise in explosives, it took him less than five minutes to construct a realistic-looking bomb using the remaining nine Semtex bricks, the detonator, its controller, and the items he had taken from his rucksack. He placed the device with its controller in his rucksack, hoisted the rucksack onto his back, grabbed his briefcase and left the cabin cruiser. No one stopped him as he left the port area—the officials at the gate simply ignored him.

Once on the street, he hailed a passing taxi and soon arrived at the office of the company that had supplied the bodyguards for Mustapha's visit to Beirut. The helpful clerks organized three powerful-looking bodyguards plus an armored black Cadillac, similar to the one that his predecessor had used. An hour later, Hashim bin Baba walked into the arms warehouse of Sheikh Mansour ibn Aziz Arabiya. He was still wearing the rucksack containing the device he had constructed. His three armed bodyguards accompanied him.

Hashim walked with an arrogant swagger to disguise the fact that he was greatly concerned that Sheikh Mansour might outsmart him. He knew that only an exceptional person could survive for decades as a highly successful arms trader.

"*As-salamu alayka* (peace be unto you), *habibi*!" Mansour said, his perennial broad smile in place. "What can I do for you? Please come into my office. I'll order us some cardamom-flavored coffee."

Hashim bin Baba placed his briefcase on the floor next to an upholstered armchair, took off his rucksack, put it next to his briefcase, and sat down; his bodyguards arranged themselves behind him. Hashim suddenly realized that, when they saw him taking the bomb out, his own bodyguards would wrestle it from him before he could press the red button. Worse, fearing for their lives, they might shoot him the moment they caught sight of the device. Then the thought struck him that it would be extremely dangerous for him even to mention fake Semtex in front of his bodyguards. Sheikh Mansour would probably order his men to kill all four of them as they left his office in order to protect his secret and, therefore, his life.

So Hashim turned to the three men standing behind him and said, "Please wait outside."

They looked at one another, shrugged their shoulders, and slowly left the room. From the expressions on their faces it was clear that they saw no point in people hiring highly trained armed escorts and then sending them out.

When the door was closed, Hashim turned to the arms dealer. "Sheikh Mansour, I've come to ask you to replace the Semtex that you sold Mustapha with the real thing."

"What do you mean? What I sold your friend is 'the real thing,' *habibi*. Of course it is—what else could it be?"

"As you well know, what you supplied to Mustapha was the Israeli lookalike."

"How can you say that, *habibi*? I've been in business for over thirty years and my reputation is the finest in the Levant, the crossroads of Europe, Asia and Africa. I'm well known throughout all three continents, and no one in any of them has ever doubted my honor and trustworthiness in this way. There's no question that what I supplied to your associate is the finest quality Semtex from the factory in the Czech Republic. Here, let me show you the document that your friend signed confirming that all the goods I supplied to him were precisely what he'd ordered."

Mansour opened a desk drawer. As he did so, Hashim bin Baba took the bomb out of his rucksack. It came as no surprise to him when he looked up and saw the large shiny revolver in Mansour's hand.

"You damn fool, put that device down," the arms dealer ordered.

He spoke louder than he had intended, because the door suddenly burst open and the three bodyguards rushed into the room with their weapons at the ready. Sheikh Mansour dropped his gun onto his desk, raised his hands, and looked meaningfully at the device bin Baba was holding in his left hand, with the index finger of his right hand touching the red button. The men immediately understood the situation; two of them kept their guns trained on Mansour while the third pointed his weapon at Hashim.

"Move your hand well away from the button and then slowly lower that thing onto the floor," the third bodyguard ordered.

Hashim bin Baba realized that all was now lost. This was the end of his efforts to obtain the Semtex that the IFJLP so badly needed to wage violent jihad. He knew what the penalty for failure was but he had no choice. He obeyed his bodyguard's command and took his finger off the red button. As he leaned forward in his armchair to place the device at his feet, a pair of Sheikh Mansour's guards ran into the office. They saw that two of Hashim's escorts were pointing their handguns at the arms dealer. The third, much to their surprise, had his weapon pointed at Hashim bin Baba, whose bent-forward body and upholstered chair blocked their view of the bomb, now almost on the floor.

"Drop your guns!" one of the guards shouted. Hashim's escorts hesitated. The other guard fired a warning shot and three handguns hit the wooden floor at almost the same instant.

Hashim spun his head round. He saw the two guards, weapons pointed at his now unarmed escorts. Months of pent-up frustration and anger instantly transported him into a state of incandescent rage. "Sheikh Mansour," he screamed, now totally oblivious of the fact that publicly disclosing that the explosive was the Israeli lookalike could have potentially fatal consequences for him, "you're a liar and a thief! I'm going to demonstrate to you that the Semtex you sold us is fake. I press the red button here, and—"

The blast instantly killed all the men in the office and set off the other explosives and ammunition stored in the warehouse. Huge flames stretching to twice the height of the roof consumed all combustible materials. An hour later all that was left of the arms empire of Sheikh Mansour ibn Aziz Arabiya was a smoldering blackened shell enclosing piles of twisted metal.

CHAPTER THIRTY-ONE

"Ilan," the Director of the Mossad said, "I'm trying to decide whether to fire you or award you a medal."

"Please fire me," Ilan replied nonchalantly. "Then I won't have to spend the rest of my life switching lookalike and Semtex, trying to remember all the time which is which. They look identical, they smell identical, so how I can be expected to know which is which?"

"I agree," Haggai Eshkolot said. "One of these days you're going to get it wrong. But before you accidentally blow yourself up, would you kindly tell me all about the Semtex on Krotonos. From the beginning, please—the whole story is more than somewhat confusing."

"The 'whole story,' as you put it, started in London, where the IFJLP acquired a supply of Semtex. Their financial backer, a banker from Saudi Arabia, paid for it; we're still trying to find out how his agents transported the explosives to England. Anyhow, the executive committee of the Islamic Front arranged to send suicide bomber Suleiman Haroun from Yemen to London. We found out about it from a CIA operative. As you know, we snuck into the safe house in Wembley while Haroun was sleeping and replaced the actual Semtex in his suicide vest with the lookalike, but with a small admixture of the real explosive. We also replaced the detonator controller with an identical-looking one that operated by radio. So, when Haroun pressed the red button on his controller, nothing happened. But when I sent out the correct radio signal, Haroun and his colleagues were killed. Which was a pity—we could have learned a lot of useful information if the British had interrogated his three friends."

"And what did you do with the real Semtex?" Haggai Eshkolot asked.

"I'm not sure you want to know."

"Oh, yes, I do."

"Well, first we had to wrap a brick in fresh plastic. When the Palestinian terrorists pushed the end of the detonator into one of the Semtex bricks, they pierced the blue plastic film. That didn't cause a problem—the plastic formed a sort of seal around the detonator. But when we removed the detonator, we created a hole in the wrapping and we quickly noticed a strong smell of bitter almonds. So we used some of the plastic film that we received from the team in Israel to rewrap that brick. Then, there's a room in the Israeli Embassy in London—"

"You were quite right the first time," Eshkolot interrupted. "I don't want to know."

"Good. Then I won't tell you. Now, where was I? Oh, yes, Haroun's bomb killed the members of the London cell of the IFJLP, and we had their Semtex. And best of all, we saved hundreds of lives by switching the Semtex and the lookalike.

"The chief character in the rest of the story is that evil genius Abdul Rahman ibn Sultan. The New Palestinian Agricultural College was entirely his idea and a truly brilliant idea it was, too. In his book *The Innocence of Father Brown*, G. K. Chesterton wrote: 'Where does a wise man hide a leaf? In the forest. But what does he do if there is no forest? He grows a forest to hide it in.' Abdul Rahman wanted to hide his school for Palestinian terrorists, and therefore he built a school for Palestinian farmers to hide it in.

"He knew all about the bugging of the United States Embassy in Moscow, so he instructed his men to protect the building against Israeli eavesdropping devices. Unfortunately for him his underlings didn't take his warnings seriously, and fortunately for us we were able to plant microphones just about everywhere. Following standard operating procedure, we embedded surveillance devices that utilize the latest technologies, including spread spectrum and burst transmission, so the IFJLP weren't able to detect them with the third-rate radio frequency receiver one of their people bought in America. In fact, without a Juke Box they had no hope of finding our bugs.

"Getting into the agricultural college was easy. All it took was one case of Stock 84 brandy. Any time that we wanted to visit the partially completed building to plant covert listening devices, one of us walked in through the hole in the fence around midnight and left a bottle for the elderly night watchman in his room. By one o'clock he was lying on the floor, dead drunk.

"Abdul Rahman was single minded and dedicated," Ilan continued. "He was convinced that the agricultural college was bugged, even though some of his colleagues thought he was paranoid. After months and months of trying without success to make his fellow members of the executive committee believe that we'd installed listening devices in the college, he finally managed to convince Mustapha and persuaded him to send Hassan Ali ibn Bakran Al-Husseini to Britain for a three-week exchange visit at the Queen Victoria College of Agriculture. That operation didn't go too well either, so they killed Abdul Rahman. Mustapha took over as leader, but the Hellenic Spartan League murdered him when he came back to Krotonos with the weapons.

"The others on the executive committee of the IFJLP, including Mahmoud ibn Laban and Hashim bin Baba, continued to refuse to even consider that the agricultural college might be bugged—after all, they'd swept the building twice using the detector that Mahmoud had bought in America. So the two of them didn't hesitate to sit in the rector's office of the college and discuss their plan to reacquire their cabin cruiser, sail it to Beirut, and force Sheikh Mansour to exchange the lookalike for genuine Semtex. We flew from London to Krotonos in a private jet with the actual Semtex that we'd stored where you don't want to know about it, hired a fishing boat, headed out to the cabin cruiser, and switched the lookalike and the Semtex. Not just any Semtex, mind you, but the very same bricks of

Semtex that we'd taken from the IFJLP when we broke into their house at 235 Swinderby Road, Wembley for the second time and were now returning to them."

"Yes," Eshkolot replied dryly, "honesty is always the best policy. But I interrupt you. Please proceed."

"There's not much more to tell. Hashim did precisely what he and Mahmoud had agreed. He exploded a rucksack bomb in Sheikh Mansour's office, clearly oblivious to the fact that we'd swapped the Semtex. Hashim was an unwitting suicide bomber, the second one in this saga."

"I assume you're referring to Heracles Stavridis as the first."

"Yes," Ilan confirmed, "but there was a significant difference. As a result of Sheikh Mansour switching the Semtex, Heracles's life was saved but Mansour himself was killed. There's some sort of poetic justice there. Or perhaps poetic injustice."

"Forget about poetry, Ilan," the Director said. "Your job is to protect Israel against her sworn enemies. Which leads to my next question. You went to Krotonos and replaced the lookalike Semtex in the boat with the real thing."

"Yes, I just told you I did," Ilan replied.

"Did it ever occur to you that Sheikh Mansour was protecting Israel by not giving the actual Semtex to the IFJLP, whereas you did the opposite? Didn't it bother you that you were giving a load of genuine Semtex to a Palestinian organization that carries out violent jihad against Israel? An organization that had proved its deadly intent to wage Holy War by sending Suleiman Haroun to London and equipping him with a suicide bomb to blow up Waterloo Underground station?"

"Of course I thought of that," Ilan responded. "But everyone knew that the orange stuff in the cabin cruiser was the lookalike. After all, there was that article in *The Times* that was reprinted by news media all over the world. Even the Greek government did nothing whatsoever about the cabin cruiser and just left it moored offshore from Argos Beach. They'd read the inspection report and decided that there was nothing more that they needed to do."

"What inspection report?"

"Well, the day after Heracles confessed to the bombing, Lieutenant Cosmatos meticulously examined the cabin cruiser from stem to stern and wrote a report."

"I understand about the Semtex lookalike," Haggai Eshkolot said, "but why did the Greek authorities leave the weapons and the ammunition in the cabin cruiser after reading about them in the report?"

Ilan laughed. "Because there was nothing about either the weapons or the ammunition in the inspection report. Lieutenant Cosmatos stated that he'd discovered a secret hold that lay under the saloon floor of the cabin cruiser and that inside the hold were small ammunition boxes containing the Semtex lookalike. And that was that. Heracles's accusations against Cosmatos were certainly forwarded to the Greek police, but the charges 'disappeared' for a while until pressure from the top forced the Greek National Intelligence Service to investigate. But no one put two and two together and realized that it was essential to thoroughly re-inspect the cabin cruiser."

"I see. Now let's get back to my original question, which was: Why did you present Israel's enemies with a supply of real Semtex?"

"As I just said to you," Ilan replied, "the whole world knew that the bricks stored in the hold of the cabin cruiser were the lookalike, even the Islamic Front for Jihad and the Liberation of Palestine. So neither they nor anyone else would consider for a moment using the lookalike for anything other than a dramatic demonstration in Sheikh Mansour's arms warehouse. And what a dramatic demonstration it turned out to be."

AFTERWORD

This story is a work of fiction. Where the settings of this story are actual places, we have described them as accurately as we could. Other locations, including the islands of Krotonos and Lagoneia, are fictional, as are the Al Fazi Mosque and Hadji Ali Square in Athens.

The description of 2,3-dimethyl-2,3-dinitrobutane (or DMDNB for short) is accurate, but Amir Frishman and his eponymous detonator are figments of our imagination. The RSA (Rivest–Shamir–Adleman) public-key cryptosystem is widely used today; RSA++ does not exist.

Every character in *Bakerloo Line* is imaginary and bears no relation to any actual person, living or dead. Furthermore, every crime-related issue, without exception, is completely fabricated. In particular, the Hellenic Spartan League does not exist. Also, all actions ascribed to members of the Greek, Israeli, Lebanese, and British military, Coast Guard, intelligence, police, immigration, and other law-enforcement agencies are totally fictional, and are in no way intended to reflect actual actions of members of the military, Coast Guard, intelligence, police, immigration, and other law-enforcement agencies of those countries or of any other country.

Steve Schach
Sharon Stein

ACKNOWLEDGEMENTS

We would like to thank Howard Aksen, Rosalind Fischl OAM, John Gallo, Joe Kensell, Johan Koeslag, Jill Selikowitz and Jane Wolfers for taking the time to read earlier versions of the manuscript and for their many constructive suggestions. We are most grateful for their help.

We warmly thank our developmental editor, Michael Mann, for his meticulous reading of the manuscript and his helpful comments and suggestions. Once again it has been a real pleasure to work with our publisher, Jennifer Chesak, of Wandering in the Words Press. And for the fifth time, we thank her for designing a striking cover.

STEVE SCHACH

After twenty-six years as a professor at Vanderbilt University in Nashville, Tennessee, Steve Schach, a Cape Town, South Africa native, recently moved to Sydney, Australia. Before he began writing thrillers, Steve wrote thirteen best-selling software engineering textbooks, which are used in universities all over the world. Down Under, Steve intended to become a full-time grandfather, and limit his intellectual activities to solving cryptic crossword puzzles and avidly watching *Sesame Street* with his grandchildren. However, the urge to write proved to be far too strong to overcome. Wandering in the Words Press has previously published four of his thrillers, most recently *A Matter of Trust* in 2014.

SHARON STEIN

Sharon Stein is a pediatric radiologist. Born in Cape Town, South Africa, Sharon was a professor of radiology at Vanderbilt Children's Hospital in Nashville, Tennessee and an examiner for the American Board of Radiology. She is a former president of the Southern Pediatric Radiology Society. In 2009 Sharon moved to Sydney, Australia, with her husband, Steve Schach, to be with their grandchildren. She is an accomplished cook and baker who loves to share her recipes and techniques. This is her second thriller co-written with Steve Schach; Wandering in the Words Press published the first, *Coopers Island,* in October 2013.

www.ingramcontent.com/pod-product-compliance
Lightning Source LLC
Chambersburg PA
CBHW061326170626
46817CB00001B/329